THE
SILVER
SCALPEL

THE
SILVER
SCALPEL

Nancy Baker Jacobs

G. P. PUTNAM'S SONS   *New York*

G. P. Putnam's Sons
Publishers Since 1838
200 Madison Avenue
New York, NY 10016

Library of Congress Cataloging-in-Publication Data

Jacobs, Nancy Baker, date.
   The silver scalpel / Nancy Baker Jacobs.
      p.   cm.
   ISBN 0-399-13834-X
   I. Title.
PS3560.A2554S54   1993   92-41849 CIP
813'.54—dc20

Printed in the United States of America
1 2 3 4 5 6 7 8 9 10

For my dear friend, Martha Humphreys

1

Flames of crimson and orange shot up as the roof exploded. The roar was as loud as a jet plane taking off, followed by a sonic boom. A wave of heat slapped me hard across the face as inky black smoke billowed toward the pale evening sky. I stepped back behind a waist-high sign at the edge of the tiny lawn while sparks showered the soaked and muddied grass around me. Inhaling a lungful of acrid smoke, I coughed.

A window at the front of the building blew out and, for what seemed like a full minute, it rained splinters of glass. There was no way the Fire Department could have responded quickly enough to save this building. The fire was spreading much too fast. I only hoped nobody had been caught inside.

I'd seen a few arson jobs in my time and this looked like one of them. The single-story structure was burning evenly on all sides, a sure sign that somebody had set fires at several points almost simultaneously. And there was a lingering stench of burnt petroleum in the air.

I watched from the sidelines as two young fire fighters fought valiantly with a wildly bucking fire hose, struggling to keep it aimed at the center of the raging blaze. The stream of water turned to hissing steam as soon as it reached the flames. Half a dozen other fire fighters, dressed in rain gear and high black boots, slid on the muddy ground as they pulled their hoses around the sides of the building. Another siren split the air and reinforcements with pickaxes scrambled off a red truck pulling up to the scene.

I looked around me and saw the fire's heat reflected in the faces of the crowd that had been drawn by the flames. By turns their faces went from white and brown to shades of copper, gold, and bronze. Behind us, the red and blue lights of the emergency vehicles flashed and their radios spit out ear-splitting static, giving the scene a surrealistic effect.

By the flickering light, I read the words on the faded sign that shielded me from the shooting debris—"Women's Medical Center"—and felt a quick pang of sadness. Not that this place had any particular meaning for me; I didn't live here in St. Cloud, and I'd never even seen this building before tonight. It was nothing more than sheer chance that I was standing here now. But the torching of yet another women's clinic was depressing and more than a little frightening.

I'd driven up to this Central Minnesota city earlier in the day only to wait four long hours for the chance to serve a subpoena on a local builder. The roof of a room the guy'd added onto a house last fall had collapsed, sending a young woman to the hospital with a broken back. Now the victim was filing suit against the builder and her attorney had hired me to serve the papers.

When I wasn't able to find the builder at his latest construction site—a half-built mini-mall that didn't look any too sturdy—I found out where he lived and camped on the doorstep of his old brick apartment building until he came home. He was less than thrilled to see me. But luckily, he limited the immediate expression of his displeasure to a stream of four-letter words. I'd heard them all before, so I climbed into my Honda and split.

On my way out of town, I stopped at The Magic Vegetable, a Chinese vegetarian restaurant I'd read about, for an expense account dinner of mushrooms masquerading as meat. My favorite sort of fare. Particularly when I didn't have to cook it myself.

As I was leaving the restaurant, I smelled smoke floating on the early evening air. I hadn't driven three blocks before I heard sirens behind me, so I pulled over and let the speeding fire trucks pass. Four fire engines and a police car quickly blocked the road ahead of me, so I shut off my motor and got out for a better look. Flames were already leaping skyward from the low, wood-frame structure.

A crowd began to gather until there were at least a dozen other people standing there with me watching the clinic's demise as the building's charred timbers crashed inward and new flames licked the sky.

I wondered if the arsonist was among them. Many arsonists are known to admire their handiwork. There were three men dressed in denim work clothes and two women in business suits, along with an assortment of people I recognized from the restaurant down the street. None of them looked particularly guilty, just curious. A teenage couple held hands, while two young boys in Little League jackets ran around the edges of the crowd, sharing the sense of excitement. The fire was probably the highlight of this little group's week.

Local Channel 3's mobile van screeched toward the curb. It jerked to a stop and a cameraman and a young blonde woman in designer jeans and a Donna Karan jacket leaped out onto the wet ground. The reporter charged toward the fire fighters, but she was quickly ordered back behind the safety lines.

The blonde looked around and spotted me at the edge of the crowd of onlookers. Thrusting her microphone in my face, she asked, "Did you see what happened, ma'am?" I wondered when I'd grown old enough to be addressed as "ma'am," instead of "miss."

"Sorry," I told her. "I got here right after the Fire Department, but flames were already shooting through the roof by then. This fire's been spreading very, very quickly." There was a sound like thunder as the entire south wall of the clinic fell in, sending a shower of sparks skyward. The crowd oohed and ahed, as though they were being treated to Fourth of July fireworks.

The cameraman circled around so that his shot included me standing in front of the clinic's sign, with the burning building in the background.

"What are your feelings as you watch this building burning?" The blonde looked concerned and genuinely interested in my response, but I couldn't help feel that her pose was simply the feigned one of a good professional. Her makeup and hair were a little too perfect for me to trust. Still, she'd asked for my opinion; I was happy to give it.

I looked directly into the lens of the minicam on the cameraman's shoulder and spoke loud enough to be heard above the crashing and shouting behind me. "As a woman, I'd just like to say that this sort of thing really makes my blood boil."

"Why's that?"

"This place used to be a women's medical clinic," I said, "and it sure looks to me like it was firebombed."

This was a little more than the blonde had been prepared for. Until I told her, I don't think she was aware that the burning building was a clinic. A true purveyor of contemporary TV journalism, she was more interested in packing her report with emotional impact than factual detail. She asked me my name and occupation, and relayed that information back to Channel 3's studio. Off camera, she told me that her taped segment on me would make the local ten o'clock news and that their network affiliate in the Twin Cities would probably pick it up, too. Then she scurried off to try once more for a statement from the overburdened fire fighters.

I didn't stick around to see whether or not she got it. I headed for my car, hoping I could make it home to St. Paul in time to see my own comments on the news. I never said I wasn't a ham at heart.

At closing time the next day, I was finishing up some paperwork in the office. I had missed seeing what Andy Warhol would have called my own personal fifteen minutes of fame—actually fifteen seconds would be more accurate. It was almost eleven o'clock by the time I'd arrived home, but two friends had left messages on my phone answering machine, saying they'd caught my virtuoso performance. One of them told me that the blonde newswoman's introduction of my segment had identified me as "Devon MacDonald, a St. Paul private investigator who happened on the scene."

I peered out the window at the traffic crawling along Grand Avenue and frowned. The sky was nearly dark and the street was slick with rain. A crack of thunder shook the building and a split second later, a flash of lightning turned the roofs of the cars below an eerie shade of green. It was a typical Minnesota spring thunderstorm, and I wasn't looking forward to going out in it.

My partner, Sam Sherman, had taken the afternoon off to visit his daughter, Lael, who was about to deliver her first baby. Paula Carboni, our receptionist at Sherman and MacDonald, Private Investigators, had left early to pick up her fiancé at his dental office. They had a four-thirty appointment to interview a wedding consultant. So I was alone in the office and the job of closing up was left to me. I set the phone machine to take calls and checked one last time for faxes. I was buttoning my raincoat when I heard footsteps on the stairs.

The young woman who burst into the office a moment later was out of breath and shivering. Her thin blue jacket was completely soaked, and water dripped from her long, straight, tobacco-brown hair. "You're Devon MacDonald, aren't you?" she gasped. I nodded. "Thank goodness you're still here. I ran all the way from the bus stop."

This waif of a girl told me her name was Monica Hammond and that she'd taken three buses to my St. Paul office from Southeast Minneapolis, near the University of Minnesota. I invited her in, took off my raincoat, then plopped tea bags into two mugs of water and put them in Sam's microwave to heat.

"I saw you on TV last night," she said. "You looked like a kind person. Understanding. I didn't think you'd yell at me or call me names." She pushed a wet brown strand of hair behind one unadorned ear. Her face was heart-shaped, with sharp cheekbones and a narrow nose.

"I try not to yell at people any more than I really have

to." The girl did not return my smile. "Why don't you just sit over here and tell me what this is all about."

"Well, it's like this. When Kerry didn't show up when she was supposed to and then I saw the fire on TV, I didn't know what to do. 'Specially after I heard today about those two dead women. But then I remembered seeing you and what you said. And I thought, you being on TV like that had to be an omen, or fate or something like that. I just knew you were the one who—"

"Whoa! Hold on a minute, Monica. I don't have a clue what you're talking about. What dead women? And who's Kerry?"

"You know, the women who died in that fire in St. Cloud. The radio said they found two dead bodies inside."

"Oh, Lord." I'd been stuck here in the office all day and hadn't heard the noon news. I felt bile rising in my throat. Swallowing hard, I forced my thoughts back to my young visitor. "I don't get it. What's that fire got to do with you, Monica?"

"Guess maybe I better start at the beginning." Monica took a deep breath, but it didn't stop her from shaking. Wearing no makeup, her lips blue with cold, she looked painfully young to need a private investigator. "Kerry's my sister," she told me. "She's younger than me, just turned sixteen, and she was coming down to the Cities to see me, but she wasn't on the bus like she said. I waited and waited, but . . . I—I'm just so scared something awful happened to her." She lowered her hazel eyes and I noticed that she had lush, thick lashes. As tears slid down her cheeks, I noted her eyes were her prettiest feature.

I handed her a mug of tea and patted her damp shoulder. "It'll be okay, Monica, trust me. I'm sure your sister will turn up." I figured the younger girl had simply missed her bus, or maybe she'd gone off with her friends and lost track of the time. Teenagers are always doing things like that. Finding Kerry Hammond would probably be a piece of cake. "Just tell me what happened, nice and calm."

Monica took a gulp of her tea and looked up at me, her

cheeks streaked with tears. "I think Kerry might've been in that abortion clinic when it burned," she said. "I'm scared they burned my sister to death."

A chill crawled down my spine. Maybe this case wasn't going to be such a piece of cake after all. "Why? What on earth makes you think your sister would have been in that clinic last night?"

Monica hugged her wet jacket to her thin shoulders. "The . . . the last time I talked to Kerry, she asked me if I knew how a friend of hers could get an abortion. She said her friend wasn't eighteen yet, so she couldn't just walk in and get one. She needed a note, a . . . what do you call it?"

"Parental consent form?"

"Right, parental consent."

Minnesota vigorously enforces its law requiring minors seeking an abortion to have the consent of at least one of their parents, or else a judge. "And this friend didn't want to tell her parents she was pregnant?"

"Right. Kerry said this girl's parents would kill her if they ever found out."

"And you think Kerry really was talking about herself."

Monica nodded solemnly. "I—I don't know for sure, but—"

"When your sister asked you about getting an abortion, what did you tell her?"

"I said I didn't know exactly how it could be worked out, but we could talk about it when she got down here. I told her there might be places where they don't check your age, or where you could use a fake ID. I thought if Kerry was talking about herself, maybe she could use my ID—I turned eighteen last fall."

I questioned Monica carefully, trying to determine why she thought Kerry would have gone to that particular clinic if she sought to terminate a pregnancy.

"That's the one where I got my birth control pills," she said, her palms smoothing her damp skirt over her knees. "It was the only one anywhere near where we live."

"Still, if Kerry wasn't eighteen, the clinic wouldn't have

been able to help her without your parents knowing about it and signing off."

"I—I don't know. That's just the only thing I can think of. Maybe she thought she could convince the people at the clinic that she was older or something."

"Or maybe Kerry just got delayed and missed her bus. Have you called home to see whether she left on time, or—"

"Oh, no! I couldn't do that. Kerry couldn't tell our folks she was coming to see *me*. They'd never let her come."

I heated two more mugs of tea and extracted Monica Hammond's story one piece at a time. She told me that her parents had thrown her out of the house more than a year ago, while she was still a senior in high school. She'd made her way to Minneapolis, where she worked nights in a pizza parlor in Dinkytown, near the University, to support herself. "Maybe it's none of my business," I told her, "but just what did you do?" I couldn't picture this frail-looking teenager transgressing in any way that would even remotely warrant her parents kicking her out of the house.

She chewed her lip and avoided my eyes. "It—It was because of the pills."

"Pills?" Monica certainly didn't look like a drug abuser, much less a pusher, not that looks were always a giveaway.

"Yeah, the pills, the birth control pills. My mom found them in my purse."

I felt like I'd gone back in time. Did parents still throw their daughters out just because they had a sex life? Sure, the average teenage girl's folks might not be thrilled at the prospect, but still, this was the nineties. And just how had Monica's mother "found" birth control pills in her daughter's purse anyway?

The picture that slowly emerged was a bleak, depressing one. Monica told me she was the oldest of Herman and Mary Hammonds' eight children. Kerry was their third. The Hammonds' lives seemed to consist of school, work on the family farm near Newton Prairie, and church, not necessarily in that order. Invading the children's privacy went with the territory, as did brutal punishments for even the smallest transgressions. The parents seemed to believe wholeheartedly that sparing the rod would spoil the child—it said so, right there in the Bible. Monica told me her banishment from the family farm had been preceded by a beating that left her black and blue for a month. No wonder the poor kid was worried about people yelling at her and calling her names, or worse. She'd grown up with that sort of treatment.

"Kerry wasn't allowed to see me or even talk to me," Monica confessed. "None of 'em were. But Kerry used to sneak out on Wednesday nights after church and call me from a pay phone in town. She—Kerry was the only one in the whole family that ever cared about me." Monica brushed away fresh tears. "She told everybody at home she was going to church camp in Wisconsin for the school break. You know, the kind where you camp out in the hills and pray all the time. But she really was gonna stay with me. So there's no way I can call her at home, I just can't. And you've gotta promise me you won't tell Mother or Father on her, either. Swear it."

I swore.

Monica rose and handed me her mug. "You'll do it, then? You'll find Kerry?"

I nodded.

She gave me a photograph of her missing sister, a posed, school portrait kind of thing. "This was taken last fall. It's the only one I've got." Kerry was lighter than Monica, with ash blonde hair and blue eyes, and exceptionally pretty. Monica's features were sharper than Kerry's, perhaps because she was so thin. Yet the family resemblance was clear. "I don't have much money, but you can have what I've got," Monica said. "And I can pay you a little more each week." She pulled three damp, wrinkled bills from her jacket pocket and handed them to me. There were two twenties and a ten. Sam would have my head for taking only a fifty-dollar deposit on a missing persons job, but I didn't care.

Monica said she had to leave to catch her bus; her work

shift started at eight and she couldn't afford to lose her job. But it was still pouring out and I didn't have the heart to let her stand out in the rain again. I bundled her into the Honda and drove her home.

2

By morning the storm clouds had headed east, the sky was clear and blue, and the air held the promise of spring. I came into the office early to clear my desk and fill Sam in on our new missing persons case before I drove north to Newton Prairie, the Hammonds' home town.

A quick look at my calendar reminded me that I'd scheduled an appointment to look at real estate during my lunch hour today. I'd earned a twenty-five-thousand-dollar bonus from an insurance company a few months back for solving a bank embezzlement case, the first real folding green I've ever had. With my divorce now final, I thought I should try to put some stability—financial if no other kind—into my life. At thirty-three, it seemed about time I did something sensible. In this economy, twenty-five grand should buy me a down payment and closing costs on a two-bedroom condominium in St. Paul, maybe even one with a real, working fireplace. But my search would have to wait for now. I called my real estate agent and postponed my appointment.

As I rang off, I heard Sam come in. I picked up the large box I'd brought from home this morning and carried it into his office. It had taken me half of last night to wrap my bulky gift for Sam's expected grandchild—I'd used pink and blue paper, and added cascades of curly ribbons and a bunch of balloons on top and I had to admit I was rather proud of the result. I didn't know my partner's daughter terribly well, but a little something to welcome her first child clearly seemed to be in order.

"Here." I smiled and thrust the package toward Sam's rotund form. "This is for Lael from me. It's an infant safety seat for the car. She'll need it to bring the baby home from the hospital."

Sam shot me a suspicious look and kept his hands firmly by his sides. You'd have thought I was trying to hand him a bomb with a lighted fuse.

"What's the matter? Here, take it."

He raised his double chins and thrust his hands into the pockets of his moth-eaten brown cardigan sweater. "The baby's born, the doc says he's okay, he's got all his parts in all the right places, *then's* time enough for presents."

"You're kidding." I'd ordered the baby seat weeks ago, and raised hell with the store when it hadn't been delivered by the date the baby was expected to make its appearance. The car seat finally arrived yesterday, with the kid already a week overdue. And now Sam was telling me this was too soon.

He avoided looking at me. "You expect too much, you tempt fate, it shits on your head every time."

"Oh, for heaven's sake, Sam. What kind of superstitious garbage is that?"

He mumbled something about Jewish traditions and some nonsense about how making too many preparations for the birth of a baby is roughly the same as guaranteeing the child will be born blind, or missing a limb or two, or even dead. I argued, but Sam wouldn't budge. Feeling deflated, I carried the gift back into my office and stowed it on top of my file cabinet. Far be it from me to do anything that might cause a problem for Lael's baby. I already felt personally responsible for far too many of the world's ills.

Maybe Sam was embarrassed about his reaction to my gift, or maybe he was just preoccupied with worry about Lael, but when I filled him in on the Hammond case, he didn't even ask me how Monica intended to pay for our services. Playing my own little game about not tempting fate, I didn't bring up the soggy fifty bucks.

Sam's mood lightened as he began to concentrate on our client's family problems instead of his own. "So I'll see what I can do about getting ID's on the dead women. You headin' north?"

"Yeah, I'll take a look at the girls' home, see if Kerry's still there."

I needed a few supplies to take with me, some documents to help me camouflage my true identity. It obviously wouldn't do for me to show up on Herman and Mary Hammond's doorstep and present myself as a private investigator from St. Paul: "Howdy, folks, don't mind me, I'm Devon MacDonald, woman detective, and I'm looking for your daughter, Kerry, who may have disappeared while trying to get an abortion she didn't want you to know about."

I had Sam help me dummy up some phony college scholarship application forms on the computer; he understands the concept of desktop publishing a hell of a lot better than I do. The results were actually not too bad; with our new laser printer, the forms looked reasonably genuine, certainly as good as anything printed locally in Newton Prairie, Minnesota.

I threw away the top copy—the one smeared red with jelly from the doughnut Sam shoved into his face when he thought I wasn't paying attention—and put the rest of the forms, along with some course catalogues from local colleges, into my briefcase. I put on my coat and stuck my head into the door of Sam's office on my way out.

"I'm leaving that baby car seat in my office, Sam, on top of my file cabinet. I won't make you give it to Lael now if it makes you nervous. But if she has her baby today, I want you to promise you'll come back here and get it for her. I swear I'll never forgive you if she leaves that hospital without it."

Sam may have his own superstitions, but they can't hold a candle to the one I have about keeping children as safe as possible whenever they're in or around cars. My only son was killed by a drunk driver a few years back. You don't get over something like that.

Sam gave me a sheepish nod.

"I'm taking that as a solemn pledge," I said, heading out into the morning sunshine.

3

I drove northwest on I-94 toward St. Cloud, following the path of the Mississippi River. Traffic thinned out as I left the outskirts of Minneapolis and headed through the suburbs and beyond to an area populated with small farms. The fields were bare now, as they always were in early spring in Minnesota, giving the landscape a gray, almost dead look. Patches of dirty snow could still be seen on the ground in sheltered and shaded spots. But it wouldn't be long before the trees began to bud and the first green shoots poked their way through the wet, rich soil.

Some people find this part of the season depressing, as winter's pristine snow melts to reveal fall's dead brown foliage beneath. But I like it. The air temperature finally warms to a bearable level, even in frigid Minnesota, and I'm all too aware that spring's new growth, no matter how beautiful, how necessary, will soon throw me into the sneezing fits of hay fever. For a few short weeks, I can breathe easily.

Near St. Cloud, I turned off I-94 and took county roads west through more desolate-looking farm country into central Stearns County. I followed Monica Hammond's directions, circling just north of the town of Newton Prairie and heading past a small lake to the Hammond family farm.

The mailbox at the edge of the county road was my marker; someone had painted the word "Hammond" in uneven black letters along its side. I turned onto the unpaved private road leading to the farm house. It was about a quarter of a mile long and bordered by fields that were naked except for an occasional oak tree. A small herd of cows huddled together against the wind on the horizon. I drove slowly and carefully, avoiding the ruts and water-filled potholes that could break the Honda's axle if I hit them at too high a speed. Three black crows scolded me as I drove, but otherwise the place seemed quiet.

The house was a dingy, weathered white, badly in need of a new coat of paint. It had a broad front porch, the kind where I could picture old folks sitting in their rocking chairs on a warm summer evening, and it was surrounded by oaks planted at least a hundred years ago. A gray barn and a chicken coop were visible at the northwest corner of the yard. I heard cackling from the direction of the chicken coop, but otherwise an overwhelming silence pervaded the place.

I parked in the yard, climbed the front steps onto the porch, and searched for a doorbell. I didn't find one, so I settled for knocking on the edge of the screen door.

A teenage boy with a pimply complexion and crewcut blond hair pulled open the door and appraised me with curiosity. I suspected that not too many strangers ventured onto this property. "Hi, is Kerry Hammond at home, please?"

"Nope." He leaned a shoulder against the door frame. "Who're you?" The youth's social graces were certainly impressive.

A woman's voice called from the back of the house, "Who is it, Mike?" As the boy turned toward the direction of the voice, I could see past him into the room. Two young girls, about six and eight years old, were in the living room area. They wore dark wool skirts that covered their knees, long socks, and matching sweaters. Their clothing had a home-made look. One held a feather duster and the other a floor mop with a handle several inches taller than she was. The girls stopped their chores to stare at the stranger at their door.

"I'm Devon MacDonald," I told the youth called Mike. "I came to see Kerry about a college scholarship."

"It's for Kerry, Mom," he called. "About school."

"When do you expect her back?" I asked.

A heavy, buxom woman in a brown paisley print house-dress charged through the living room. "Marsha, that table's not gonna dust itself. Floor neither, Patty." The two young girls didn't utter a word; they went back to their chores, sneaking occasional looks at the front door when their mother wasn't watching. I smiled at them, but their faces remained grim.

"What's this about Kerry and school?" the woman demanded, pushing the screen door open. Her short frizzy hair looked like the product of a bad home permanent and her face was bare of makeup. She did not invite me in, so I stood on the porch, holding my briefcase. I began to understand where Mike had gotten his training in etiquette.

"I'm Devon MacDonald," I repeated. "From the Women's Equality Scholarship Fund. Your daughter Kerry was recommended to us as a strong candidate for one of our college scholarships, so I—"

"Who recommended her?" The woman did not seem pleased. A third daughter, this one no more than three or four, streaked across the floor from the same part of the house where the woman had come. She grabbed the hem of her mother's dress and tugged on it.

I came up with what I hoped was a plausible story. "One of the teachers at the high school gave us Kerry's name, I think. I don't recall which one right—"

"Bet it was that Lundberg woman."

"I don't remem—"

"Just like her, stickin' her nose in."

"*Mom*-my." The little girl pulled harder on her mother's skirt. "I wanna—"

Mrs. Hammond rapped her knuckles sharply on top of the child's head; I winced as she stumbled backward and began to whimper. "You see I'm busy, Lucie. Go on back in that kitchen *now*, before I give you a good lickin'." Lucie slunk away; the poor little thing obviously was still learning how to toe the line in this family without complaining. I saw now how a house could have so many children in it, yet be so devoid of their natural chatter and laughter.

I glared my disapproval of the woman's abuse, but held my tongue about it. I wasn't here as the parent police. "I'd like to have Kerry fill out an application, Mrs. Hammond. You *are* Kerry's mother?"

"Yeah, I'm Mrs. Hammond. Kerry's my third. Got eight kids in all, five girls and three boys. A real houseful. Gotta keep a firm hand when you've got that many." At least the woman had noticed my disapproval and felt it necessary to explain a little about her theory of child raising. As though that would make the smallest difference in her children's lives once I was off the property.

I propped my briefcase against my hip and opened it. "Well, then, with so many children to educate, I'm sure some scholarship money to help with Kerry's college expenses would be welcome." Reaching inside the briefcase, I pulled out one of the application forms Sam had helped me print. "I can start this application now. Then, if you'll just tell me when I can come back and see Kerry, I can get the rest of the information I need from her and get this into the works."

"Save yourself the trouble."

"What?"

"We're not interested."

"But you don't understand. I'm not here to sell you anything. This could mean money, *free* money to help your daughter with her—"

"I understand just fine, miss. I know what a scholarship is. But my daugher's not goin' to college."

"But—"

"But nothin'. We're a Christian family and we don't go along with this women's lib stuff. When the time's right, my Kerry'll find herself a good, God-fearin' boy, get herself married, and keep a good home with as many children as God sees fit to give her. The way the Bible teaches."

"Going to college doesn't mean she won't get married or have children, Mrs. Hammond. In fact, it might—"

"The answer's *no*. No daugher of mine's goin' off to the city, gettin' her head filled with ideas from no college. You got money to give away for school, lady, you find some for my son Mike here. He's goin' to the seminary, be a pastor someday."

The corners of Mike's mouth curled into a smirk. Apparently he enjoyed his superior standing among the Hammond children, and why not? I felt myself getting more and more angry on Kerry's behalf. "The Women's Equality Scholarship Fund is for females only, Mrs. Hammond. The rules specify that quite clearly."

"Then, like I told you, we're not interested."

"Still, I'd like to hear what Kerry has to say about it." This was getting downright silly. Here I was, getting pissed off because this female relic of the dark ages wouldn't let her daughter apply for a scholarship that didn't even exist. Still, her attitudes toward her daughter's future and women in general made my blood boil.

"Like Mike told you, she's not home. Gone to church camp for the school vacation. But she wouldn't tell you no different. Kerry's a good girl, never a lick of trouble from that one."

Little do you know, I thought, stuffing the application form back into my briefcase. At least I wouldn't have to worry about the Hammonds' discovering my paperwork was fake. And I had learned what I'd come here to find out— that Kerry Hammond was indeed missing. "Thanks for your warm hospitality," I said, unable to resist injecting a note of sarcasm into my farewell. I snapped my briefcase shut, turned on my heel, and stalked back to my car.

As I U-turned and headed past the front door, I saw Mike Hammond still standing at the door, supervising my departure. He didn't wave good-bye.

4

As I left the Hammond farm, I headed toward Newton Prairie. A sign at the edge of town announced the population at nine hundred and eleven. I suspected that might be a bit high, judging from the fact that maybe twenty percent of the buildings along the town's main street were vacant.

Krauss Hardware had managed to survive the recession, or the flight to urban areas, or whatever it was that ailed this town. Wheelbarrows and lawnmowers perched hopefully on the sidewalk outside the store's front, waiting for warmer weather to make them necessary and a better economy to make them affordable.

Milly's Dress Shop hadn't fared as well as the hardware store. Its sign was broken and its windows boarded up. A small office building and a candy store had suffered the same fate.

A beauty shop on the right seemed prosperous enough, though. Two elderly women with pink curlers in their hair sat in the front window, in clear view of anyone passing by. And Bud's Diner—its garish blue lighted sign was missing a couple of letters, making it read "Bu 's Di er"—was hopping.

I pulled into Econogas, one of the town's two gasoline stations, filled up the Honda, and used the pay phone at the edge of the parking lot. The receiver was icy against my ear and a brisk wind from the north set me to shivering as I punched in the numbers of my phone credit card.

Paula put me through to Sam, who sounded like he was eating something. My description of my chilly welcome at the Hammond farm was accompanied by Sam's rhythmic chomping.

He swallowed and put in his two cents. "Ya ask me, that kid we're lookin' for probably got fed up and ran away. Could hardly blame her."

"I can see why Kerry'd want out of that family, but why would she flake out on her sister? According to Monica, they were very close."

Sam didn't have an answer for that one. He agreed that I should stick around town for a while longer and see what I could find out about Kerry Hammond. "Got something for you on this end," he told me. "Lemme just find my notes here." More smacking sounds echoed over the phone line.

I sighed, picturing Sam licking something gooey off his fat fingers. Catsup dripping off a forbidden hamburger. Or maybe ice cream. My partner was truly incorrigible when it came to watching his diet, an exercise of no small importance for an overweight man who'd barely survived two heart attacks in recent years. But I was getting tired of scolding him, something that never did a damned bit of good anyway. At least Sam had given up smoking his beloved cigars, which probably did as much to improve my allergies as his heart condition. I was learning to be grateful for small victories.

The whine of an air compressor being fired up in the gas station's garage pierced the air and paint fumes quickly assaulted my nostrils. Pollution was inescapable these days. I stuck a finger in my ear to block the noise as Sam came back on the line.

"Here it is," he said. "Got an ID on one of them women died in the fire. A Dr. Janet Gilman, head sawbones at the clinic."

"Okay, makes sense that one of the doctors would be at the clinic after hours. What about the other woman?"

"That's a little harder. St. Cloud P.D. says everybody else that works at the clinic's been accounted for. They let slip that the second dead woman was a lot younger than the doc, but that's all I got out of 'em."

"You didn't mention Kerry Hammond's name to them, I hope."

"I look like I got loose lips?"

"Just checking. After meeting the mother, I think Monica's fear is probably justified. Kerry could be in real trouble if her parents ever find out she lied to them. Somehow I don't think unmarried pregnancy and abortion are the kind of things their type would forgive easily."

"Yeah, well it ain't gonna be me that squeals on them girls. You just watch who you're shootin' your mouth off to, petunia."

Touché. We agreed to touch base later.

5

Listening to Sam's munching and crunching reminded me that I hadn't had lunch yet. I headed back through town and stopped at Bud's Diner.

Bud's seemed to be riding out the recession with relative ease, at least this week. It was nearly filled, mainly with teenagers looking for a way to spend their school vacation. It was an old-fashioned sort of eatery, complete with booths upholstered in worn red Naugahyde, a cigarette-burned tan Formica counter with blue plastic stools, and a real jukebox. The tunes listed were an eclectic mix of country and western and pop, the latter tending more to Amy Grant than Madonna. Just a clean, all-American town, Newton Prairie. No dirty little secrets here.

The only unoccupied booth hadn't been cleared after its previous customer, but I grabbed it anyway. I pushed aside the remains of somebody's burger and fries, and grabbed the plastic-covered menu. Its offerings were real middle America: hamburgers, meat loaf, beef pot pies, pork chops with applesauce, Bud's Special Short Ribs. Since I no longer eat red meat, my choices narrowed fast, to either fried chicken with mashed potatoes and gravy—probably dripping fat, not to mention the calories—or a dinner salad. I opted for the dinner salad and a side order of toast.

While I waited for my food to arrive, I eavesdropped shamelessly on the three teenage girls in the next booth. Their high speed chatter was gossipy and ranged from quick assessments of the boys they knew to the clothes worn by any local girl who wasn't around to the latest fad diets to movie stars. I found it refreshingly normal after the artificial silence at the Hammond house.

My lunch arrived. If you can call a wedge of iceberg lettuce topped with a slice of anemic pink tomato and drenched in catsup-and-mayonnaise dressing a lunch. The toast was only slightly more promising—tanned Wonder Bread with a pat of congealed butter in the center of each slice. I picked up a piece of toast and chewed on a corner. A hamburger was beginning to sound better and better.

As I picked at my food and observed my fellow diners, I sipped my tea. It wasn't bad; luckily, there's not much anybody can do to spoil a tea bag dunked in hot water.

Two of the girls in the next booth left, declaring their intention to check out the baseball practice up at the school. A "real stud" named Ryan was expected to be there. The third girl remained behind, quickly burying her nose in a recent issue of *People* magazine with Princess Diana on the cover. When I was her age, my girlfriends and I read movie magazines with the same sort of gusto; I wondered what ever happened to *Photoplay* and *Modern Screen*.

"Excuse me," I said, leaning toward her. No reaction. I raised my voice. "Excuse me, miss."

The girl raised her eyes and stared over the back of her booth. "You talking to me?" She had short, dark hair and enormous blue eyes ringed with heavy black eyeliner and mascara. But her nearly flat button of a nose kept her from being technically pretty.

"Yeah. Just wondered if you could answer a few questions for me."

"About what?" She appraised me with suspicion. Her mother had probably warned her never to talk to strangers.

I smiled, trying my best to rejuvenate my "kind, understanding" television image, which had recently enticed Monica Hammond to trust me. "I'm Devon MacDonald, from the Women's Equality Scholarship Fund in St. Paul." I explained that I'd driven up earlier in the day to complete a scholarship application for a local girl who'd been recommended to us. "I went to her home to talk to her, but she wasn't there. And I got the strangest reaction from her mother when I told her about the scholarship. You go to the high school here, right?"

She nodded.

"Well, I was just wondering whether you might know this girl."

Her eyes grew wider in anticipation of a juicy piece of gossip. Who knew what added status the information I was about to divulge might give her with her friends. "Prob'ly. I know just about everybody in Newton." She bit her lip and waited for me to name names.

"The girl recommended for the scholarship is Kerry Hammond. You know her?"

"Sure. I know all the Hammonds."

"Great, then you'll be able to help me." I laid some cash on my table, then moved myself and my cup of tea to her booth. The girl told me her name was Wanda Kirchner and that she was a sophomore at the high school, a year younger than Kerry. I described my earlier meeting at the Hammond house. "I've never had this happen before, somebody telling me they're dead set against their daughter's getting an education," I told her. "I really hate to leave town without knowing whether this is what Kerry wants, too. I mean, lots of times girls don't agree with their parents, right?"

Wanda nodded conspiratorily.

"You know where I could find Kerry?"

"Uh uh, sorry. I think I heard something about her going to some kind of religious retreat over the break, in Wisconsin or Iowa or someplace. I didn't pay much attention. The Hammonds are all real religious."

"I got that idea from Mrs. Hammond. She told me the son, Mike, is planning to be a minister."

Wanda rolled her eyes skyward. "Mike, yuck! What a nerd."

"Does Kerry buy into this religion stuff?"

"I guess so, sort of. I mean, I really don't know. All the Hammonds go to church a lot, so I s'pose Kerry believes in it. Lots of people in Newton go to the same church, but not everybody takes it so serious."

"What do you mean?"

"You know, like you can't wear makeup or dance or wear shorts in public, bullshit like that. Like you can't have any fun, or else it's a sin."

I had some ideas about how Wanda defined having fun and suspected that a lot of religions might not approve. But that conflict was as old as time. "Sounds pretty dismal for a teenage girl," I said. "Kerry isn't even allowed to wear makeup?" I wished I'd worn more myself, to help me create something of a bond with Wanda.

"Well, sometimes she puts on a little at school, not too much. You know, in the girls' lav, but her parents aren't s'posed to know. They're pretty weird about stuff like that." She twisted a seed pearl ring on her finger.

"Boy, I can't blame Kerry. I think if I were a teenager with strict parents like that, I'd probably just learn how to sneak around behind their backs."

Wanda giggled. My understanding act was beginning to pay off. "What do you know about what Kerry wants for her future? Did she ever mention plans to go to college?"

"Not really. We're not best friends, thought, and besides, Kerry keeps pretty much to herself. Ever since Lucas split, anyway."

"Who's Lucas?"

"Lucas Drew, Kerry's boyfriend. At least he used to be her boyfriend, but they broke up."

"And he left town."

"Yeah. He's a couple of years older, graduated last year. Worked up at the feed store for a while, but I guess he didn't like it much. Everybody figured he and Kerry were gonna get married when she graduated, but then Lucas just took off."

"Why?"

Wanda shrugged. "What I heard is he had this idea about being an actor." She leaned closer and spoke in a near whisper. "Lucas Drew is a real hunk. I mean, he could be Tom Cruise's younger brother." Her eyes glowed with appreciation of Tom Cruise. "I think I heard he went to Hollywood. Or maybe it was Broadway."

"And Kerry was upset?"

"Who wouldn't be? I mean, God, how would you feel if your guy just took off like that?"

I allowed as how I would be devastated if my own personal hunk left town without me. Actually, it had happened to me once and I honestly had been devastated. Every once in a while, I still was. "Did Mr. and Mrs. Hammond know about Kerry's relationship with Lucas?"

"God, no. At least I don't think they knew Kerry and Lucas had anything really serious going on. I mean, they could only see each other after school and at church things, when Kerry's parents figured she was with a whole group of us kids."

In other words, they sneaked around behind the Hammonds' backs. Monica's fears that her younger sister might be pregnant began to seem justified. I wondered whether Kerry had told her sister about Lucas. "You know anybody who might know more about Kerry, like maybe where I could find her? I just hate to blow off this scholarship because of her family. For all I know, Kerry might want it."

Wanda tugged on the neck of her lilac sweater. "She's pretty tight with Sarah Percival. Maybe Sarah could tell you something." She gave me directions to the Percival girl's house.

Wanda also identified the teacher Mrs. Hammond had accused of poking her nose into Kerry's future and the Hammond family's business; the despised "Lundberg woman" was named Linda and she lived in a big yellow house on Main Street, near the edge of town. Wanda told me that

Miss Lundberg, who taught English composition and doubled as the school counselor, was "pretty cool, for a teacher."
I suspected that was high praise from a fifteen-year-old.

I thanked Wanda and stood up. As I slipped my arms
into my coat, I noticed Mike Hammond coming through
the front door of Bud's Diner, carrying a large envelope.
He joined two other young men in one of the booths. One
looked several years older than Mike, broader shouldered,
with sandy hair and thick, black-rimmed glasses. The other
was about nineteen, tall and broad-shouldered, with a
protruding Adam's apple and cauliflower ears. On my
way out, I caught Mike's eye and gave him a little wave. He
gave me a cursory nod of the head, but did not return
my smile. I was inclined to agree with Wanda that Mike
Hammond showed all the signs of being a nerd. As did his
two friends.

As I pushed open the door, somebody dropped a quarter
into the jukebox and Tammy Wynette launched into her
rendition of "Stand By Your Man." Maybe someday someone will record "Stand By Your Woman." I wondered
whether it would find an audience.

6

Sarah Percival's younger brother, a freckle-faced boy of
about eight, answered the door and told me his sister was
baby-sitting three doors down the street. He pointed out a
two-story gray house with blue trim. "I think Sarah's gonna
be there for supper, too, 'cause we're havin' pizza tonight.
Pepperoni. Sarah hates pepperoni. My mom never lets me
have pepperoni on it when Sarah's home." Just another in

the long list of reasons younger brothers have for resenting their older sisters.

"Thanks." I laughed and headed down the street.

Sarah Percival was surprisingly small for a high school junior. At under five feet tall, she couldn't have weighed more than eighty-five pounds. She reminded me of the many Olympic gymnasts, who at the same age still haven't developed a sign of breasts or hips. But Sarah had a foghorn of a voice. "Suzy, turn down that TV. Now!" she yelled. "Somebody's at the door and I can't hear." Her small charge, a girl of about five, leaped to obey. The cartoon show she'd been watching was instantly muted.

I stood on the porch and presented my cover story through the closed screen door. Maybe in a large city my efforts for the Women's Equality Scholarship Fund would have been greeted with more suspicion. But here in Newton Prairie, no one seemed to wonder why someone like me would go to such lengths to track down a potential scholarship applicant. I wanted to think my success was entirely due to my superb acting ability and the way I presented such a professional, yet caring image. But the real reason was probably that folks here lacked a certain amount of sophistication. Their gullibility clearly worked to my advantage.

After I had identified myself and my mission, Sarah invited me inside and led me to the kitchen. We sat at a round white table while she shoveled Cream of Rice into the mouth of a baby boy strapped to a high chair. It occurred to me that the girl hardly looked big enough to lift this chubby infant, but maybe she was stronger than she looked. I hoped so, for both their sakes. "Open up, Denny-poo. Just a few more bites," she urged in her gravelly voice. Denny-poo used his small pink tongue to push out most of the soupy white mess, but Sarah was ready for him. She deftly scraped off the rejected cereal with her spoon and pushed it back into the baby's mouth. "Swallow it, sweetie pie. You want to grow up big and strong like your daddy, don't you?"

I described my visit to the Hammonds' farm and my reservations about leaving town without talking directly to Kerry Hammond.

"Gosh, I don't know if Kerry wants to go to college or not," Sarah told me between spoonsful. "Me and her never talked much about college."

"Know where I can find Kerry right now? This scholarship could be worth maybe forty, fifty thousand to her over four years."

Sarah's brown eyes widened. "Fifty thousand *dollars?* You're kidding!"

"Nope. Even public colleges cost between ten and fifteen thousand a year these days, Sarah, when you add up tuition, books, and living expenses."

"Wow, I never realized. Guess it's a good thing I'm going to secretarial school, huh? It's only a year and I can live at home and commute to St. Cloud if I get my own car." She wiped the baby's chin with the corner of a towel and handed him a hard brown cookie that resembled a dog biscuit. "My mom and dad promised me one for graduation if I get my grades up. I have to pay my own insurance and gas, though, so I'm saving up."

That seemed a fair tradeoff to me. "Great. Now, about Kerry. If you know where I can find her. . . ."

"Kerry swore me to secrecy, but—" Sarah thought for a moment, pushing a long brown strand of hair behind one ear. "Promise you won't tell?"

I nodded.

"Kerry'll really kill me if she finds out I told. I mean, she's already mad at me. And her folks can't ever know about any of this."

"My lips are sealed."

Sarah leaned closer, as though to impart a secret. But the way her voice carried, I suspected she could be heard throughout the house. Maybe even outside. "Kerry told her folks she was going to church camp—it's a campout, so she figured it'd be hard to check up on her. But she really took the bus to see Monica in Minneapolis. Monica's her older sister."

I realized I'd been holding my breath and exhaled slowly. I was back to square one. Sarah told me about Monica Hammond's banishment from her family; her version was roughly the same as the one I had heard from my client. I commiserated, then took notes as Sarah told me where Monica could be found; I couldn't think of a logical excuse not to.

I thanked Sarah for her help, pushed back my chair, and stood to leave. She got up, lifted baby Denny onto her left hip, and led me though the living room toward the front door. The baby's weight didn't seem to bother her a bit.

Sarah stood aside as I pushed open the screen door. A chilly draft entered the room. "By the way, you said Kerry was mad at you," I said. "What for?"

"Oh, just that abortion thing. It wasn't anything serious. I don't know why she got so mad."

I caught my breath and kept my hand on the door handle. "What do you mean, 'that abortion thing'?"

"Oh, nothing, really. I mean, me and Kerry belong to Kids for Life and everything. I guess she just wasn't thinking straight."

"What happened?"

Sarah shifted the baby to her right hip. He grabbed for her hair with gooey fingers. She tilted her head away from his reach. "Well, it was like this. Kerry said she knew this girl who was pregnant and she wanted to get an abortion. But she couldn't get one 'cause her parents wouldn't let her. Kerry said she wanted to help this friend of hers, but she didn't know what to do."

"And she wondered if you'd know how to get around the parental consent law?"

"I guess so. But she shoulda known better. I told her to back off. I mean, she'd go straight to hell if she ever helped somebody kill a baby and she knows it." Sarah pulled a tissue from her pocket and wiped little Denny's fingers gently. "It was really weird of Kerry to even say something like that. But she started yelling at me and said I didn't know what I was talking about."

"Maybe it's just that this was a really good friend of hers," I said. "Maybe she just wanted to help her."

"By getting this girl condemned to the eternal fires of hell? Some help!"

I kept my opinions to myself. "You said you and Kerry belong to something together. What is it, some kind of club?"

"Oh, yeah, K.F.L. Kids for Life. It's a pro-life group our church started, and now it's all over the country. I mean, that's what I just don't get. It's not like Kerry doesn't know what's right or something. Me and her even picketed with K.F.L. once. And I remember one time when she said she was gonna adopt a whole bunch of babies when she grew up. So they could have a good home and wouldn't end up murdered."

"It's hard to argue with that kind of ambition."

"Yeah, but then she stopped going to K.F.L. and she started talking weird sometimes."

"When was this?"

Sarah wrinkled her brow. "I think it was maybe sometime in January that she stopped going to K.F.L." More than two months ago. "She always came into town on Wednesday nights, that's when K.F.L. meets. Her folks wouldn't let her quit. But she'd just sit up at the diner. Or use the pay phone there to call Monica."

"You don't know why she wanted to quit the group?"

"She wouldn't tell me. Once she started crying when I kept asking her about it. So I just let her alone. I mean, she's my best friend. She'll tell me when she's ready to."

"And when did you two have this fight about the girl who wanted an abortion?"

"Oh, that. Just a coupla days ago." The baby began to fuss. Sarah bounced him up and down and he quieted. She had a good touch with children, firm yet loving. "But I'm not worried about it. Me and Kerry been best friends since seventh grade. She'll get over it."

As I left young Sarah with the two children, I couldn't help but ponder her naive certainty that her views about birth and death were the only correct ones. How convenient it must be to see life with such simplicity, as either all black or all white.

Chances were Kerry Hammond was now learning the world had a few gray tones. Unless she was already beyond learning anything.

I felt sorry for my client's younger sister. Sorry for her probable circumstances and sorry that the friend she'd tried to turn to was Sarah Percival. If Kerry was, indeed, pregnant and trying to get an abortion, she'd certainly come to the wrong place for help. I just hoped a trip to the women's clinic on the wrong day hadn't cost her her life.

7

As I drove back through the main part of town, I spied Mike Hammond once again. He and his two buddies from the diner were busy posting crimson flyers on telephone poles and storefronts up and down Main Street.

I pulled into the curb across the street from the gas station and waited for the youths to move on down the street. When they had rounded the corner and were out of sight, I climbed out of the Honda and read one of the xeroxed signs they'd posted.

EMERGENCY MEETING TONIGHT
Kids for Life and Adults for Life
8 P.M. Community Fundamentalist Church

Because of the recent closing of the St. Cloud Family Planning Clinic, K.F.L. and A.F.L.'s abortion protest campaign will be redirected. Reverend Ed will issue new assignments tonight. All members are expected to attend. New members welcome.

The anti-abortionists certainly weren't wasting any time getting their new show—whatever it was—on the road. And it pissed me off that the tone of the flyer was so misleadingly benign. An uninformed reader would have no clue that the "closing" of the St. Cloud clinic in fact referred to an arson fire in which two women had lost their lives. It also seemed way out of line that plans for the anti-abortionists' next attack were obviously well underway when neither of the murdered women had been laid to rest yet; one of them hadn't even been identified by the police.

I raised my right hand and shaded my eyes against the mid-afternoon sun as I peered down the street. There was almost no pedestrian traffic in town now. It seemed unlikely that these posters would draw much of a crowd to tonight's meeting. But I suspected they were simply the final piece in a well-organized notification campaign. Surely there would be telephone lists and housewives spending their afternoons calling the members to let them know of the changed plans. These flyers were probably designed to attract prospective new members; I wondered what I might learn about Kerry's whereabouts if I attended the meeting. I wanted information about the missing girl, but the thought of going to that meeting made my stomach clench. I felt like an unarmed soldier about to hike through enemy territory.

While I stood thinking about whether I wanted to show up at the meeting, I saw a dark-haired young woman come out of the beauty shop half a block down the street. She glared angrily in the direction in which Mike Hammond and his friends had disappeared. Then she stood for a moment, reading the flyer posted on the front of the building. Suddenly she reached for the red paper, ripped it down, and crushed it into a ball. Then she stomped back inside the shop.

Maybe Newton Prairie had one pro-choice resident after all. Or maybe the woman simply didn't like people posting flyers on her beauty shop.

I crossed the street to the gas station and used the pay phone. Monica Hammond wasn't at her rooming house. I tried the number of the pizza restaurant where she worked.

I held on for a good five minutes before Monica came on

the line, sounding out of breath. "I've only got a minute. They get real mad at us if we use the phone here."

"I'll try to hurry. I just wanted to let you know that Kerry isn't at the farm. Your family thinks she went to that church camp and her best friend thinks she's with you. I'm going to try to find the bus driver, to see if she ever got on that bus heading for Minneapolis. But first I wanted to ask you about a teacher your mother mentioned, a Miss Lundberg."

"Yeah, right, Linda Lundberg, she's the school counselor."

"I told your mother I'd come up here to talk to Kerry about a scholarship application, and she assumed that Linda Lundberg had sent me. She didn't much like that idea, either."

"She wouldn't. My folks don't like Miss Lundberg much. 'Specially since she helped me out that time."

"What time?"

"After they beat me up, and I didn't know where to go. I mean, I didn't even have any place to sleep. So I went to Miss Lundberg's house and she let me stay with her for a while, 'til I came down here. She told my folks she'd report them to the child welfare if they gave me any more trouble."

"She sounds nice."

"She's great." Monica's voice took on a wistful tone. "I wish my mom was more like her."

"Do you think Kerry might have confided in Miss Lundberg? If she was pregnant and wanted an abortion, I mean."

"I—I dunno."

"The reason I ask is that I'd like to talk to Linda Lundberg, to see if she might know where Kerry went. But the thing is, there's no way I can fool her into believing I'm there about a scholarship. The woman is a teacher and guidance counselor and she's not going to buy that story. If I tell her the truth, can we trust her to keep her mouth shut?"

There was a pause on the line. "I already gave table ten their check. Just give me one more second," Monica said to someone in the background. She came back on the line. "I think Miss Lundberg would be cool, if you tell her you're working for me. Just let her know how important it is."

"So I have your permission to tell her?"

"Yeah, sure. Whatever. Just find Kerry real soon, please. I'm worried half to death." There was more commotion on Monica's end of the line. "Sorry, I have to go now or I'll get fired." She put down the receiver and the line went dead.

8

I found Linda Lundberg with a paint brush in her hand, changing the trim on her house to the color of weathered cedar. Her hair was tied up in a navy-and-white bandana and her face was half hidden by a pair of enormous sunglasses.

"Sorry about this," she said, gesturing at her paint-spattered jeans and University of Minnesota sweatshirt. She grinned and dropped the brush back into the paint can. "Every time I get a few days off from school, I seem to spend them trying to keep blight from taking over this place."

"Whatever you're doing, it's obviously working. It all looks wonderful to me." The house was yellow, two stories high, with a big bay window on the second floor. Its black roof looked relatively new, and a used brick chimney jutted up from its peak. The front of the house boasted a covered screened porch that ran the full width of the structure. I felt a pang of envy that a single woman only a few years older than I had managed to buy and maintain a place like this. I consoled myself with the fact that prices in Newton Prairie were far cheaper than in the state capitol. But still, this house had to be worth at least as much as the kind of condo I'd recently been longing for. I made a vow to resume my search for a home I could call my own as soon as I got back to St. Paul.

When I explained that Monica Hammond had sent me, Linda Lundberg invited me inside and offered me a cup of coffee. I waited in the living room while she washed the paint from her hands and made coffee. Despite the traditional look of her house's exterior, she had chosen modern furnishings. I sat on one end of a cream-colored cotton sectional, facing the stone fireplace. The carpeting here was a pale grayish blue that matched the oversized throw pillows on the sofa.

The square oak and glass coffee table in front of me held the most recent issues of *Time* and the *New York Times Book Review,* plus an Anne Tyler novel with a fringed bookmark protruding from its center.

Linda Lundberg came back into the room carrying a tray with a silver coffee carafe, two cups, a sugarbowl, and creamer. Slung around her neck was an old blue bath towel. She'd removed her bandana and brushed out her copper-colored hair, which was cut short to frame her round face. She was not a beautiful woman, and her body was probably two sizes larger than the current style, but her face showed character. I expected she would be considered more and more attractive as she aged. Or is it that society has more relaxed standards of beauty for older women, so more of us manage to qualify?

She put the tray down on the coffee table, then spread the towel on the seat of the sectional across from me. "Don't want to get paint on the furniture," she said, carefully positioning herself on top of the towel. "So, how is Monica these days?" She poured coffee into a flowered china cup and handed it to me. "I often think about her, but I haven't heard from her in months."

"Working in a pizza restaurant near the U and scraping by." I explained my mission to find Kerry Hammond as concisely as I could.

"So you think Kerry went looking for an abortion? Lord, Kerry Hammond is one of the last girls I'd expect to find herself in that kind of trouble. She's always been so studious and quiet, a very pretty girl, but not the kind who seems particularly interested in boys."

"The abortion is one possibility. We're not sure that's what happened. All we really know is that she wasn't on the bus she was supposed to take to Minneapolis and she hasn't been heard from since." I blew gently on my coffee to cool it. "That, plus she told both her sister and Sarah Percival that she was trying to help an underage friend who wanted an abortion. Sarah thinks Kerry meant just what she said—that a friend of hers was in trouble. But Monica suspects her sister might have been talking about herself. Especially in view of what's happened since."

Linda drew a deep breath and exhaled slowly. "I wish I could help you, but Kerry never confided anything in me. I always found her to be very tight-lipped, shy really."

"Well, it was a long shot at best. Monica and I hoped she might have come to you for help. Assuming she really was looking for someone to help her get an abortion."

Linda chewed her lower lip and stared at her hands for a moment before she spoke. "I don't discuss my private views at school, so I suppose some of the students might think I'd be willing to help in that kind of situation . . . that I'm pro-abortion. But the truth is, I'm really not."

I warmed my hands around my cup. "I don't think I've ever met anybody who was."

Linda met my gaze. "Was what?"

"Pro-abortion. It's hardly the same as pro-choice. I've always agreed with Ellen Goodman, the columnist. She says women don't want abortions the way they want a new dress or a weekend in Paris. They want abortions more like an animal caught in a trap wants to gnaw off its own foot."

She smiled. "I see your point, really I do. Still, if Kerry had come to me for my opinion, I would have counseled her to have her baby . . . not to have an abortion."

"I see. Do you belong to this group that's meeting in town tonight? Adults for Life?"

"Lord, no." She drained her coffee cup and put it back

on the tray. "Look, my personal views are my personal views. I guess you could call me a raging moderate. What I mean is that I can't think of any circumstances under which I would have an abortion myself, but I certainly don't believe in harassing women who think differently. And I don't think abortion should be made illegal, either. I'm old enough to remember what happened when getting an abortion was against the law."

"Me, too. But the fact is that abortion *is* virtually illegal in Minnesota for girls like Kerry, who can't get their parents' help. Look, *I* wouldn't want to face the Hammonds. Look what they did to Monica."

"More coffee?" Linda offered. I declined, pleading a low tolerance for caffeine, but she poured herself a second cup. "Look, I can sympathize with pregnant teens, but even if I felt differently about abortion, there's no way I could stick my neck out to help them, not when doing that's illegal. I'd be fired in a minute, and lucky if they didn't prosecute me."

"You're probably right."

"But don't misunderstand me. I think the Hammonds' child-rearing techniques are atrocious. They run their home like some kind of fascist state. In my opinion, there's nothing much worse for children, except maybe total neglect."

"It always amazes me how people can abuse their kids and then rationalize that it's for their own good."

"You got that right." Linda smoothed the blue towel with her right hand. "I try to do what I can to help when I see that one of our students has an abusive home situation. But I can't step over that legal line. When Monica came to me for help, it was the Hammonds who were breaking the law, not me. So there wasn't really much they could do to me."

"Except maybe complain to the principal."

"Yeah, well, they could have. But I threatened them with the child welfare people if they didn't back off."

"So Monica told me. She was really grateful to you."

Linda's face broke into a broad grin. "I was happy to help. I've got plenty of room here."

"Does the high school give the kids any sex education?" I asked.

Linda rolled her brown eyes skyward and sighed. "Wish we did. But the school board doesn't want to fight people like A.F.L., so they ignore the issue. There's a group of us teachers who keep telling the board that we've got to take a stand on this. If we don't teach our students about sex and birth control, we're going to get more pregnant students. More doomed teenage marriages. More abortions. Maybe even AIDS one of these days. 'Cause the fact is that the parents just aren't educating their children about sex or condoms or anything."

"Do you know a young man named Lucas Drew?"

"Sure, Luke grew up in Newton Prairie, went to school here. I had him in my sophomore composition class. But he doesn't live in Newton Prairie anymore."

"Somebody told me he used to be Kerry's boyfriend."

Linda picked up a paper napkin and wiped an invisible spot off the coffee table. "Now that you mention it, I do remember seeing Kerry and Luke together after school once or twice, but he graduated last year, so they were never like some of the students who pair off constantly in the halls." She laughed indulgently. "You know, I get to feeling like the sex police sometimes, the way I have to tell some of these kids to stop pawing each other in public or serve detention hours."

I was a schoolteacher myself once, before my son Danny died and I could no longer face being around small children all day. "One possibility is that Kerry followed Lucas . . . to wherever he moved. Particularly if she found out she was pregnant after he'd already left town. Or maybe even if she wasn't having his baby; she could have figured she'd be able to get him back if she went after him. Only thing is, I don't know why she wouldn't have let her sister know . . ."

"Could've been too embarrassed. Or maybe she figured she'd let her family know where she was after she and Lucas were already married."

"Married at sixteen. What are the chances of that succeeding?" I shook my head. "Look, Linda, do you have an address for Lucas? I'd really like to contact him and see if he knows where Kerry is. You could save me a lot of legwork."

"I can probably get it. I'll call his mother right now and tell her I've got something to send him from school, or that we're updating our alumni mailing list or something."

"I'd really appreciate it, and I know Monica would, too."

"Hey, whatever I can do to help." She left the room for a few minutes. When she returned, she told me, "Nobody answered. I'll try again later."

"Thanks." I put my empty coffee cup on the tray, crumpled my napkin and tossed it inside the cup. "Think for minute, will you? What if a girl from Newton Prairie were pregnant and afraid to tell her parents? Is there some way she could get an abortion without letting them know?"

"I don't think so. Not anymore."

"What do you mean, not anymore?"

"Well, there was one girl last year, Kitty Sue Boswell. She was fourteen and she found somebody to abort her. Only problem was, he didn't do such a hot job." Linda shuddered visibly. "Poor kid bled to death. Her parents found her in her bed the next morning, unconscious in a pool of her own blood."

"Christ."

"She died later that day."

"Tell me they caught the guy."

"To tell the truth, I'm not sure. I remember a few weeks later a former army medic was arrested in St. Cloud for performing abortions on underage girls. But I don't know if they ever convicted him for Kitty Sue's death."

"So she could've gone to somebody else."

"Could have. But I hope not."

So did I. I thanked Linda and told her I'd call her tomorrow for Lucas's address.

"Fine, I'll try to call Mrs. Drew for it again tonight."

I pulled one of my cards from my purse and handed it to her. "If I don't reach you tomorrow, or if you have any other thoughts about Kerry Hammond, please call me."

Linda Lundberg took the card and put it into her jeans pocket. She held my hand firmly for a moment at the door. "I really do hope you find Kerry. And that she's safe. God, she's so young."

But not too young to die, I thought, as I walked back to my car.

9

It was dark by the time I arrived at Community Fundamentalist Church. The parking lot was nearly filled, mainly with older American cars and an assortment of pickup trucks. The building wasn't large as churches go, but Newton Prairie wasn't a large town. It was one story, made of tan bricks with a massive lighted cross rising from the center of the peaked roof.

As I entered the double glass doors, handwritten signs directed me away from the main chapel and down a flight of carpeted stairs to a community room in the basement. There I found rows of white folding chairs, with an aisle down the center, all facing a podium at the front of the room. Behind the podium was a huge poster fastened to the wall with masking tape. At first glance, the photo on the poster reminded me of the head of an ancient man. But I quickly realized it portrayed instead a fetus that had been severed in two. In large red letters across the top of the poster were the words: "Abortion Kills Babies."

About half the seats in the room were already taken. I sat on the left side toward the back, where I could see those already seated and watch to see who came in, yet, I hoped, remain inconspicuous.

After a few minutes, a heavy blonde woman in a brown

tent dress with a ruffled hem took the chair to my right. "You're new here," she said, her massive hips crowding into me as she sat down. I shifted as far to the left on my seat as I could.

So much for my remaining inconspicuous. "I saw the posters in town and thought I'd come and see what this is all about."

"Praise Jesus."

I nodded, unsure of the proper response.

"A.F.L. always needs new members," the woman confided. "With thousands of poor little babies dying every day in all them abortion mills, the good Lord needs every soldier he can get to save 'em. This is war, y'know."

"Hmm." I found it difficult to remain noncommittal, but starting an argument in these surroundings wouldn't help me or my client. "I don't know whether I'll want to join yet. I only came to hear what this is all about."

The woman smiled broadly, reached over and squeezed my hand. "Just wait 'til you hear Reverend Ed speak, dear. That man can convince anybody of the need. He speaks with our dear Lord's own words."

"That so?" I extricated my hand from the woman's damp grasp, but she didn't seem offended. I'm not big on body contact, at least not with total strangers.

"Are you saved?"

"What?" I stared at the dark mole on her left cheek.

"Are you saved? Have you accepted Jesus Christ as your personal savior?" The mole bounced up and down as she spoke.

"Uh—" I felt a tightening sensation around my throat. What was the right answer? If I said yes, I might become embroiled in a conversation I couldn't carry on adequately. If I said no, I feared I would be seen as the enemy. I tried changing the subject, but my attempt was pretty feeble. "Goodness, it's already five minutes past starting time."

"I didn't think you were saved, dear. The Bible says there are only two kinds of people in the world, the saved and the unsaved. Only the saved go to heaven. But it's not too late.

I'll pray for you." And she actually did, right then and there. The woman bent her head and closed her eyes and I could see her lips moving rhythmically. I was relieved that I couldn't hear her words. After a minute or two, she raised her head and opened her eyes. "Jesus loves you, my dear." There was no doubt in her voice and her face now wore a glow, a look of complete happiness. She'd done her good deed for the day, done her best to save one more soul.

I asked myself how I could be frightened by someone so ready to pray for my salvation. Yet I was. The zealots in the Crusades probably prayed for people's souls, too, right before they executed them for heresy.

I wondered what would happen if I revealed myself as a feminist, a believer in allowing every woman complete choice and control over her own body? Would she and her fellow A.F.L. members resort to something stronger than prayer to convert me to their thinking? Certainly somebody had resorted to violence at that St. Cloud clinic a couple of nights ago.

I breathed an audible sigh of relief when my companion spotted some people she knew across the aisle and excused herself to speak to them. I shifted back into the middle of my chair and plopped my purse on the seat next to mine. With luck, it would act as a barrier, protecting my personal space.

I noticed Mike Hammond enter the room with the other two young men who had helped him with the posters. The youth with the black-rimmed glasses led the way toward the front of the room, as a dozen pairs of eyes followed the trio's progress. Mike paused for a moment to speak with a thin, gray-haired man seated on the aisle. The woman next to the man turned her head and I recognized Mary Hammond. So the man with her had to be her husband, Herman Hammond. But Mike didn't sit with his parents. He and his cronies removed a white satin ribbon cordoning off the front row and sat there. It was clear that they rated a place of honor.

Little Sarah Percival came in soon afterward, accompanied

by two other teenage girls. Apparently her baby-sitting job
had lasted only for the afternoon. The three chose seats
halfway toward the front. Wanda Kirchner, the girl I'd met
at the diner, did not come, nor did her two friends. Maybe
they were too busy with the "stud" from baseball practice.

Suddenly the air was pierced by music. A recording of
"What a Friend We Have in Jesus" blared from the loud-
speakers at the front of the room. Everyone still standing
scrambled for seats and a number of people began to sing
along. I counted nearly sixty people in attendance.

As the tune ended and the music died away, a huge man
with a full head of white hair rushed down the center aisle,
his long black robes billowing behind him. The famous Reverend Ed must have been six feet six and weighed two-fifty.
"Praise the Lord!" he shouted. Everybody stood up. When
the preacher reached the podium, he raised his hands, palms
downward, then slowly lowered them to his thighs. In unison, the crowd took their seats.

"We have work to do, my friends. The Lord's work." Reverend Ed's cadence was that of an old time revivalist
preacher or a southern politician. I would have thought it
a bit flashy for rural Minnesota, but the crowd ate it up.
Reverend Ed's hands flew in the air like a couple of hyper-
active birds. Gold rings on at least two fingers of each hand
flashed in the overhead lights as he shouted, "We must not,
we cannot rest."

"Hallelujah," said the crowd.

"As we come together here tonight, as we pray together
for divine guidance, our hearts cry out. We weep for the
children, the babies who are dying by the hundreds of thousands. We give our solemn vow that children like this dear
little one will never be forgotten." He grasped a Bible in one
hand and waved the other at the poster behind him, sounding near tears. As the sleeve of his robe fell back, I spotted
a heavy gold bracelet circling his right wrist. "Jesus asks,
Jesus *demands* that we stop this holocaust."

"Praise Jesus."

"We gathered here tonight have the ability, we have the

means, we have the *will* to save these precious young lives, my friends. We know it takes sacrifice. And we must sacrifice . . . until we bleed our veins dry with the effort. But we do not despair. When Judgment Day comes, my fellow Christians, we will be prepared. The Lord our God will not forsake us."

"Amen."

I wondered how the crowd knew the proper responses. I mean, who told them when to shout "Hallelujah" instead of "Praise Jesus" or "Amen"? Maybe they were cued by Reverend Ed's many hand signals, movements that certainly drew the eye, but which I couldn't interpret.

From behind his podium, Reverend Ed produced four wooden baskets lined with crimson satin. He handed one each to Mike Hammond, his two friends, and another young man in the front row. "Due to recent events, my dear friends, we must now take our message farther from home. Our buses will not run on prayer alone. They need gasoline. The presses will not print on good intentions alone. It costs dollars to produce and mail our message proclaiming God's word. Dig deep into your pockets and give as generously as you can."

"Hallelujah."

These were plain working folks for the most part, farmers and small-town merchants and their wives and children. Yet when the offering basket reached me, it contained mostly twenty-dollar bills, even a couple of fifties.

I begrudgingly put in a dollar. I didn't want to be conspicuous by putting nothing in the basket, but I didn't want to be responsible for putting too much gas in those buses, either. Assuming that the money would really go for gas. I suspected that a good percentage might go straight into Reverend Ed's pocket. Who knew when he'd need another gold bracelet. Or more padding in a Swiss bank account. After all, what I was seeing here tonight was just the tip of the iceberg. As Sarah Percival had told me, K.F.L. and A.F.L. were national organizations, with the flamboyant Reverend Ed at the helm.

The meeting lasted another half hour, during which Reverend Ed preached diligence against just about every liberal thinking group out there—not only the reviled abortionists, but feminists, gays, Communists, and children who didn't follow their parents' and the Bible's teachings. The longer he spoke, the more alienated I felt.

Finally, the minister announced the cancellation of the previous arrangements to picket at the St. Cloud clinic. If he offered a prayer for the souls of the two women who had died in the clinic fire—or even mentioned their passing—I must have missed it. Still, there was no admission of any complicity by Adults for Life or Kids for Life in the fire. No attempt to take credit for ridding the world of evil. The arson was presented as nothing more than an act of God, an example of God's vengeance against those black souls who would kill babies.

St. Cloud might be out, but Reverend Ed had no intention of allowing his anti-abortion forces to rest on their laurels. He outlined new plans to picket a family planning clinic in Minneapolis two days hence. He requested volunteers to make the trip, telling them to come forward and give their names. His wife, Helen, a six-footer with salt-and-pepper hair drawn back into a severe bun, stood ready to take their names and hand out assignments.

Volunteering seemed to pose no problem for these folks. I might have been the only one in the room not clambering to sign up for one of the buses. No doubt about it, Reverend Ed was preaching to the choir here. I could feel the energy level in this room and recognized that most of these people saw this mission as the most important effort of their entire lives. They identified themselves as soldiers in a religious war against abortion and homosexuals and women who didn't keep to their proper place. They believed they were truly "saving lives." And I didn't doubt for a minute that most of them would be willing to die in their holy war if they became convinced that their God wanted them to. But would they also be willing to kill the enemy?

I asked myself whether Kerry Hammond could have been

a member of this group, whether she could have believed
in their mission, and then turned around and tried to find
an abortionist to solve her own problem pregnancy. Certainly, she wouldn't have been the first person to change her
mind when an abstract moral concept actually hit home. But
I really couldn't know the answer.

All I knew was that she was missing, and I began to wonder
whether she might have confided in the wrong person in
Newton Prairie. Might someone in this room have impris-
oned her somewhere, perhaps even killed her, to keep her
from submitting to the mortal sin of abortion?

No, I told myself, even these people couldn't be that il-
logical, that fanatic. Or could they?

As the others scrambled toward the front of the room to
sign up for the Minneapolis-bound buses, I sneaked out the
door and up the stairs to the parking lot.

10

I sat in my Honda, watching people emerge from the
church, get into their cars, and exit the parking lot. The fat
woman who had prayed for my soul wedged herself behind
the wheel of an old Chevy and drove off. Sarah Percival and
her friends waited on the church steps for a few minutes
until a man I assumed was one of the girls' fathers came to
pick them up. Mr. and Mrs. Hammond left together, without
Mike. Finally, the parking lot was empty except for my
Honda, two other cars, a van, and a truck.

Reverend Ed's wife, Helen, came through the church door
alone, carrying her notebook, and got into the passenger
seat of a dark red, recent model Cadillac. It was clearly the

most expensive car in the parking lot. She sat and waited. Apparently the preacher was still busy inside, but his wife's presence was no longer required.

When ten minutes had passed and neither Reverend Ed nor Mike Hammond and his cronies had emerged from the church, I got curious. I drove out of the parking lot and left the Honda on the street about half a block away from the church. Then I doubled back and sneaked through the parking lot on foot, doing my best to avoid letting Helen see me. I crept through the thick darkness surrounding the church and around the side of the building.

Light from the basement windows of the meeting room cut slivers across the dormant brown grass of the church-yard. But a glance down through one of the windows showed me that the room's only inhabitant now was an elderly janitor with a push broom. I spied a particularly bright rectangle of light glowing from the back of the low brick building, though. I walked toward it across the damp, spongy ground, being careful not to intrude into the light and reveal my presence to anyone inside.

The illuminated window belonged to an office. I could see an oversized walnut desk and walnut-paneled walls in-side. Reverend Ed sat at the desk in a high-backed burgundy leather chair, facing the window. Behind him was a massive oil painting of Jesus Christ, his long fingers tented in a po-sition of prayer. The portrait served to make the big minister look even more imposing.

Seated across the desk from Reverend Ed on wine-colored velvet upholstered chairs were Mike Hammond, the guy with the eyeglasses, the one with the Adam's apple, and a fourth man, who sported a thatch of carrot-red hair. The four all had their backs to me. The night was cool and the office window was closed so that, from where I stood, I could see Ed's mouth moving and his fist occasionally pounding the desktop, but I could not make out what he was saying.

I stole closer to the window and stood with my back against the building, near the edge of the window frame. From this position, I could no longer see into the room without moving into the wedge of light and risking being seen by Reverend Ed, but I could hear better. At least the preacher's booming voice now came through loud and clear.

"—crazy enough to torch a clinic, I don't want to hear about it!" he yelled. "I *do not* want to know. As far as I am aware, A.F.L. and K.F.L had nothing to do with that business. *Nothing!* And that's the way it's going to stay. Understand?"

There was a low, rumbling sound, probably someone else speaking, but I couldn't make out his words. The others had their backs to the window and their voices didn't have the resonance of Ed's.

"I don't care!" Ed replied. "You think I'm going to risk my whole operation because one of you little twerps gets trigger happy?"

More rumblings.

"That's better. Now, I'm dog-tired, and this meeting is over. Let me leave you with one thought, my young friends, and only one thought. *I* run this organization. *Me,* Reverend Ed Beale, pastor of Community Fundamentalist Church. That means I call the shots, *all* of them. From now on, you boys don't take a leak around here 'til I tell you to. Got it?"

Apparently they got it. There was a little more rumbling, then the window went dark.

I scurried back toward the front of the church, just in time to stand in the shadows and watch the four young men emerge. Mike and the two poster hangers got into a vintage Volkswagen beetle with a shiny pumpkin-colored paint job. The guy with the eyeglasses was behind the wheel. The fourth youth climbed into a Ford pickup.

Reverend Ed emerged last, locking the glass doors behind him. Apparently the janitor slept in the church, or else he would leave by another door. Ed climbed in beside his wife and, without a word to her, started the Cadillac's engine and sped out of the parking lot.

I waited until they'd all left before heading toward the road and my own car.

11

The main street of town was nearly deserted now. Newton Prairie had no barroom, a fact that probably sent most people who lived here home fairly early. The only sign of life was a few night owls in Bud's Diner. At suppertime, I'd eaten an order of Bud's fried chicken and had to admit it tasted pretty good. It sure beat the dismal lunch I'd had there earlier in the day. It was no mystery why people like Sam love grease so much. Too bad it tends to hit human arteries like quick-drying cement.

As I drove down Main Street, I saw a figure emerge from the beauty shop, key in hand. I recognized the dark-haired woman I'd seen there earlier in the day. As she put her key in the door lock, I pulled into the curb behind a parked Dodge station wagon and got out of my car.

"Hi there. Wondered if I could ask you a few questions."

"Maybe. I guess so. About what?" The woman was a couple of inches shorter than I am, probably about five feet five or six, with regular features. At closer range, her black hair looked too dark for her complexion. If she'd left it her natural color, she'd probably have looked about twenty-five; with the black shoe polish effect, she appeared closer to thirty.

"I'm Devon MacDonald, from St. Paul," I told her. "I didn't have anything to do tonight and I was sort of curious, so I went to that anti-abortion rally up at the church." I forced a laugh. Keep it light, Devon. "Truth is, I've never been to anything quite like that before." The woman watched me with what looked like interest, but she didn't speak. "I couldn't help but notice earlier that you tore down the meeting poster from your storefront, and—"

"Yeah, what of it? It's my shop, ain't it?"

"Hey, sure it's your shop. Listen, I'd've done the same thing if they tried to put one of those signs up on my business."

She relaxed a little. "Sorry, didn't mean to snap at you. Been a long day, with the payroll to get out and all. My name's Tammy Myers."

"Glad to meet you, Tammy. Listen, you've obviously got roots in this town, and maybe you and I think alike about a few things. What can you tell me about this Reverend Ed and his anti-abortion organizations?"

"Why do you want to know?"

"Just curious, I guess. I wondered what they're up to."

"Like what?"

No way was she going to make it easy for me. "Look, Tammy, what I want to know is how many people around here belong to A.F.L. and K.F.L.? How many members do they have nationwide? Ever hear about any violence they might be connected to? That sort of thing."

"I—I can't tell you about that kinda stuff. Alls I know is, if I were you, I'd stay away from Ed. He comes across like a good man, a Christian and all, but—Well, he ain't necessarily everything he seems."

"What do you mean, Tammy?"

I heard a car engine behind me and saw Tammy's eyes leave my face and dart over my shoulder. A look of fear spread across her face. As I turned and followed her gaze, the two of us were caught for a moment in the glare of low slung headlights slowly approaching.

"I—I gotta go," she said, clutching her purse and hurrying toward the Dodge. She started the station wagon's engine and pealed away from the curb while I stood watching.

The car whose headlights had pinned us against the beauty shop passed me at a snail's pace, then drove in the same direction Tammy had gone.

It was the orange VW bug.

12

I wasn't sure I would learn a great deal more about Kerry Hammond's whereabouts here in Newton Prairie, but I had one vital task left to accomplish. I planned to be at the bus stop outside Bud's Diner by ten-fifteen the next morning to meet the daily bus to Minneapolis. There was always a chance that the bus driver might remember whether Kerry Hammond had gotten on his bus and, if she had, where or with whom she got off.

I took a room at the Sleepytime Motel. A half mile out on the county road, it was the only motel anywhere near Newton Prairie. My bed sagged in the middle and there were brown iron stains from hard water in the sink and bathtub, but at twenty-four dollars single, the price at the Sleepytime was right.

Stripped to my bra and panties, I lay in bed with my back bent into a comma for what seemed hours. Sporadic traffic passed by on the old county road outside my window, but it wasn't the noise that kept me from sleeping. It was my churning thoughts.

I couldn't shake the feeling that there was something going on in Newton Prairie that went far beyond my first impression. Something sinister. I had a hunch that, as Tammy Myers had warned me, Reverend Ed Beale and his Christian organizations weren't quite what they seemed. At least it was obvious that the big minister's anti-abortion enterprises paid him well; he certainly didn't drive a Cadillac and deck himself out in gaudy jewelry on his salary as pastor of Community Fundamentalist Church.

But, then, he wasn't the first minister to get rich preaching that others should sacrifice. Witness Jim Bakker and Jimmy

Swaggart and the rest of the televangelists. Certainly there was a fortune to be made from all the gullible believers out there. So Reverend Ed had found a way to proselytize and profit without his own personal broadcast audience; he simply used the U.S. Mail.

Although I might find Reverend Ed's enterprise distasteful, I reminded myself that there was nothing necessarily illegal about it. And it was a far stretch from greed to murder. Profiting from the anti-abortion movement didn't necessarily make him a terrorist.

I thought a lot about the snippets of conversation I'd overheard coming from the minister's office. My instincts told me that one or more of the young men in the minister's inner circle had been involved in the St. Cloud clinic firebombing, and that Reverend Ed's reaction to the news showed he hadn't liked the idea. But what I'd overheard was no real proof of anything.

And maybe my instincts were wrong. Perhaps one of the young men had merely expressed admiration for whoever torched the clinic and Reverend Ed had responded by warning his own followers to keep their matches in their pockets.

Truth was, these people were alien to me, both too simple and too complex to analyze. I didn't understand how they thought. I had no way to judge, for instance, whether Reverend Ed truly believed in the cause that brought him wealth, or if he was a complete charlatan. Or maybe something in between.

I realized with a shiver that, if the men from her church found out about Kerry Hammond's pregnancy, she might actually be better off if they were total phonies. True religious fanatics had been known to kill or imprison in the name of their cause, while money grubbers were more likely to stick to efforts where they could turn a shady profit.

The fact that Kerry Hammond's brother was so active in the group I'd visited tonight bothered me, too. Yet I couldn't decide exactly what that boiled down to. Had Mike Hammond followed his sister to St. Cloud? If so, could he really have been cold-hearted enough to torch the abortion clinic while she was trapped inside? I just couldn't buy that. The kid might be a budding misogynist, but Kerry was his sister. Surely, that had to count for something.

Assuming that Mike really had helped torch the clinic, it seemed more logical that Kerry's presence there that night was a bizarre coincidence.

It was also possible that Mike himself had not participated in the St. Cloud firebombing, but that one or more of Reverend Ed's other protégés had. The pimply-faced Hammond boy might well be applauding the act of terrorism without realizing that his sister could well be one of its victims.

If, of course, Kerry Hammond really was at the abortion clinic the night it was hit. I reminded myself not to jump to that conclusion. Sam still didn't have an ID on the second fire victim, and she might not turn out to be Kerry at all.

There had to be a better than even chance that Kerry never went to that clinic in St. Cloud. The girl could have found a back alley abortionist to do the job, someone who wouldn't give a hoot about her age if she had enough money to pay him. Or maybe she was never actually pregnant in the first place; the story about a "friend" might be true. My head began to ache with all the possiblities.

I finally fell asleep after convincing myself that I'd been looking so hard for some kind of crime that I'd let my imagination run away with me. Reverend Ed was probably just a small-town pastor who'd found a way to make a buck on the side; he wasn't necessarily a figure of evil. His inner circle was undoubtedly nothing more than a handful of young men going nowhere in a no-account town, young men who'd gotten drunk on their first sip of power. Tammy Myers hadn't really been frightened away by the orange VW; she'd simply found me nosy and pushy, so she used the passing car as a handy excuse to get away from me. And Kerry Hammond had probably gone off with a friend and forgotten to notify her sister; she would soon turn up safe and sound, with a logical if irritating explanation for where she'd been the last few days.

In the morning, I stood for a long time under the stinging hot needles of the shower, until the muscles in my back unkinked and I began to feel human again. At least the Sleepytime had a generously large water heater. I used the toothbrush and toothpaste I'd bought yesterday at the Newton Prairie market and dressed in the same light wool pants and jacket I'd worn when I came to town. Someday I may learn to pack for an overnight stay every time I leave town, but I haven't yet. So I'm frequently stuck wearing the same outfit I wore the previous day.

I pulled my long reddish blonde hair back into a ponytail, clipped it low on my neck, and applied what little makeup I carry in my purse. There, I thought, inspecting myself in the mirror. I would pass muster, at least for Newton Prairie. Luckily, I was a long way from New York or Paris and the standards of beauty here were achievably low.

I gathered together my things, tossed my room key onto the old mahogany dresser, and emerged into the early morning sunshine. As I walked toward the Honda, I caught my breath. The poor old car was listing to one side and resting hard on its wheel rims.

I darted forward and dropped to my knees next to the Honda. Someone had slashed all four tires.

I felt almost as if an old friend had been violated, and all my negative thoughts of the night before came back in a rush. Frightened, I realized I was marooned here, at least for the moment. I looked around the parking lot, but saw no one watching or waiting for me. I breathed a little easier.

Still, someone had sent me a clear message.

13

As I walked the half mile into town, I felt certain I knew who had tried to intimidate me by carving up my tires. It had to be one of the young men in Mike Hammond's tight little group. Nobody else would have any reason to vandalize my property. And I found the idea that I'd been the victim of random vandalism too bizarre to consider seriously.

I had more trouble figuring out exactly *why* Mike and his cronies had it in for me. Had they discovered that I'd eavesdropped on their meeting with Reverend Ed and thought I overheard more than I actually did? It was certainly possible they thought I knew something that could implicate them in the St. Cloud clinic fire and the murders of the women inside, and thus were warning me to back off.

Helen Beale could have seen me sneak around the back of the church and then told her husband about it. He could have let the others know sometime afterward—somehow I couldn't quite picture the huge minister bent in two, slicing up my tires himself.

Or maybe it was just my empty Honda parked down the street from the church that had sent somebody's imagination into overdrive. Mike Hammond would have known it was my car; he saw me driving it away from his family's farm earlier in the day.

On the other hand, the reason for my ruined tires might be far less ominous than somebody's fear that I could implicate him in arson and murder. It could be as simple as my being labeled a "women's libber" after my visit to the Hammond farm, plus my attending the anti-abortion rally last night. That sequence of events could well be enough for those young punks to figure I was a spy for the enemy camp and, therefore, a fair target.

My conversation with Tammy Myers outside her beauty shop after the meeting could have worried them, too. Did Tammy have something to tell that somebody in that orange VW didn't want revealed?

To tell the truth, warning me off—for whatever reason—was precisely the wrong tactic for those young hoodlums to use with me. My ruined tires only made me that much more curious to find out what they were up to. But I reminded myself that I hadn't come to Newton Prairie to find out who firebombed the abortion clinic, unless it had some connection with Kerry Hammond's disappearance.

I decided I could poke around in those ashes later, if I had time, but finding Monica's sister had to come first on my agenda. Which meant I had to be at the bus stop in less than an hour, or I'd have to wait another full day to talk to the bus driver.

I stopped at both gas stations and talked to the attendants. The first place didn't normally sell tires but, under the circumstances, the owner said he could special order me a set from St. Cloud; it would take two or three days to arrive. That was not my idea of a great option.

The second station had what I was looking for, at highway robbery prices. I found this option only slightly more attractive than the first, but I was in no position to haggle. I handed over my MasterCard and reluctantly signed a receipt for well over six hundred bucks. I consoled myself with the knowledge that at least I was lucky to drive a Honda and not a Cadillac like Reverend Ed's. Tires for a monster like his probably would've set me back a cool grand at this place.

It was almost ten by the time I reached the bus stop outside Bud's Diner. An elderly woman was standing there alone, a Dayton's shopping bag and a brown suitcase with wheels and a leash nestled close to her low-heeled, navy blue Enna Jetticks.

"You goin' down to the Cities, too, dear?" she asked me,

her right hand twisting a button on her lightweight navy coat.

"No, ma'am, I just need to talk to the bus driver."

A look of confusion crossed her wrinkled features, but she was too well bred to press me for an explanation.

The bus pulled up right on time and rested at the curb, belching inky black diesel fumes into the cool morning air. I waited while the driver, a thin man whose youthful, unlined face was at odds with his balding head, stowed the old woman's suitcase under the passenger section of the vehicle. He checked her ticket and helped her slow ascent up the three steep stairs leading to the bus's interior. The driver wore a plastic nametag pinned to his maroon uniform that identified him as Eldon Reedy, Transportation Supervisor. I looked around, but couldn't spot anyone he might be supervising.

"You drive this route last Monday, Mr. Reedy?" I asked him as soon as the old woman was out of earshot.

"You bet, ever' Monday to Friday."

"Good, then maybe you can help me." I pulled Kerry Hammond's photograph from my purse. "This girl was supposed to get on here on Monday and get off in Minneapolis. You recognize her?"

He took the picture from me and considered it carefully. "She in trouble or somethin'?"

"I certainly hope not. Problem is, she never made it to Minneapolis, and her family's worried sick."

"Ran away from home, huh?"

"They don't think so. They're more frightened that something happened to her between here and there."

He tilted the photo toward the sun. "Hmm, dunno what to tell ya. Girl looks familiar, but I couldn't swear to nothin'."

"I'll settle for your best guess." I shot him a pleading look. "It's really important."

He handed the photo back to me. "Monday, huh? Lemme jes think a minute." He ran a hand over what was left of his fine, light hair. "That's the day before the big rain, right?"

"Uh huh."

"Thought so. It was cloudin' up pretty good on Monday. Let's see. 'Member I had two little kids ridin' unaccompanied from Fergus Falls clear to Minneapolis that day. Company offers the unaccompanied minor service and the parents like it—visits to divorced dads or grandma and grandpa, that sort of thing. But it's us drivers that gotta keep them kids from gettin' themselves hurt or tearin' the bus apart. These two were a coupla real terrors, too, lemme tell ya. Runnin' up and down the aisle like they were at some school playground."

"I can see where that kind of thing would be hard on the drivers." I showed him the photo again. "Were you having trouble with those kids when this girl got on?"

Reedy chewed on his lip. "Yup, that's it. Now I remember her. Just didn't recognize her at first from this picture. Had her hair different, I think."

"Good. She got on here?"

"Yup. Had a ticket all the way to Minneapolis, just like them little boys. Then I 'member she sat down with 'em in the back of the bus there and told 'em a story for near an hour."

"But she didn't ride all the way to Minneapolis?"

"Nope. Asked me, could she use the first part of her ticket, just as far as St. Cloud, then take a later bus the rest of the way."

"So she got off in St. Cloud."

"Yup. Company policy says she shoulda bought two tickets, one from Newton Prairie to St. Cloud, and a second one from St. Cloud to Minneapolis. Company makes more that way. But this girl was such a big help with them kids, I fixed her ticket for her."

"Hey, thanks, Mr. Reedy. You've been a big help yourself."

"You bet. Just hope she's okay. Don't like to think about nothin' bad happenin', not to a nice kid like that."

I didn't like to think about it, either, but Kerry's having gotten off the bus in St. Cloud was definitely not a good sign. It made her sister Monica's initial fear—that Kerry had been killed in the clinic fire—all that much more plausible.

14

I had a plate of scrambled eggs and hash browns at Bud's, then picked up my newly shod Honda at the gas station and headed for St. Cloud.

I wandered through the bus station, Kerry's photograph in my hand, asking people who worked there if they remembered seeing her. The shoe shine man leaned back in his imitation leather chair and sneered at me. "Whadya think, lady, I got nothin' better to do than remember every chick comes through this joint?"

I moved on.

I was batting zero after talking to the ticket seller, a popcorn vendor, and the matron who cleaned the women's room. My last hope seemed to be the guy at the newspaper stand.

He squinted at Kerry's picture. "Pretty little thing, ain't she? When was this little gal s'posed to be here?" he asked.

"Monday morning, about eleven, eleven-fifteen. Might've been here again later that day or the next, too, catching another bus out."

"Sorry, I don't remember seeing her myself, but ya might ask Molly. She was on all day Monday."

"Okay, where do I find Molly?"

"That's her over there, on her break. The dark-haired gal eating the popcorn." He pointed across the waiting room to a middle-aged woman wearing a green plaid shirt and black pants. She sat on one of the tan plastic chairs, reading a paperback book she held open in one hand. Her other hand busily plucked pieces of popcorn from a large box she had wedged between her knees and shoved them, several at a time, into her mouth.

"Thanks." I crossed over and took the seat next to hers. "Molly?"

She looked up at me and swallowed, then dusted some stray popcorn crumbs from her chin. They fell onto her black pants, making them appear lint-covered. "Yeah?"

"Hi, I'm Devon MacDonald. Your co-worker at the newsstand thought you might be able to help me out."

"Sure, what is it?" I showed her Kerry's picture and explained my quest for information. Molly placed a bookmark in her book—a battered copy of Jack Olsen's *Predator*—and concentrated on the photograph. "Another blonde, huh?"

"What do you mean?"

"There was somebody came around a couple of months ago, looking for a teenage girl. She was a blonde, too."

"Do you know if they ever found her?"

" 'Fraid not, but I've been keeping my eye out ever since."

"Find out anything?"

Molly put the popcorn box on the floor and grimaced. "God, but there's a lot of real sickos out there, you know. Guys like this one—" She waved her book in the air. "Like that Ted Bundy fellow, the Hillside Strangler, Manson and his crazy bunch of druggies. We've even had one or two of these psychos around these parts. Can't get away from them." She leaned closer, as if to confide a secret. "Got to tell you, I worry about all these young girls, traveling by themselves, the way they do nowadays. It's not safe."

I suspected Molly might be reading too many true crime books, but I didn't say so. "You're saying that men hang out here in the bus depot, waiting to pick off girls like this one?"

"Can't say that for sure; it's just that I've been keeping my eye out since that fellow came through looking for that other girl." She picked up the popcorn box and held it out to me. "Here, want some?"

"No, thanks. I just ate."

"Only thing I've really seen around here that looks odd is six, maybe seven different girls about the age of the one you're looking for. They get off their bus and stand around here, waiting for somebody to meet them—"

"And?"

"Well, the thing is, it isn't just men who meet them, so it's probably all right. Sometimes it's a woman alone comes to get them, sometimes it's this woman along with either another woman or a man."

"Always the same woman?"

"Almost always, anyway. The thing is, you can tell by watching them, none of these girls know the person who's meeting them by sight. I mean, it's not like they're watching out for their grandma or aunt or somebody they're going to recognize."

"Any idea what it's all about?"

Molly put a piece of popcorn into her mouth and chewed it slowly. "If it was a man meeting them, I'd figure he was probably a pimp looking for new girls to put on the streets. Or maybe a rapist who'd figured out some way to lure naive young farm girls to the city. But, I don't know. Maybe these kids are just coming to a local girls' school, or maybe they're here to take a look at St. Cloud State or something. Probably wouldn't even notice them, except for that guy who came around looking for the other girl."

Or except for reading so many books like the one she was reading today, I thought. Molly impressed me as a woman with an active imagination. "What about this particular girl, then, Molly?" I held up Kerry's photo once more. "She look at all familiar to you?"

"Can't say for sure. So many people come through here. She looks like somebody I might've seen, but so many of these kids look alike to me these days." She laughed. "Guess I'm getting old, to have to admit that."

"How about if this girl had a different hairdo? Think you might recognize her if she had her hair tied up in a ponytail or something?"

Molly shook her head. "Sorry. Just can't say one way or the other. Look, I'll keep my eye out for you, give you a call if I see her. Will that help?" She sounded eager to take on the task.

"Sure, thanks, that's nice of you." I handed Molly one of my cards.

"Private investigator, huh?" Molly looked impressed.

"That's me."

"Must be exciting, huh? Finding missing persons and that sort of thing."

I felt I should tell Molly some war stories, offer her some excitement before she returned to her job at the news stand. But I wasn't feeling much like a crack private investigator at the moment. "Sometimes it's exciting work, yes. But there's also a lot of research and paperwork that goes with it."

"Gosh, you're lucky."

Molly was right; I was fortunate to have a job I loved, a fact which I sometimes forgot. Particularly when I was feeling like a failure. Like right now. To date, I'd spent the best part of two days out of town. I'd run up bills for gas, meals, and a night in a motel on a case that probably would never pay more than the fifty dollars I'd already collected. I'd managed to make some knife-wielding youths nervous enough to cost me more than six hundred dollars' worth of tires. And I knew almost nothing more about Kerry Hammond's whereabouts now than I did before I left St. Paul. Still, I loved what I did for a living, and most people I'd observed were unhappy in their work.

As I walked out of the bus station, I looked back over my shoulder. The next bus was just pulling into the station. And Molly had gone back to her book, munching her popcorn as she eagerly read all about a man who got his kicks preying on women.

15

I made it back to the office by late afternoon. Paula was seated at the reception desk, working with her usual dedication to the job. "Look at this, Devon," she whispered excitedly, as I came in the door. She pointed a sculptured fingernail—painted a pearly mauve this week—at a photo layout in the issue of *Today's Bride* that she'd been reading. "Isn't this just the cutest cake you've ever seen in your whole life?"

"Cute" wasn't a word I often used to describe a cake, unless maybe it was one decorated for a small child's birthday party. I leaned over her desk and looked at the photograph of a gigantic wedding cake. It was at least five feet high, with plastic columns between the layers to make the cake stand taller. There wasn't a wedding cliché missing from its decoration, either. Everything from love birds to garlands of pink and white roses, from an open Bible to the inevitable plastic replicas of the bride and groom was there. How precious. Well, why not? There certainly was plenty of space for all of it. "Hmm, it's even got a little piece of sheet music down there in the left hand corner," I said.

"It's the 'Hawaiian Wedding Song.' See the adorable little ukulele next to it? I wonder if Piatti's Bakery could copy it for my reception. What do you think?"

I took another look. "I bet they could." For the right price, they'd manage to copy the Eiffel Tower in whipped cream, complete with pigeon droppings.

Paula ripped the page from the magazine. "I'm gonna stop off at Piatti's on my way home from work and talk to them about it."

"Good idea." I looked through the open door into Sam's office. It was empty. "Where's Sam?"

"Oh, that's right. He said to tell you if you got back. Lael had her baby about eleven this morning and he went running off to the hospital."

"Oh, good! What did she have?"

"A boy. Nine pounds, six ounces."

"Ouch!"

"You can say that again. But Lael's a pretty big girl, thank God."

"Everybody healthy?"

"Yeah, except maybe Sam. He's a nervous wreck. Called around noon and said he'd try to get back in before the end of the day."

I hung up my coat and went into my office. My eye fell instantly on my baby gift for Lael, still sitting on top of the file cabinet. "Shit!" I shouted.

Paula stumbled in on her black patent leather spike-heeled shoes. I never could understand how she could stand to wear those treacherous things, but she obviously thought they were sexy and was willing to pay the price. "What's the matter, Devon?"

"I told Sam I'd kill him if he didn't give this to Lael before she left the hospital with that baby, and I meant it."

"Oh, yeah, Sam mentioned it when he called. I guess it's my fault."

"*Your* fault. How's that?"

"Sam said he forgot to bring it with him this morning when he went tearing out of here. He wanted me to hide the box so you wouldn't see it when you got back."

I swore under my breath. "Leave it to me. I know just where to hide it." I picked up the pink-and-blue be-ribboned cube. Noting that the balloons I'd tied to the top were starting to lose their oomph, I carried it into Sam's office and plopped it squarely in the middle of his desktop.

There was a small pile of phone messages waiting for me on my desk. Including one from Linda Lundberg. Embarrassed, I realized that Sam wasn't the only one getting senile around here. With all the hassle over my car this morning, I'd forgotten to call back the Newton Prairie teacher to see if she'd been able to get Lucas Drew's address. But luckily, her memory was better than mine. Paula had written down Lucas's address, on a street in West Hollywood, California.

Another message was from Meredith O'Connor, my real estate broker. I returned her call and made an appointment to look at two properties that evening. "You're really going to love the second one," Meredith told me. "It's the cutest little place you've ever seen."

I wondered why all of a sudden "cute" was the adjective of choice around here. "Just as long as it doesn't look like Paula's wedding cake," I said.

"What?"

"See you at seven." I hung up.

By the time I had returned the rest of my phone calls, I heard Sam come into the outer office. "Pictures!" he shouted. "I've got pictures of Aaron Sherman Cohen, nine pounds, six ounces, and the smartest kid in that hospital."

He lumbered into my office, a selection of fuzzy Polaroids gripped in his fist. The grin on his face was so wide that I couldn't stay angry with him about the gift. I oohed and ahed over little Aaron, a chubby, bald, red-faced infant who looked remarkably like his maternal grandfather. I privately hoped he would outgrow it. "You're right about his IQ," I teased. "There it is spelled out right on his little plastic bracelet."

"Whadya mean? That's just his ID num—"

I broke into a laugh and Sam joined me. "Thought you had me goin' for a minute there, eh, sweet pea?"

When he spotted my gift sitting on his desk, Sam raised his hands as if to ward off blows and turned to face me. "I'll get it to the hospital before Lael and the baby check out tomorrow, Devon, promise. Just got a little excited this morning and forgot, that's all."

He looked so contrite and embarrassed that I felt compelled to forgive him. "Just don't let me come in tomorrow morning and find that thing still sitting there."

I filled Sam in on my trip to Newton Prairie and he commiserated with me about my tires, agreeing that one or more of Mike Hammond's group probably had done the deed. "Tough luck, kiddo. Sounds like they got their own little teenage mafia up there." But he didn't offer to reimburse my loss from Sherman and MacDonald's coffers, and I didn't ask him to, for fear that would lead to a discussion of how much money this case was likely to bring into the agency.

We weren't very close to having solved it yet, either. Sam's efforts yesterday had brought us no closer to finding Kerry Hammond than my own. "Called every hospital between here and the kid's home town," he told me, moving my gift to a spot on the floor, next to his coatrack. He sat down behind his desk, took a fat cigar from his pocket, unwrapped it, and stuck it between his teeth. A blue strip of paper circling the cigar proclaimed, "It's a Boy!" "Nobody answerin' our girl's description's checked into any of 'em."

"You covered all the hospitals in St. Cloud, too? The bus driver sounded sure that Kerry left his bus there."

"Every last one of 'em." Sam chewed on the end of his still-unlighted cigar. "But I do have one piece of info that oughta cheer up the sister."

"Yeah?"

"Cops finally ID'd that second body from the fire. Turned out to be an office machine *mavin* came in to repair the computer or the Xerox or somethin'. That's why the lady doc stayed late that night, 'cause this girl was still workin' on whatever machine it was that broke. Anyway, bottom line is, the dead girl ain't our client's little sister."

"That's a relief." But it didn't solve the mystery of where Kerry Hammond had gone. "I think the boyfriend is probably our best lead now. If Kerry found out she was pregnant, it makes sense she'd have gone after him. I've got his address and phone number; I'll check him out."

"You're on."

"Got a project for you, though. Just to follow up on a hunch of mine."

"Shoot."

"I'd like you to check the Stearns County property rolls for any pieces of property owned by Reverend Ed Beale,

Community Fundamentalist Church, or Beale's two anti-abortion organizations. I'd like to start getting an idea of just how much wealth the good minister's managed to rip off the faithful."

"What's that got to do with our case?"

"Maybe nothing, maybe plenty. I don't know yet."

"Listen, petunia, I don't wanna find out you're stickin' your nose into who set that fire, ya hear? It's got nothin' to do with that girl we been hired to find, and that means it's got nothin' to do with you."

"Just check the property rolls, will you, Sam? It's not going to take you half an hour on the computer."

He leaned over and spit his soggy cigar into the waste-basket. It landed with a thump. My partner exudes such class from every pore that I frequently can't avoid being impressed. "I know you," he complained. "You get your female dander up and next thing—"

"Sam! Just check the goddamned property rolls."

"Okay, okay, guess I owe ya that much. Just make sure you keep your *tuchis* covered on this one, daffodil. These guys can get nasty, they think you didn't get their warning, they think you're still pokin' your nose in their business."

Believe it or not, the same thought had occurred to me. But no way was I going to admit that to Sam.

16

Monica Hammond was predictably relieved when I called her rooming house to let her know her sister hadn't been in the St. Cloud fire. But she begged me not to give up the search before I found Kerry.

"What do you know about a boy named Lucas Drew?" I asked her.

"Luke?" I know him. He was in my class at school, at least we had English together one year. Never liked him much."

"Why not?" I spotted Sam on his way out of the office and gave him a wave good-bye. He stuck his head in my door to show me that he was carrying my gift, just like he'd promised. Paula had already sneaked out, undoubtedly anxious to talk to her favorite baker.

"Luke was always really into himself," Monica told me. "Like I remember one thing he did that really stank. He was going with Cindy Weber our senior year, but he dumped her right before homecoming, and she was supposed to be in the royal court and everything. Cindy had this awesome dress she saved up for—real silk from China or Hong Kong or someplace. She got a new hairdo, the whole works. But she couldn't get another date for the dance that late, so she had to stay home."

"Poor kid, how humiliating for her."

"Yeah, she just about died."

"I heard Lucas was Kerry's boyfriend."

"You're kidding."

"No. A girl named Wanda Kirchner told me that Kerry and Lucas were an item until a couple of months ago, when he left town. Went to Hollywood to become an actor."

"*That* sounds like something he'd do. But, I don't know about him and Kerry. She might've mentioned his name once or twice, now that I think about it, like one time she said she thought he was pretty cool. But . . . Geez, you think Lucas is really the one?"

"Who got her pregnant?"

"Yeah. I mean, if she *is* pregnant. I could be wrong about that. I sure hope I'm wrong."

"If what Wanda told me is true, Lucas may very well be the guy. Wanda made him sound like a real heartthrob. Said he looked like a young Tom Cruise."

"Lucas? I remember he had zits and greasy hair."

"A lot can change in a year. Maybe his skin cleared up

and he discovered shampoo. You got any new ideas about where Kerry might have gone?"

"Wish I did. Luke Drew, huh? I gotta think about that."

I promised to keep Monica informed of my progress, but warned that I wouldn't be able to devote full time to finding her sister. Sherman and MacDonald had other cases on its docket. Luckily, most of the other cases could afford to pay for our services, but I didn't tell Monica that.

From the phone book, I got the number of the Minneapolis women's clinic Reverend Ed's groups had targeted for the next day's blockade and dialed it. The clinic receptionist put my call through to Dr. Barbara Hansen, the director. I told her who I was and what I'd learned about the Newton Prairie group's plans to blockade her clinic.

She thanked me for calling, but said, "We've got other sources, so we already knew. From what we've heard, there are three or four different groups all merging on us tomorrow, so we've got our volunteers all set."

"Be extra careful," I warned. "There's nothing I can prove, but I think some of these Newton Prairie people are the ones who torched that clinic up in St. Cloud Monday night."

A choking sound came over the line. "Those hypocritical bastards! God, I'd like to see somebody torch *them!*" I heard an intake of breath. "Sorry. It's just that my friend Janet was in the clinic that night. She—She died there."

"Dr. Gilman."

"Right. We'd been friends since medical school. Jan was such a good person, so brave, and now she's gone because of those cowardly—What a waste."

"I've got to give you credit. It must take guts to keep a clinic like yours open nowadays."

"Ha! You don't know the half of it. Those people picketed Jan's house for a week once—this is her *home* I'm talking about, not the clinic. Fifteen, twenty people went up and down her street, day and night, shouting and carrying signs, telling her neighbors she kills babies for a living."

"You're not serious."

"Wait 'til you hear what they did to me. Three of those sons of bitches actually went to my daughter's junior high and passed out these flyers that said Jody Hansen's mom murders little children."

"What crap. What's your daughter got to do with your work?"

"That's my point. These people don't care whether Jody has anything to do with my work or not. If embarrassing her at school gets me to stop doing abortions, they figure they've succeeded. Any means to their end."

"Like torching a clinic with two women inside."

"Sure. It worked, didn't it? Janet Gilman's not going to be doing any more abortions."

"Just don't let them do the same thing to you."

"Organized picketing we should be able to handle all right. As long as plenty of volunteers show up. Truth is, we don't even have any abortions scheduled for tomorrow. So those stupid fanatics are coming all this way to try to block women from getting prenatal care and birth control advice. We had two breast exams scheduled for tomorrow, too—indigent women who found lumps and are hysterical because they don't have regular doctors or health insurance. There's no way they can afford private medical care. I don't know if they'll still show up, though, once they see the picket line they'll have to cross. Say, we can always use another volunteer. How about helping us out?"

I begged off. I planned to try to sneak over there to see which of Newton Prairie's leading citizens were on the picket line, but I didn't want them to see me. I promised to introduce myself if I made it. "I'll let you know if I find out anything more about who killed your friend, too."

My final call before leaving the office was to Lucas Drew's West Hollywood number. Apparently it was not his private line.

A gravel-voiced man answered. "Lucas Drew? He's the new guy, right? Hold on a minute." There was a clunking sound as he dropped the receiver, probably onto a table. It was followed by an ear-splitting baritone yell: "Lucas! Lucas Drew! Telephone!" As I rubbed my sore ear, I developed a new respect for fiber optics.

I held on. And on. No one ever returned to the phone. I hung up and redialed. The line was busy. When I tried again five minutes later, it rang six times before another young man answered. His hacking cough made me suspect I'd roused him from a sickbed. I explained that I was calling long distance, trying to reach Lucas Drew, "the new guy."

"Don't think I've seen him around today."

I wasn't about to give up that easily. "Listen, the person I'm really interested in talking to is Lucas's girlfriend. You know if she might be there?"

I waited through a coughing fit. "Which one?"

Great. "Her name's Kerry Hammond."

"Doesn't sound familiar." Cough, cough. "What's she look like?"

"Long blonde hair, very pretty, sixteen years old. She's from Minnesota."

There was a pause on the line. Surprisingly, this time it wasn't accompanied by a hacking sound. Maybe he was drinking a glass of water. "Yeah," he said finally. "I think I know the girl you mean." My heart made a tiny leap of hope. "Haven't seen her around today, either."

I finally had to settle for leaving my name and two phone numbers—both the office number and my home number—for Lucas. "Please tell him it's urgent that he call me back. He can call me collect, at any hour, day or night."

"Sure thing, lady. I'll leave him a note."

"And see a doctor about that cough, huh? Could be something ser—" There was a click, and the dial tone buzzed in my ear. For some reason, I had trouble feeling confident that Lucas Drew would ever return my call.

17

"Now *this* is a kitchen to die for." My real estate agent, Meredith O'Connor, was showing me the second of the two condominiums on our evening agenda.

The first had been a complete disaster. It was billed as a "fixer-upper townhouse with a breathtaking view of the Mississippi River." It turned out to be in Lilydale, a suburb of St. Paul located on the far shore of the river. When spring comes to Lilydale, its residents often find themselves battling the Mississippi's life-threatening floodwaters. This spring had been relatively dry, so it was obviously the best possible time to unload this turkey on some unsuspecting sucker.

The townhouse needed fixing up, all right. As I walked through the first floor, my jaw dropped—it was a shock to be reminded that some people lived like this even outside the slums. The gold carpets were stained and riddled with cigarette burns, and I counted no fewer than four fist-sized holes in the flimsy plasterboard walls. As if that weren't enough, the downstairs bathroom door listed to one side, having been pulled nearly off its hinges.

"I know it's a little on the tacky side right now," Meredith said, smiling brightly, "but just think of the potential. And you haven't even seen the view yet." Meredith was a small, perky blonde, a perennial optimist. There were times when she got so cheerful that I had an urge to belt her in the teeth just to see her smile wilt. But she had sold more property than anyone else in her real estate office in the last year, so I suppressed my urge. If I really wanted to buy a condo, I told myself, someone as successful as Meredith was the obvious choice to help me find the right one.

I allowed myself to be dragged upstairs to see the view of

the Mississippi, which was allegedly available from the master bedroom window. On closer inspection, I realized that, at best, a sliver of water would be visible over the peaked roofs of the complex across the street . . . *if* I hung my head out the window and *if* there happened to be a full moon out, which there wasn't.

But it wasn't the misrepresented view that made up my mind. I tried to like the place, honest I did. Particularly since Meredith assured me the owner would accept as much as twenty thousand dollars below his asking price. I figured twenty grand could buy a lot of fixing up. So I went back downstairs to give the kitchen a second look. The dark room exuded a rancid odor reminiscent of rotten cantaloupe. The stove would have to go; it would take a chisel to clean that oven and three of the four burners wouldn't light. The vent fan was dead and the cracked Formica countertops would need replacing, too.

I was opening a cupboard, thinking it might be easier to tear this place down and start over—unfortunately, not a viable option with an attached property—when something gray and furry scurried out of the cupboard and over the top of my foot. I jumped back reflexively, my heart in my throat.

But it was almost worth being startled half to death just to see Meredith's reaction. The field mouse tried to dart between Meredith's legs. It hit one of her ankles, then careened across the greasy linoleum floor, crashing into the wall. Meredith's perpetual smile froze to her teeth as she grabbed her chest, propelled her hips onto the countertop, and released a shrill sound that seemed to come from her toes. One leg of her pantyhose snagged on a cabinet handle and shredded instantly.

Meredith's scream seemed to revive the momentarily stunned creature; it righted itself and made a beeline for the baseboard beneath the sink, where it squeezed its body through a narrow crack in the wood and disappeared.

I started to giggle. Meredith shot me a look of sheer hatred, which only made it worse. I laughed harder and harder, barely able to contain myself as Meredith raced for the front door.

Now we were inspecting the second condo. This one was on the third floor of a converted apartment building east of downtown. "Walking these stairs will keep you in great shape," Meredith told me, her usual perkiness fully restored. I was used to walking up to the third floor, which is where the tiny apartment I'd been renting in Ramsey Hill was located. But whether I wanted to do that for the rest of my life was another question.

The kitchen "to die for" was, indeed, a vast improvement over the Lilydale toxic dump. It was clean and neat and all the appliances were nearly new, but like the rest of this place, it was terminally cute. Little white French bunnies galloped over a blue background on the wallpaper edging the ceiling. The countertop had its own selection of baby animals preserved for posterity on every fifth or sixth tile. And the tiny dining area was decorated in pale pinks and blues, with ruffled café curtains at the windows.

There was no smell of rotting cantaloupe in this place. Here, every room was perfumed with an appropriate odor: spiced apple for the kitchen; pine for the living room; mint for the bathroom; lavender for the two bedrooms. This trick was evidently accomplished by using some little plug-in devices that heated perfumed wax, sending its smell out into the air. My sinuses began to throb and I could feel a sneeze coming on.

I walked across the living room, opened the patio doors, and ventured out onto the balcony for a breath of fresh air. It was a dark night and everything across the street was black, except for one rectangular lighted area where two men were using implements that looked a lot like pickaxes. "Hey, Meredith. Come on out here a minute. Look over there." I pointed at the square of light. "What're those guys doing?"

She squinted into the distance. "Oh, that's nothing, really," she assured me. "They do the digging at night, that's all.

But they only use hand tools, so it's quiet. It won't bother you a bit."

"They dig at night, huh?" I began to understand why this obviously superior place was in the same price range as the Lilydale disaster area. I turned to examine my real estate agent's face; her eyes were blue and blank, but the corners of her mouth still edged upward slightly. "Tell me, Meredith, just what are those guys digging?"

I thought I detected a tiny flash of embarrassment before her blinding professional smile returned, but I couldn't be sure. "Oh, just graves," she said cheerfully.

18

I picked up a mushroom-and-artichoke-heart pizza on my way home. Its garlicky odor quickly escaped the box on the passenger seat and permeated the interior of the Honda, but I didn't mind; the honest if pungent smells of garlic and cheese sure beat the chemical variations on pine and lavender I'd been subjected to at the cemetery-view condo.

I grabbed my mail from the box on the front porch, tossed it on top of the pizza carton, and trudged up the outside stairs to my third-floor digs. As I opened the front door and set the pizza box down on my little round dining table, I realized this place still looked pretty good to me. Especially after tonight's colossal waste of time.

My compact little apartment used to be the servant's quarters of an old mansion in the historic Ramsey Hill district of St. Paul. The building long ago was carved up into rental units of various sizes, mine being the smallest. But, even in its chopped-up state, the place had far more character than many more modern buildings.

My tiny home was cramped, even for one person, but I could see oak branches whenever I glanced out my windows—a green view in spring and summer, burnt orange in fall, grayish brown and white in winter—and my rent was less than three hundred dollars a month. After I left my teaching job and my husband walked out on me with most of our money in his pocket, I couldn't afford anything larger.

But now that I had a little money in the bank and Noel was history, I'd begun to think about having a larger place, one I could really call my own. Finding my dream home, however, was quickly becoming a major pain in the butt. In addition to tonight, I'd wasted two nights the previous week, examining places that were too expensive or too far from the office or had some other fatal flaw.

In the mood for some music, I put a compact disc of Itzhak Perlman performing Beethoven's Violin Concerto on the stereo. The timeless melodies echoed against the walls and ceiling, adding an extra touch of class to my gourmet meal of pizza eaten from the box.

I read my mail while I ate, my frequent substitute for dinner conversation. It was the usual melange of bills and ads, except for one pale aqua envelope that I saved for last. Dessert for the mind.

With only one slice of pizza left, I wiped the grease from my fingers and lips, picked up the envelope I'd been saving, and tore it open. Inside was a greeting card, a romantic photograph of a silhouetted man and woman walking hand-in-hand on a deserted beach, the sun setting into the fiery orange water behind them. I opened it and read the printed message, "Thinking of You Always." The card was signed "Love, Doug," and underneath his signature, Lieutenant Douglas Winthrop had written, "Hoping that something (could it possibly be *me*?!?!) will bring you back to California soon. I've found a great new restaurant I know you'll love. It's *very* romantic. Can't wait to show it to you."

I smiled. I'd met Doug a few months ago on the Monterey Peninsula, where I'd become involved in a murder case. He was the Carmel Police Department's investigating officer on the case. To my mind, Lieutenant Winthrop, a widower, was incredibly sensitive, and sexy, too, especially for a cop. Maybe it's because he lost his wife—she died of ovarian cancer a few years back—and I'd lost my son, so we shared a common bond of personal loss. But I'd like to think we shared a lot of interests and values, and a dose or two of plain old-fashioned animal attraction as well.

Now Doug and I talked on the phone about once a week and he frequently sent me cards and notes to let me know he was thinking of me. Receiving one never failed to raise my spirits. Doug had even managed to spend a weekend with me in Minnesota in early February, where he'd been introduced—not entirely happily—to real winter weather. But it was hard for us to see each other, with his work schedule and my work schedule and two thousand miles between us—the most common dilemma of the modern working couple. Holding his card, I realized I missed him. Maybe too much.

At the same time, I could almost feel myself stepping into my suit of emotional armor—that steely stuff that keeps me from getting hurt again—and zipping it up to my chin. I wondered if Doug might be a major reason I'd embarked on this search for a condominium. After all, if I bought property in Minnesota, if I sent my roots here even deeper, then I couldn't fall in love with a blond cop from California, could I? Right. So how come I couldn't stop thinking about him?

Picturing Doug's intelligent blue-green eyes and heart-meltingly broad grin, I walked into the bedroom and propped up his card on top of my chest of drawers, between my grandmother's silver hairbrush and a framed photo of my son, Danny. There, now I could glance at it while I lay in bed. Maybe it would even bring me pleasant dreams.

At that moment, I had to admit I felt very, very tempted to take off a day or two and fly west to visit this man I found so attractive. Had young Kerry Hammond done something similar? Had she gone to California to find the man she loved, the father of her expected child?

I went into the bathroom and turned on the taps over the bathtub, adjusting the water's temperature until it was almost too hot to bear. Just the way I like it. I let the water run to fill the tub and went back into the living room, which is all of about six paces away. On the stereo, Perlman was winding up his performance. In the mood for more romantic violin music, I placed a CD of Tschaikovsky's Violin Concerto into position to play next. This time Isaac Stern would do the honors.

Despite the music and the pleasant respite brought by Doug's card, though, my work kept creeping back into the corners of my mind. I felt terribly frustrated that I hadn't yet been able to find Kerry and that I had so few ideas about where she was. I felt a genuine sadness for both her and her sister, too. When they handed out families, those poor kids had definitely been standing in the wrong line.

I wondered how I would have handled a pregnancy at the age of sixteen. And what my own parents would have said if I'd gone to them with that kind of problem.

I added some bubbles to my bathwater—plain, old-fashioned Ivory dishwashing liquid. It's not perfumed, so it doesn't bother my allergies, and to my mind it works every bit as well as that smelly five-dollars-an-ounce stuff the department stores sell. When there were mounds of white fluff covering the entire surface, I stripped and slowly lowered myself into the steaming water.

I lay back in the water, thinking about my mother and father, dead for more than a decade now. They were certainly not religious fanatics like the Hammonds; they seldom if ever went to church. But that didn't mean they didn't raise me to be hyper-vigilant about what the neighbors would think of every little thing I did. They did a good job, too; it took me years of living as an adult and a round of psychotherapy to learn not to give a damn about what the neighbors think.

My sex education probably wasn't a helluva lot better than Kerry's and Monica's, either. It had consisted mostly of warnings not to "go and get yourself in trouble like that no-good Thelma." Thelma was a distant cousin of my father's who, at fifteen, had been sent off to a home for unwed mothers. Her baby—I never found out if it was a boy or a girl, and I'm not sure Thelma ever knew, either—was put up for adoption. As a young girl, I'd never quite figured out how Thelma had gotten herself pregnant; I always thought it took two to make a baby, but you'd never know that from my family's lectures.

Thelma's disgrace happened during the sixties, when abortion was still illegal and dangerous. By the time I was fifteen, though, Roe versus Wade was already the law of the land and abortion was more readily available than it is now.

I realized that I might make a very different decision now than I would have at sixteen. Having had a child of my own and then having lost him gave me a different perspective. Now I had a better sense of what I might lose through an abortion. At thirty-three, I would be far more able to care for a child, too. Still, there were far worse things to my mind than having an abortion. One of them was a woman's giving birth to a child for whom she could never feel anything more than resentment and anger.

If I'd gone to my parents for help at sixteen, I suspected that they—unlike Kerry's parents—would have pushed me into having an abortion, whether I wanted one or not. And they would have made sure I had the surgery long before the rest of the community ever learned of my problem, too. Then Mom and Dad never would have let me forget how thoroughly I had disappointed and disgraced them.

No, asking my parent's help definitely would not have been a comfortable option for me. So I probably would have done almost anything to avoid confronting my family about my pregnancy. And Kerry Hammond's folks were a thousand times more threatening than mine had ever been. To what lengths would she go to keep them from knowing?

I soaked in the bathtub for a long, long time, listening to the violins and thinking about men and women having babies together, and not having them. About loving each other and the children they made together, and about not loving them. About the choices we think we would make, and about those other choices that we really do make, when the chips are finally down.

The only conclusion I came to was that love and sex can get to be a real mess. Sometimes even a dangerous one.

19

The protesters began arriving outside the clinic by ten o'clock the next morning. They came by bus, car, truck, anything that would carry them. I'd arrived half an hour earlier and introduced myself to Dr. Barbara Hansen and her staff. Now I waited inside the clinic with a group of about fifty women pledged to defend the place against attack, as well as to escort patients through the picket lines and into the clinic building.

"Here they come," Barbara said. "Let's get our first shift out there before they get too close." About half of the women's defense team rushed through the clinic's front door. Each member wore an oversized white T-shirt pulled over her regular clothing. The T-shirts were printed with a picture of a wire coat hanger and the words "Women Will Never Go Back" on the front; on the back, they said, "Another Vote for Choice."

The pro-choicers, ranging in age from their late teens to their late sixties, arranged themselves shoulder-to-shoulder across the front of the building, each woman placing her arms around the waist of those next to her to form a human fence against the protesters.

There only to observe, I had no part to play in the clinic's defense, except maybe to identify some members of the attack team. I'd come to find out firsthand what was going on here and to see who I recognized from the Newton Prairie rally. Then I planned to get back to my work, which this morning included serving a subpoena on a doctor in downtown Minneapolis for one of Sam's workman's compensation investigations.

By now, three buses had pulled into the curb across the street. Each was like a clown car from the circus, carrying far more people than I'd ever have believed possible. I recognized some of those emerging from one bus, a small yellow vehicle designed to transport no more than about twenty. Reverend Ed Beale's wife, Helen, stepped off first, followed by at least forty others, some of them very small children, some of them elderly.

There was no way all of those people could have ridden sitting down inside that bus; more than a dozen must have stood in the aisle during the entire trip from Newton Prairie—more than two hours. Obviously the group hadn't felt it necessary to observe the seat belt laws. If I asked them about it, they would probably claim to be following a higher law, or they'd spout some nonsense about God keeping them safe, as though human beings bore no responsibility for their own safety.

I saw the fat woman who had prayed for my soul step shakily down the steps of the bus. She was wearing the same brown tent dress she'd had on at the rally in Newton Prairie the other night, topped now by a short, dark blue quilted jacket. She stood for a moment, holding her hand over her heart and gulping in air hungrily.

Mary and Herman Hammond got off next. Herman was carrying their smallest daughter, the little girl called Lucie, the one I'd seen Mary strike. Herman set the child down on the sidewalk, where she looked around, a fragment of pink blanket clutched tightly in her left fist and a bewildered expression on her face.

The shiny orange VW beetle was there, too, as was the Ford pickup truck I'd seen leaving Community Fundamentalist Church after Reverend Ed's late night meeting. The pickup's bed now carried six or seven young men—one of them was Mike Hammond—who rode with their knees pulled up under their chins. Wedged in between them was an assortment of picket signs.

Reverend Ed was there, too, of course, arriving at the wheel of his dark red Cadillac. Three gray-haired men rode with him, certainly enjoying a far more comfortable method of transportation than the minister's wife had taken.

I counted three more buses and at least two dozen cars, delivering about three hundred people in all. Although Dr. Barbara Hansen had warned me that several anti-abortion groups were converging here today, I was stunned by the sheer size of the turnout.

As the defense team stood their ground, the protesters gathered together across the street. They pinned signs saying "Christians for Life" and "Abortion Kills Children" to each other's backs. Now both sides were in uniform, so there would be no confusion about which team they were on.

Reverend Ed waved his arms, calling for his group's attention. I couldn't hear his words, but it was obvious that he was offering a prayer. All but the smallest children stood quietly, their heads bowed. When they'd finished praying, Mike Hammond and the others from Reverend Ed's inner circle began to hand out the picket signs.

I saw Mike hand a picket sign to his little sister and I swore under my breath. He pried her scrap of pink security blanket away from her and stuffed it into his jacket pocket. Then he wrapped her tiny fingers around the wooden pole attached to her sign, which displayed the same head of a dead fetus I'd seen at the church rally. "Abortion Kills Babies" was printed in red ink along the bottom.

Poor little Lucie had all she could do to hold the bulky sign upright as, flanked by her beaming parents, she marched back and forth in front of the clinic.

A crew from a local television station arrived and began to tape Lucie's trek. Whoever was in charge of the anti-abortionists' public relations campaign was right on target; they'd managed the perfect photo opportunity for tonight's six o'clock news.

A silver-haired woman standing next to me whispered, "Now that's child abuse if I ever saw it."

She would get no argument from me. I felt a hand at my elbow. "Devon, come with me a minute," Dr. Barbara Hansen said, "there's someone here I'd like you to meet."

I backed away from the window and turned to face the doctor. When I met her earlier, I was surprised to see that she was much smaller than I'd pictured her during our phone conversation. I'd figured the kind of woman who'd withstood the harassment Barbara had described to me should be substantial in size. But Dr. Hansen was no more than five feet one and very slender, with chestnut, pixy-cut hair.

She led me back into the bowels of the clinic. "Room B isn't being used today, so I put Claire in there. It'll give you two some privacy." We entered a room dominated by a leather examining table, its metal stirrups extended. Along one wall was a counter with various examining and surgical instruments laid out on a clean white towel—a stethoscope, two or three scalpels, forceps, a dilator, a glass cylinder filled with cotton-tipped swabs, a microscope, and a couple of those clamp-like gadgets used to do Pap smears. After spending so many hundreds of hours at the hospital while my son Danny was in a coma, I'd learned to hate and fear places like this. My stomach felt queasy.

A woman with puffy red eyes sat on a chair in one corner. As she brushed a strand of gray-streaked brown hair away from her forehead and got to her feet, I could see she was half a foot taller and a good fifty pounds heavier than Barbara. It was obvious she'd been crying.

"This is Claire Hooper, Devon," Barbara said. "Claire's a nurse. She worked with my friend Janet up at the St. Cloud clinic."

Claire and I shook hands. "Hi, Claire. I was so sorry to hear about Dr. Gilman."

Claire Hooper bit her lip and nodded.

"Claire left work Monday night about an hour before the fire broke out," Barbara said, thrusting her dainty hands into the pockets of her lab coat. "I was telling her about what you said, that the people who burned the clinic might be here today. Maybe you two can compare notes." She dragged over a second chair and gestured for both of us to sit down. "I'll be out front if you need me." The doctor scurried away, leaving me alone with the tearful nurse.

"I just keep thinking I should have been there instead of Jan," Claire said, "or that I should at least remember something important, some kind of clue, to help catch these guys." Her breath caught. "Jan was more than just a boss to me. I really liked her a lot. She didn't deserve what they did to her."

"Nobody does."

"Barb told me you might know who did it."

"Not really. All I can say is that I overheard a conversation, and it sounded to me like one of the people talking either burned the clinic himself, or knew who did it. But I haven't got anything conclusive."

"Oh. I guess I was hoping—"

"Look, Claire, if I find out anything useful, anything at all, I'll go right to the police with it. They're the ones who should be handling the clinic fire, not you or me."

"It's just that I want so bad to help. I—I guess I feel sort of guilty."

"You've no reason to. If you'd been there that night, we'd probably have three dead women now, instead of just two."

"I s'pose. But I was the last one to leave that night. Maybe I should've known something was wrong. Maybe I should've been able to warn them and then nobody would have died."

The nurse's face was haggard, as though she hadn't slept well in days. She was so obviously troubled that my heart went out to her. "It's too late to worry about those things now," I told her, "but maybe you can help bring the murderers to justice. Let's think a minute. Did you notice anything different when you left that night? Anything at all that didn't seem right. Like anybody milling around who shouldn't have been there."

"No, nobody was in the parking lot. There was only my car and Jan's."

"What about the other woman who was killed?"

"You mean the woman from Office Fixers. She was working on the copy machine, 'cause the paper kept jamming up on us and we had this mailing that had to go out the next day. For the annual fund-raiser. That's why we had to get the copier fixed right away. We paid overtime. Or at least we would have if—"

"Right. This repair woman, how did she get to the clinic?"

"I don't know. I s'pose she drove—"

"But she didn't leave her car in the parking lot?"

Claire thought a moment. "No. No, I'm sure she didn't. The only ones there were Jan's and mine. That's strange, isn't it? Hey, wait a minute—" She leaned her chin against the heel of her hand. "I remember now. She didn't park out back in the lot. She must have parked on the street in front, 'cause I remember letting her in the front door with this suitcase full of her tools. It was a shorter carry through the front door and I s'pose her tool case was heavy."

"Okay, that's good. Now, try to remember seeing her car out front when you left the parking lot. Try to picture the street in your mind, the way it looked that night."

Claire closed her eyes. Her breathing became so steady that I thought for a moment she'd fallen asleep. But finally she spoke. "There were three cars out front, I think. One was a green Toyota. I remember that, because my sister drives one like it."

"Good! Now picture the other two." I waited.

"A—An American station wagon, an older model. A Dodge or maybe a Plymouth. It was light, either white or beige, and there was a lot of rust on it."

"And the third car?"

"I remember now. It was an old VW, you know, a beetle."

My heart skipped a beat. "Was it orange? Bright orange, the color of a tangerine?"

Claire shook her head. "No, no, I don't think so. I think I would have remembered orange. I think this one was a duller color, like gray or tan."

"All right."

Claire pushed the errant strand of hair back behind her ear again. "How is any of this going to help find the guy who killed Jan?"

"I don't know, Claire. But it might mean something." I convinced her to call the St. Cloud police when she got back home and tell them about the three cars that had been parked in front of the clinic on the fatal night. If nothing else, it might make her feel like she'd done something to help the investigation into her friend's death.

I left Claire sitting in the examining room and made my way back to the front of the clinic. Most of the women pledged to defend the place were outside now, their arms linked, trying to create a pathway for a frightened black woman of about thirty who was trying to enter. The patient was dressed in a teal-and-white-checked business suit and carried a black shoulder bag.

"Abortion kills babies! Don't kill your baby!" the protesters shouted at her in unison.

A teenage girl grabbed at the woman's sleeve and tried to keep her from moving toward the clinic, while another held onto the strap of her purse. But she pulled away and ran. One of the picket sign carriers chased her, but was held off by two defense guards on the opposition team. A moment later, four more of the women with the coat-hanger shirts surrounded the patient and formed a protective shield while she marched slowly through the clinic's front door.

"God will condemn you!" a male voice shouted after her. "Judgment Day is coming. God remembers all sinners. You will burn in hell! You will burn in hell!"

Inside, the young woman was shaking visibly. "Lord, those people aren't fooling around out there!"

Dr. Hansen reached up and put a hand on her shoulder. "They call it peaceful protest," she said. "Did they hurt you?"

She fingered a rip in her sleeve. "I don't think so, but they sure made a mess of this jacket." The two women headed toward the back of the clinic.

It was half past eleven, time for me to go if I was going to serve my subpoena before lunchtime. I sneaked out a side door, but soon realized that I would have to make my way along the side of the building to the front to reach my car.

The defense team opened a hole in their human fence to let me pass through, but the picketers were less polite. They kept right on marching back and forth while I tried to pass. Two of them rammed me with their signs, then feigned apologies.

Screw this, I thought. I led with a shoulder and barged through the human barrier. One woman staggered as I hit her and I stepped hard on somebody else's foot, but I no longer cared.

"Baby killer!" a woman shouted at me. I wondered how simply being inside a women's clinic had earned me that label. I turned and saw angry faces surrounding me.

Mike Hammond stood still, staring at me. He raised his hand in a fist and mumbled something I couldn't hear. I don't think it was, "Have a nice day."

As I broke free of the crowd and sprinted back to my car, I heard sirens in the distance. The police were finally on the way.

20

I served my subpoena, took some photos at the scene of an auto accident we suspected had been staged for the insurance money, interviewed a witness in an embezzlement case, and then drove past the women's clinic. The picketing and praying were still going on outside the building, if at a less frenetic pace than before. Half a dozen police officers now stood observing the scene, leaning against their squad cars and chatting among themselves.

When I returned to the office, I found Sam on his way out and Paula already gone for the day.

"My new grandson comes home from the hospital today," Sam announced, grinning. "Rose's got the whole *mishpocheh* comin' by tonight to get a look at him." He set down the two overflowing Toys "Я" Us shopping bags he was carrying.

"Glad to see you're not planning to spoil the kid, or anything."

"Picked up a coupla things at lunchtime, that's all. This's Lael's first, ya know. They need everything."

I leaned over and peeked inside one of the bags. On top was a child-sized baseball mitt made of real leather. Very practical, something no red-blooded, two-day-old American male child should be without, particularly with spring training just around the corner. I wondered whether Sam had bought a miniature Minnesota Twins uniform to go along with it.

I started to laugh, then bit my lip as I noticed a wounded look creeping into my partner's eyes. I managed to show what I thought was considerable maturity by stifling my impulse to tease him. "Give little Aaron a big fat kiss for me, will you? And say hi to Rose and the others," I said. I checked my phone messages. They were all routine, and none was from Lucas Drew. "Nothing from California yet?"

"Nope. Not a thing on the Hammond case while you been out. Them property listings you wanted'll be ready Monday morning, but that's all I got."

Sam and I briefly discussed several of our pending cases and I promised him I would compile my expenses for our latest workman's compensation case before Monday. As always, he was anxious to bill the client as soon as possible. Also as always, my missing paperwork was the last thing holding him up.

It was clear that Sam intended to spend the weekend away

from the office, and I couldn't blame him. It wasn't every day he had a new grandson to drool over. I felt a brief pang of pity for Lael and her husband, wondering whether they'd planned on quite such intense grandparenting from Sam and Rose this early in the game.

After Sam left, I tried Lucas Drew's West Hollywood phone number once more. This time no one answered. A plan began to form in the recesses of my mind. I assured myself that this was, after all, Friday afternoon, and I didn't need to be back in the office until Monday morning. If I flew to California to check out Lucas Drew, I'd still be working on the Hammond case, right? Nothing too guilt-producing there.

The way I saw it, the fact that I'd also be in a position to see Doug Winthrop for a few hours could be taken as a sort of bonus.

One or two more rationalizations later, I was dialing Northwest Airlines for reservations. Six hours after that, I was boarding the red-eye to Los Angeles.

21

Lucas Drew's address was just north of Melrose Avenue in West Hollywood. It was a three-story Spanish-style house that had seen better days. Its tile roof was cracked and portions of the white stucco exterior were chipped away. The lawn had long since succumbed to the drought or neglect or both. And the ancient fire escape on the side of the building was warped and rusty.

I pulled my rental car into the curb across the street and read the three parking signs attached to a metal pole, one on top of the other. The first prohibited parking between four and six o'clock any afternoon. The second allowed two-hour parking from eight in the morning until four in the afternoon, Monday through Friday. So far, so good. The third warned that I must display a resident's permit to park after ten at night and on weekends. It was now eight o'clock on Saturday morning; if I didn't live here, I couldn't park here.

I made a U-turn at the corner and found the same restrictions posted for the other side of the street. The hell with it. After an all-night flight, during which I'd had a maximum of one hour's sleep, I was too tired for this nonsense. I pulled into the driveway that ran along the side of Lucas's house and parked behind a vintage Mustang. If its owner needed to get out, he'd just have to come looking for me.

There was only one doorbell, so the building apparently was not divided into separate apartments. I pressed it and heard a buzzer sounding inside the building. No one responded. I rang continually until a young man leaned out of an open second story window and stared down at me. He was nude from the waist up. "Shut the fuck up, willya?" he hollared. "We're trying' to sleep up here."

"I'm looking for Lucas Drew. You him?"

"No, I ain't him."

"Is he home?"

"How the fuck should I know?"

"You could try looking."

"Hell, lady, I didn't get home 'til after four."

"Me, either, but I haven't lost my sunny disposition. Tell you what. You get Lucas down here and I'll stop ringing the bell. Deal?"

"Shit." The window slammed shut. I rang the bell again, then waited. Two minutes later, I rang it again, then waited again.

After I'd repeated this process half a dozen more times, the door was finally opened by the rude guy from upstairs. He was wearing a pair of tight Levis and nothing else. His blue eyes were bloodshot, his dark hair disheveled. "Top of the stairs, last room on the right. I heard voices, but he wouldn't open up. Think he's got a date up there."

"Thanks. I'll try not to interrupt anything important."

My host let me in, then disappeared up the stairs ahead of me. Footsteps pounded overhead, then a door slammed.

The rooming house smelled musty, as though no one was in charge of cleaning it. As I passed the second floor landing, I saw a telephone mounted on the wall. A small writing desk and chair stood next to it. Half a dozen phone messages were littered across its surface. I wondered whether the ones I'd left for Lucas Drew were among them. I also wondered how an aspiring actor like him could ever hope to find work using this system of communication.

I climbed to the third floor and walked toward the back of the house, past the open door of a bathroom. Dirty bath towels lay in a heap on the floor and the sink was spattered with toothpaste. Someone's razor lay on the back of the toilet, next to an open can of Gillette Foamy.

I found the last room on the right and knocked on the door. "Lucas, I have to talk to you," I said quietly. "It's important. Please open up."

"Who's there?" a voice from inside asked.

"My name is Devon MacDonald. I'm a friend of Monica Hammond's."

The door opened a crack, revealing a tall young man dressed in jeans and a T-shirt advertising some rock group I'd never heard of. "I'm Luke Drew, but this isn't a good time." He glanced nervously over his shoulder. He was too tall for me to see past him, but my guess was that he had a woman in his bed and didn't want me to see her. Could it be Kerry Hammond?

"Look, I'm sorry to wake you up, but I came all the way from Minnesota to see you and I'm not leaving until you and I have a little talk." He winced. He was a handsome fellow. Maybe not quite the Tom Cruise lookalike he'd been billed to be, but close. On the other hand, maybe Tom Cruise didn't look this good without his makeup and the right lighting. I've heard that Hollywood magic does wonders to make heartthrobs out of some pretty ordinary-looking people. "It won't take very long, I promise."

"Okay, I guess it's all right, but not here. Give me two minutes. I'll meet you in the living room."

I went back downstairs. I cleared myself a place on the worn maroon plush sofa and sat down to wait. The two latest issues of *The Hollywood Reporter* were lying next to me, but I decided to rest my eyes rather than read them.

Luke had combed his hair and put on shoes by the time he entered the living room. Some of his Midwest manners had apparently stayed with him. "What's this about?" he asked.

"Kerry Hammond has disappeared and her sister is very worried about her."

His blue eyes widened. "Disappeared? Kerry? What happened?"

"We thought she might be with you."

"Why would—I mean, Kerry's a great kid, and she and I are real good friends. . . . But I haven't seen her in a couple of months. Haven't even talked to her since before I left Newton." He appeared genuinely bewildered.

"Let me be blunt, Luke. Monica suspects—I mean, there seems to be some evidence that Kerry might be expecting a baby."

"Jesus Christ, Kerry—I don't believe it." He bit his thumbnail. "You don't think I—" I said nothing. "You *do*, don't you? Oh, God, this is just too much."

"I went to Newton Prairie, Lucas, and I asked around. People told me that you were Kerry's boyfriend, until you left town."

"Kerry and I are friends, good friends. We're not lovers."

"So you never slept with Kerry?"

"Hell, no. She wouldn't have let me, even if I wanted to. Not with all that religious stuff her family kept shoving down her throat. Sex just wasn't—Well, Kerry doesn't think it's right to have sex before marriage."

"I'd like to believe you, Luke, but—Look, if Kerry is here

with you, I'm not going to tell her parents on her. I just want to let Monica know she's all right."

"But she's *not* here. I don't know where she is."

"When I called here a couple of days ago, Luke, one of the guys who answered the phone told me you had a blonde girlfriend. Mind telling me who she is?"

The bewildered look was back. "I haven't got any girlfriend. I mean, I know a couple of girls from my acting classes, but—"

"Ever bring any of them here?"

"Sure, a few times. This place is pretty much of a dump, but at least it's got a big living room. We've been rehearsing some scenes from Tennessee Williams, from *Cat on a Hot Tin Roof* and *Glass Menagerie,* stuff like that." He shook his head. "One of those girls is blonde—Gina Baer—but she's not my girlfriend. I tell you, I haven't got a girlfriend."

I wondered how young Lucas categorized the woman he had hiding in his bedroom upstairs. As a pickup, a one-night stand?

I heard a voice say, "See you later, Luke. I gotta get to work." Lucas's gaze darted past me. He stiffened and his face colored instantly.

I turned to see an auburn-haired young man leaning against the doorframe. He was about Lucas's age and dressed similarly, in jeans and a T-shirt.

Lucas choked out his words. "Yeah, see you later." He stared at his lap. Suddenly I got the picture. Lucas Drew had been hiding a lover in his room, all right, but it wasn't a woman. It was a young man. Lucas was gay, or maybe bisexual. Neither would play very well in Newton Prairie, Minnesota— the home town of Community Fundamentalist Church.

A couple other things I'd heard about Lucas fell into place to confirm my suspicion. If he was gay, Kerry Hammond would have been the perfect cover for him—a pretty girl people would assume was his romantic interest but who, because of her religious convictions, would never push him into having sex with her. I wondered whether Kerry knew the truth about him.

I remembered Monica's telling me that Lucas had dumped her friend the homecoming attendant right before the big dance and that now made sense to me, too. He'd probably simply panicked. Taking a girl to the homecoming dance could have put him under strong pressure to become sexual with her. Wouldn't the easiest way out be to break up with the girl?

I reached over and patted Lucas's clenched fist. "Look, I don't intend to report back to Minnesota about anything I find here, unless it has something to do with my case. All I want is to find Kerry."

"Hey, sorry to interrupt again—" The guy with the auburn hair was back. "Is that your car in the driveway? It's blocking mine."

"Yeah, sorry. I'll move it."

Lucas walked outside with me and waited while I pulled my rental car into the street, let his friend's Mustang out, then drove back into the driveway.

Lucas placed his palms against the roof of my car and leaned over to talk to me. I rolled my window down. "Hey, listen, Miss MacDonald—"

"Devon."

"Devon, then. I really wish I could help you, honest. I wish I knew where Kerry was. But I don't. And—Well, I hope you meant what you said about not letting anything get back home. I mean, my life here doesn't have anything to do with Kerry, right?"

"Right. I meant it." I handed him one of my cards. "Kerry may contact you, Lucas, as a friend. If she does, will you have her call me, or else Monica? Tell her I promise I won't go to her parents. We're just worried about her."

"Sure, thanks." Lucas shook my hand, then disappeared back inside the old rooming house.

22

I headed west out of Los Angeles on Highway 101, which veered north at Ventura and followed the coast. Doug Winthrop and I had agreed to meet in Big Sur late Saturday afternoon, unless one of us ran into a snag with our work. The drive took longer than I'd figured. As I turned west onto Highway 1 at San Luis Obispo, then headed north again past Cambria, I found myself getting groggy. Not the best condition in which to drive the winding highway through Big Sur.

I'd been at the wheel for four hours by the time I stopped at a café and gas station in San Simeon. I filled the gas tank, then downed two cups of strong black coffee. Unused to so much caffeine, I still felt tired, but now it was a wired kind of tired. At least I would face a much shorter drive tomorrow. I'd made plans to drop my rental car off at the Monterey Airport, then fly back to Minnesota from there. And I planned to enjoy plenty of relaxation in between.

Nearly two hours later, I was still winding my way up the coast toward the inn where Doug was to meet me. The scenery was spectacular: golden cliffs dropping hundreds of feet to the craggy shores of the Pacific; herds of cattle grazing on green and gold hillsides; flocks of pelicans soaring high, then stopping in mid-flight to drop straight down into the water; a cargo ship crawling across the horizon. But most of my attention was taken up in driving the treacherous road behind a fleet of snail-paced campers and trailers that refused to pull over and let faster drivers pass.

I told myself to calm down, that I was probably better off driving this road slowly, given my level of exhaustion. If Doug got to the inn ahead of me, he would wait.

As I drove, I examined my case over and over in my mind, trying to figure out what I'd overlooked. If Lucas Drew wasn't the key to Kerry Hammond's disappearance, then who or what was?

The scene at the women's clinic yesterday troubled me, because it strongly confirmed how adamant the Hammonds were about their anti-abortion beliefs. People who would force their four-year-old child to march, carrying a picket sign depicting a grisly dead fetus, were hardly wishy-washy in their convictions.

That, coupled with the Hammonds' treatment of their oldest daughter a year earlier, made me wonder whether they might have harmed—even killed—Kerry in a fit of overzealous punishment or self-righteous rage. Maybe right now Kerry was buried somewhere on the Hammond farm, beaten to death by the same parents who'd sent Monica running to her high school counselor for protection and shelter.

That theory assumed both that Kerry really was pregnant and that her parents had somehow found out about it, of course. And the pregnancy theory was looking a lot weaker now that I'd found Lucas Drew. If he hadn't been responsible for Kerry's alleged condition then who had?

I made a mental note to call Linda Lundberg when I got back to St. Paul. The high school counselor hadn't been quick to agree that Lucas and Kerry were a romantic couple. With luck, she might have noticed the girl paired off with someone else.

I had to admit that Kerry's disappearance could be a random abduction, too. If it was, I felt an extra pang of guilt that I hadn't yet been able to prove it. If she'd been lured off that bus and kidnapped, the fact that her parents still thought she was at church camp only worked against her being found in time to save her. If there still was time.

But despite my finding Lucas, my thoughts kept returning to Kerry's questions to her sister and best friend about how an underaged girl could get an abortion. There had to be a reason for her inquiries. What would a girl in her position be likely to do, besides asking her sister and friend for advice? Were there some organizations or services set up to help girls like Kerry? Or to take advantage of them in some way under the guise of assisting them? I couldn't shake a mental picture of the Newton Prairie girl Linda Lundberg had told me about, the one who bled to death following an illegal abortion.

I decided that, when I got back to Minnesota, I would try to put myself in Kerry's position, to follow her thinking processes and her footsteps and see where they led me. But for now, all I wanted was twenty-four hours of fun.

I passed Nepenthe, the famous restaurant built on property once owned by Orson Welles and Rita Hayworth. It was a redwood and glass structure perched on the cliffs overlooking the water. As I passed the crowded parking area, I began watching for the signs Doug had told me about. I rounded another bend and saw the Ventana sign on the right. There, opposite the Ventana turnoff, on the ocean side of the highway, was my marker—a newly cut road and a sign identifying the entrance to the Post Ranch Inn.

I turned in and followed the narrow road across some fields, then drove uphill to a tiered parking area. Neither Doug's car nor a Carmel PD vehicle was in the parking lot. I'd obviously beaten him here, despite my tediously slow progress up Highway 1. I pulled the rental car into a temporary parking zone and went inside the registration building.

"Hello. Welcome to Post Ranch Inn." The desk clerk was a smiling woman in her mid-twenties.

"Hi. I'm here for the Winthrop reservation."

"Oh, yes. Ms. MacDonald, right?" I nodded. "I've got a phone message for you."

She handed me an envelope. I opened it and forced my bleary eyes to focus on the note's tiny handwriting. As best I could tell, the message had been taken about two hours earlier and it read, "Just picked up a suspect for questioning. Waiting for his lawyer to show up. Make yourself comfort-

able and I'll be there as soon as I can. Love, Doug." I folded
the note and put it back into the envelope.

The clerk called for a hotel van and the driver loaded my
suitcase inside, then drove me up the final steep hill to our
room. The Post Ranch Inn wasn't a hotel in the strictest
sense of the word; it was a series of individual and double
units perched on the edge of a cliff overhanging the ocean.
Construction had been completed within the year, and
everything possible had been done to keep the place as close
to its natural setting as possible. The main construction materials used were natural woods, metals, and lots of glass.
Many of the cottages actually had sod roofs so, at a quick
glance, they appeared to be part of the landscape.

The cottage to which I was assigned was almost spartan
in its furnishings, holding only a bed, a dresser, a couple of
chairs, and a small table. But the view was a thousand percent
luxurious. One wall of the bedroom was made completely
of glass, making me feel suspended in mid-air above the vast
Pacific Ocean. I wondered how much Doug was shelling out
for this place, but decided I would probably only feel guilty
if I knew.

I unpacked and hung up my clothes, drank a big glass of
water, and opened the sliding glass doors to the balcony.
The sun was slowly sinking toward the purple fog bank on
the horizon. I sat down on a chaise lounge, leaned back, and
closed my eyes, listening to the soothing sound of the waves
hitting the rocky shore below and the occasional call of a
sea gull.

I would rest here, I told myself, just until Doug arrived.
Surely that wouldn't be long now. I felt myself drifting
off.

When I awoke, it was dark and I was shivering in the
damp, cold night air.

23

It was after ten o'clock before Doug arrived at the inn, wearing a contrite look and offering me a dozen sincere apologies. I'd had time to shower, change my clothes, and dry my hair after my nap. I felt far more rested and human than I had when I arrived this afternoon.

Doug explained that he'd been held up taking a confession from a sixteen-year-old youth who'd been caught earlier in the day while holding up a 7-Eleven store. Turned out the kid had pulled off a whole string of convenience store robberies in the Carmel area and, when apprehended, he was ready to sing. Complete with several choruses and an encore.

"The kid wants to put on a concert, I've got to be his audience." Doug placed a finger under my chin, tilted it upward and kissed my lips softly. "But God, I'd sure rather have been here with you."

I couldn't be angry with him. He'd only been doing his job, and I'd have done the same thing in his place. The truth was, we both had jobs that would never be nine to five, with weekends off.

We ate dinner at the inn's restaurant. I had a sautéed scampi appetizer, a baby greens and goat cheese salad, grilled salmon, and chocolate mousse. Doug had the same, except for the main course; unlike me, he was a meat eater, so he went for the rack of lamb with rosemary. Everything was elegant, but expensive, at least by Minnesota standards—four gourmet courses for a fixed price of forty-five bucks apiece, plus wine and tip.

"This place is incredible, Doug," I told him, "but I'm not used to being treated like rich folks. I can't help but feel a little bit guilty about all the money this is costing you."

"And it didn't cost you a dime to come all the way out here to see me, right?"

I laughed, mentally adding up my airfare and the car rental, items that certainly would never be reimbursed by Monica Hammond. "Now that you mention it, tonight may set some kind of record for the most expensive date in history."

"It's worth every penny to me." He put down his dessert spoon and we held hands across the table.

After dinner, we walked outside along the bluff for a time. Most of the fog had lifted by now. We watched the moonlight and clouds cast shadows across the water and made wishes on the canopy of stars above. The night air was completely silent, except for the low roar of the waves and the tinkling of wind chimes somewhere in the distance. I felt suspended in a magical place and time, which my hyper-vigilant self-protective instincts kept telling me had nothing in common with real life.

Watch out, Devon, just watch out, my subconscious kept saying. *Don't let this romantic setting rope you in or you'll get your heart broken.*

I shivered, suddenly feeling the damp, chilly air sink in clear to my bones. We went inside our cozy room, where Doug wrapped me in a blanket and held me tight against his chest. I felt his warm breath gently caressing my forehead and listened to his heart beating strongly, reassuringly, in his chest. We sat like that and talked for a long time.

He told me about the kid he'd interrogated that day, a misguided youngster who reminded him of his younger brother and made him sad.

I told him about Monica and Kerry Hammond, girls who made me remember a lot I'd forgotten about the coldness and stern discipline of my own family.

As Doug's fingers released the barrette holding my ponytail, then began to stroke my hair lightly, we talked about how hard it was to find the time to keep a love relationship alive when one half of a couple was a cop. Or a private investigator.

Both of us had tended to grow more cynical about life and people over the years, mainly because of our chosen professions and because of the tragic losses we'd had in our own lives. Yet we agreed we did not like being cynical. We both wanted to be emotionally open again, the way we once were.

I began to feel warmer. For the moment, I stifled my self-protective instincts, threw off the blanket, put my arms around Doug's neck, and kissed him full on the mouth. He tasted a little salty and warm and entirely pleasant. We kissed some more. Then he helped me throw off a few more things.

After that, we were too busy to talk again for a long, long time.

24

Sam was already at his desk, hard at work on the agency's monthly billing by the time I arrived at the office on Monday morning. My plane had arrived late Sunday night and I'd overslept.

"Morning, kiddo," he called to me as I hung up my coat. "Looked all over the place, but I couldn't find that expense report ya promised me first thing this morning. Musta took it home with ya, huh?"

Oh, shit, my expenses on that workman's comp case. I'd completely forgotten. "Sorry, Sam . . . " My partner wasn't smiling; billing the agency's clients always makes him grumpy, particularly when he sees how many accounts are delinquent. I apologized, explaining that I'd gone out of town for the weekend. At least I told him the part about going to see Lucas Drew in West Hollywood; I figured the rest of it was my private business.

"Jesus Christ, Devon, you actually went all the way to L.A. to see that girl's boyfriend? And then he turns out to be a *faygeleh!*" He pounded his fist on his ledger. "Who the hell d'ya think's gonna pay for that fiasco?"

"Come on, Sam. I'm going to pay for 'that fiasco' out of my own pocket, so you don't have to worry about it. I'm not asking the agency to pay one damn nickel."

"But why the hell would you—" Suddenly the deep crease between Sam's eyebrows disappeared and he broke into a broad grin. "Oh, I get it. Went to see that cop you got the hots for, didn't ya?"

"Lord, you can be crude sometimes, Sam." I felt my face getting warm. "I haven't 'got the hots' for Doug. We just happen to enjoy each other's company."

"But I'm right, ain't I? You went up to Carmel to see that Winthrop fellow."

"Not all the way to Carmel, I didn't." It wasn't a complete lie; Big Sur was twenty-six miles south of Carmel.

At least Sam was smiling now; teasing me about my love life had improved his humor. "Hey, it's your funeral, petunia. I don't care what you do with your weekends." He took a long drink of his coffee. "Just so long as ya got that expense report on my desk before lunch."

I swore under my breath. But I went into my office and slapped together the expense report. I brought it into Sam's office and tossed it onto his desktop.

"Trade ya." Sam swiveled his chair around to the computer printer, ripped off the printout, and handed it to me. "Here, take a look at this. Guess preachin' an' picketin' pays pretty good these days."

I looked over the printout of Stearns County properties owned by Reverend Edward Beale and whistled.

"Pulled up the parcels owned by Beale and his wife, plus his two anti-abortion groups. Legally, he *is* them two groups. What they own, he owns."

"Good work, Sam."

"Made a coupla calls and got some more dirt on some o' these joints, too. That house in Newton Prairie's the biggest one they got in that town, four thousand square feet. English Tudor place on the north side, just off the main county road. Got five bedrooms, four bathrooms."

"I remember driving past that house on my way out of town. It's got a big circular drive in front and a triple car garage. I wondered who owned it." I looked to see what the county assessor's valuation for the place was. "Three forty-five, huh? God, Sam, it must be a regular palace. Three forty-five would buy any four average houses in that town." Reverend Ed had managed to avoid paying property taxes on his home, too, by claiming the nonprofit organization tax exemption. I ran my finger down the list. "Find out anything about these other places here?"

"Is the Pope Catholic?" Sam puffed up his chest. "St. Cloud address is an apartment building. Six units in a blue-collar neighborhood. The Rockville addresses are two little houses, probably rentals, plus a medical building."

"A medical building?"

"Yup, small one, one or two offices. S'posed to be a good kinda income property to own, medical offices. Doctors pay their rent on time and they don't move around much."

"And what's this last one, the one with all the acreage?"

"Farmhouse and land in southern Stearns County. Dunno if it's a workin' farm or just some kinda hobby thing Beale's got. Two hundred acres ain't real big for a farm in that part o' the country."

"Ver-ry interesting."

"That's a fact, sweet pea. But what I wanna know is what all this stuff's got to do with your missin' gal."

"I don't know, Sam, I don't know. Maybe nothing at all." Still, I felt a little better after seeing this list, if only because it confirmed my gut feeling that Reverend Ed Beale was up to his armpits in greed and hypocrisy, skimming money from his so-called cause to fatten his own holdings. I folded up the computer printout and headed back to my office to make some phone calls.

* * *

Linda Lundberg was not at home, but I left a message on her phone machine asking her to call me when she came back in.

Dr. Barbara Hansen was in surgery, but she returned my call within half an hour. I asked her what kind of help might be available for a pregnant sixteen-year-old who wanted an abortion and was afraid to tell her parents.

"Legally, there's nothing we can do for her here at the clinic, not without her parents being informed. Unless she can get a judge to sign off for her, of course."

"How would she do that?"

"She tells her story to a judge who's known to be sympathetic to these cases. She convinces him that she's mature enough to make her own decisions, he signs on the dotted line, and that's all there is to it."

That process sounded easy in theory, but I was willing to bet it was a lot harder in practice. I had trouble envisioning a girl like Kerry going out and finding any judge, never mind one guaranteed to be sympathetic to her plight.

"It's not as hard as you'd think," Dr. Hansen told me. "There are a number of organizations who help these girls. Some even provide transportation to another state, if that's what it takes."

"So how does a girl find one of these organizations?"

"Word of mouth. Some of them advertise, too, mostly in the Yellow Pages or the classified ads in the newspaper. Some of the women's clinics'll put girls in touch with them, too. I know it kills me to have to tell a girl we can't help her and just turn her away. Most of these kids are already basket cases by the time we see them."

I thanked Barbara and opened the St. Paul phone book to the Yellow Pages. Then I checked the classified ads in that morning's *St. Paul Pioneer Press* and *Minneapolis Tribune*. I called all the abortion services listed, but learned little that seemed useful.

Yet I realized that Kerry Hammond's sources would have been different. If she'd been searching for this kind of help, she undoubtedly would have used her local newspaper or phone book to find it.

I dialed the information operator in Stearns County and coaxed her into reading me the listings in the Yellow Pages. Maybe it was a slow day for her, or maybe small-town phone operators are just more old-fashioned anxious to please their customers. Whatever the reason, the woman was completely accommodating.

There were only three listings of the type I wanted. The first was for the St. Cloud clinic that now was in ashes. The second was an 800 number for Planned Parenthood of Hennepin County, a group I'd already contacted. But the third interested me.

"It's a display ad, takes up a quarter of the page," the operator said. "You want me to read you the whole thing?"

"If you would, I'd really appreciate it."

"You bet. Along the top it says in big letters, 'Facing an unwanted pregnancy? Thinking about abortion?' Under that, there's smaller type. 'If you are underage, don't be intimidated by Minnesota's tough parental consent law. Call five, five, five, fifteen, twenty for confidential help.' "

"And does it give the name of the group?"

"It's just got some initials here—P.C.A. Doesn't say what they stand for."

I thanked the operator for her help and rang off. I stared at my notes— "Don't be intimidated by Minnesota's tough parental consent law." This sounded like the kind of organization Barbara Hansen had mentioned. Either that, or maybe P.C.A. was a conduit to a source of back-alley abortions for minors.

I dialed the number.

A woman's voice answered, "Planned Childbirth Association."

I identified myself as a teenager facing an unwanted pregnancy. "My boyfriend dumped me as soon as I told him about the baby and there's no way I can tell my folks. They'd kill me." I did my best to sound both young and frantic. "I want an abortion, but I saw on TV where that clinic in St. Cloud got burned down and I can't tell my folks anyway." I sniffled once or twice, hoping to sound more credible. "I saw your ad and . . . well, I was hoping you could help me out."

The voice was soothing, sympathetic. "I know just how you feel, dear. The same thing happened to me when I was a girl. How old are you?"

"Uh, seventeen."

"Well, don't you worry, you've called the right number. P.C.A. will help solve your problem." She gave me a sub-urban St. Cloud address. "Now you just come right on in here, honey, just as soon as you can, and have a little chat with one of our counselors. I promise you'll feel better about this before you know it."

"I don't want counseling. All I want is an abortion. Can you get me one?"

"We can help you with all your options. Just come on in here and see us. Do you have your own transportation or do you need a ride?"

"I've got a car, but—"

"Good, my dear. You know where we're located?"

"I guess I can find it all right, but—"

"Let's set you up with an appointment, then. What's your name, dear?"

"All I want is the number of some place that can get me an abortion. Can't you just give me that much over the phone?"

"Against our policy, my dear." I had to give the woman credit. She wasn't losing her cool for a second; her voice was just as warm and comforting as ever. She also wasn't giving me any useful information. "We always do our counseling face-to-face," she insisted. "But you don't have to worry, it's all *completely* confidential."

I glanced up to see Sam standing in my office doorway, his face grim. Had I screwed up my expense account again?

"I'll have to think about it and let you know," I said into

the phone, then quickly hung up. "What's the matter, Sam?"

"Got some news," he said, squeezing himself into one of the two narrow guest chairs facing my desk. "My contact at the Stearns County Coroner's Office just called."

"Yeah?"

"They got themselves another burned-up corpse up there. Farmer found it in a public dump somewheres out in farm country. Looks to be a girl in her middle to late teens." Sam leaned back in the chair and I heard it creak under his weight. "Somebody dumped gasoline on this kid and lit a match. Not a helluva lot left of 'er anymore."

"Oh, my God." I had a mental picture of the charred corpse and my stomach did a quick flip-flop. "Does it sound like this one could be Kerry Hammond?"

"Dunno. Ain't much to go on so far. Figure it's gonna take 'em a while to come up with an ID, considerin' the shape the body's in. Prob'ly have to go with dental records."

"How long ago did the girl die?"

"They're still workin' on that, but the early guess is two, three days max." Sam stared at his hands. The fact that he wasn't spouting his usual gallows humor worried me. I suspected he wasn't telling me everything he knew.

"There's something else, isn't there, Sam? Something that makes you think this one *is* Kerry."

" 'Fraid so."

"Well, spit it out then."

"This girl didn't die from the fire. Looks like she bled to death, 'n' somebody torched 'er after."

I felt a chill creep down my spine. "She bled to death, huh? How?"

"Coroner's bet is the kid had an abortion. Guy that done it botched this one up real good."

25

"Please God, don't let it be Kerry," said Monica Hammond for the twentieth time since I picked her up at her rooming house and we began our journey. "Please God, don't let it be Kerry." Her eyes closed now, she was using the phrase as a kind of chant.

I drove Monica north to view the remains of the girl we both feared would turn out to be her younger sister. Now I pulled into the parking lot of the medical examiner's offices, my knuckles white on the Honda's steering wheel. This was not my idea of a good time.

"Please God, don't let it be Kerry."

When I told Monica about the corpse that had been found in rural Stearns County, I explained that it could take days, maybe even weeks or months before the victim would finally be identified. Unless, of course, Monica wanted to give the authorities her sister's name. If they had that, they could get Kerry's dental records and compare them with the body. But that method of identification would require Mary and Herman Hammond's knowledge, and there was no way my client would agree.

"What if I just go up there and see if it's her?" Monica asked. "I mean, that way we'd know right away, and I wouldn't have to give the police Kerry's name, would I?"

"Look, Monica, I don't think you have a clue what you'd be getting yourself into. If you've never seen a dead body before, trust me, you don't want to start with one in this kind of condition."

"I've seen dead people before. I know what it's like." She bristled, straightening her spine and squaring her thin shoulders. "I went to Grandma Hammond's funeral when I was only five. And I bet I've gone to half a dozen more since then."

"It's not the same thing, not the same at all." Frankly, I think the peculiar American practice of viewing the corpse prior to a funeral—even when the deceased has been embalmed and gussied up with layers of wax and makeup—is little short of barbaric. When I die, I hope whoever's in charge will simply shove me into the crematorium as fast as possible. I want it all over with before anyone can comment on how "lifelike" some money-grubbing mortician has made me look in death. Anybody who wants to view something can view my ashes.

"I know it's not the same thing," Monica insisted. "I'm not stupid, ya know." There was a combative tone in her voice.

"Nobody said you were stupid. Come on, now, Monica, I know this has been hard on you. I know you're worried about your sister." I laid my hand on her upper arm, but she shrugged it off.

"I can do this, honest I can. I have to, can't you see that? 'Cause I just gotta know what happened to Kerry. This is driving me crazy."

So I allowed myself to be talked into driving Monica north to examine the Stearns County corpse. Dr. Grabowski, the assistant coroner I'd talked with earlier on the phone, led us into the bowels of the building. As we walked along the halls, I tried not to think about what might be going on behind the closed doors we passed. I stole a glance at Monica; she was pale and silent and she looked very, very frightened. I knew just how she felt.

"Just take a deep breath first," Dr. Grabowski said. "Then try to get a good, careful look at her." The three of us were standing before a wall of refrigerated cubicles that resembled a bus station locker room. But these cubicles didn't contain left luggage; each was a drawer large enough to hold a dead body. "This young woman's not in very good condition because of the fire. So you're probably going to have to look her over pretty carefully to make an identification."

Monica swayed on her feet a little. "You sure you're up to this?" I asked her.

"Yeah, sure, I'll be okay. Let's get it over with."

I nodded to Dr. Grabowski and he unlocked one of the drawers and pulled it out. A mound covered with a soiled sheet lay inside. A putrid odor assaulted my nostrils and I gagged, then forced myself to swallow.

"Ready?" the young doctor asked.

I tried not to breathe as he pulled back the sheet from the head, then from the feet, leaving it piled up over the center portion of the body. It was almost hard to believe that the charred mess underneath had until a few days ago been a live human being. The hair was now completely gone. The skin was blackened and blistered, like chicken left too long on a backyard barbeque grill. Bare bone was visible in a couple of spots, where pieces of the dead girl's flesh were missing. I didn't know whether that was the result of the fire, or if animals had been working on the corpse while it lay undiscovered in the rural dump; I didn't really want to know. Ordering myself not to be sick, I turned my eyes away and swallowed hard once more.

I watched Monica standing beside me. She was staring straight ahead now, her mouth hanging open, and she had lost all her color. "I—I—" She started to sway. Her knees buckled and she folded toward the lineoleum floor. I grabbed for her, but managed only to cushion her fall.

Dr. Grabowski and I each took an arm and carried her to a leatherette couch out in the hallway. We laid her down and raised her feet. Then the doctor held a small vial of ammonia under Monica's nose and she revived quickly, turning her head away from the sharp smell and gasping for fresh air. Or for what would have to pass for fresh air in a place like this.

"It's okay now, Monica," I said, wiping her damp brow with my handkerchief. "It's all over." *All but the nightmares,* I thought. I wouldn't press her for an identification of the body until the color began to come back into her cheeks.

When she was able, the doctor ordered Monica to sit up and bend over, with her head between her knees, until her dizziness had passed.

Ten minutes later, she looked up at me and said, "I don't think it's Kerry. That girl looked too short."

"How tall is Kerry?"

"She's pretty tall. Five-six, at least. Maybe closer to five-seven."

I left her sitting on the couch while I chased down the doctor. He checked the autopsy report. Monica was right; the corpse was only five feet one. It was definitely not Kerry Hammond.

26

I drove Monica back to her rooming house near the University of Minnesota and went home to bed. My sleep was fitful that night; I dreamed about being chased down a narrow corridor lined with smouldering bodies by an unknown man carrying a can of gasoline in one hand and a burning torch in the other. I awoke in a sweat, my heart beating wildly.

My uneasy night left me fearing that Kerry Hammond had met the same fate as the dead girl I'd seen in the Stearns County morgue. It now seemed obvious that somebody in that area of the state was circumventing the parental notification law and aborting minors illegally. Somebody whose lack of medical skill had probably killed at least two girls in the past year, including the one Linda Lundberg had told me about. I hoped that Kerry hadn't brought the total higher.

The longer Kerry was missing, the more likely it was that she was dead. And, truth was, I was running out of places to look for her. The only lead I hadn't already explored was that ad in her local telephone book. So, early the next morning, I was on my way north again, this time to check out the Planned Childbirth Association. I was beginning to feel like the bus driver assigned to the eighty-mile route between St. Cloud and the Twin Cities.

Wanting to get an early start on the drive back north, I didn't bother to go into the office at all the next morning. I just climbed back into the Honda and headed for I-94.

I found easily the address the P.C.A. telephone operator had given me; it was a small gray house in a transitional neighborhood on the west side of St. Cloud. There were no identifying signs on the front of the building.

I parked about half a block down the street and watched the house for a half hour or so. There was no movement at all until about eleven o'clock, when a new blue Chrysler Le Baron convertible pulled into the curb in front. A portly middle-aged woman in a black polyester pantsuit got out of the driver's side, and a red-haired teenage girl in jeans and a gold sweatshirt emerged from the passenger's. The girl was carrying a small black duffel bag. The older woman gestured for the girl to follow her and both of them entered the gray house through the front door.

I suspected that the woman was one of the counselors touted by the P.C.A. receptionist I'd spoken to. As I sat and waited, I pictured the red-haired girl inside the little house, nervously getting prepared to have an abortion—one that might kill her. She looked no more than fifteen, so the surgery wouldn't be legal in Minnesota even if it was performed by a licensed physician. Unless, of course, the woman in the pantsuit was not a counselor at all, but the girl's mother.

It would have been helpful if I could pass for a teenager. I was conscientious about my aerobics routines and I always tried to keep my fair complexion protected from the sun, but I had to face it—there was nothing I could do to erase nearly half my age from my appearance. Still, women in their thirties had unplanned pregnancies all the time, didn't they? If this place was in the business of performing abortions, they might be willing to accommodate someone my age, a woman who said she didn't want to travel all the way to the Twin Cities. I decided to go inside and see what I could find out.

I entered what had once been the house's living room, but now was set up as a reception area. There still was no sign posted anywhere. "Is this the Planned Childbirth Association?" I asked the receptionist, a hawk-nosed woman with unruly permed brown hair.

"That's right. Can I help you?"

"I hope so. I'm here to see a pregnancy counselor."

She looked at an appointment book that lay open on her desk. There were very few entries. "What's your name?"

"Devon, Devon MacDonald, but I'm afraid I don't have an appointment. I didn't know I needed one."

She looked up at me. Her eyes were a remarkably clear green; I wondered whether they were natural or the result of colored contact lenses. "That's all right, dear," she said. "We try to make accommodations, and we're not too busy this morning. How far along are you?" I recognized her soothing voice from our telephone conversation yesterday but, with luck, she wouldn't recognize mine.

The fact that the receptionist gave me no trouble at all about my age confused me a little. Apparently this service, whatever it was, wasn't limited to minors trying to circumvent the law. "About two months," I told her, hoping that no one here was prepared to give me a pregnancy test or, worse yet, a pelvic exam. "I'm pretty sure I want to have an abortion. Guess I'd better make up my mind pretty soon, huh?"

"Well, you've come to the right place, dear. Just have a seat over there and I'll see if Mrs. Bartz can see you." She punched three numbers on her telephone and quietly spoke a few words into the receiver. She hung up and smiled at me. "It'll be just a few minutes."

I sat down on one of the three chintz-covered chairs lined up against the wall. The mahogany lamp table next to me offered a selection of the current *Good Housekeeping* and *Woman's Day* magazines, along with a stack of old *Reader's Digests*. Nothing too radical there. Or of much interest to teenagers, either.

About ten minutes later, the woman I'd seen getting out of the Chrysler emerged from the back of the building and introduced herself as Mrs. Bartz. I followed her into a room that had once been a bedroom, but now held two desks, several chairs, and a big-screen television set. The walls were covered with large posters of babies and young children— all of them white, healthy, and beautiful. Only one of the posters showed a child with its parents; it pictured a handsome couple walking on a seashore, each holding a hand of the tow-haired toddler between them.

"Make yourself comfortable right there, Devon." Mrs. Bartz pointed to an upholstered chair placed perpendicular to her desk and directly facing the TV. "Is it all right if I call you Devon?"

I nodded, wondering why she didn't offer me her own first name.

"Now first off, let me make sure I understand everything. You say you're two months pregnant and thinking about having an abortion, right?"

"Uh huh. My boyfriend doesn't want to get married and I just don't think I can handle bringing up a baby all by myself."

"Your feelings are certainly understandable, Devon, and quite common." She leaned toward me. "But I wonder if you really understand what abortion means—" Her eyes locked onto mine. "Whether you realize that your choice to have an abortion means killing your baby, murdering your own flesh and blood." I felt my back stiffen as I began to get the picture. "I wonder if you've thought about all the other options available to you." Mrs. Bartz reached over and grabbed hold of my hand—to make sure I didn't bolt and run? She had two thick gold rings on her pudgy fingers, one set with a circle of small diamonds and the other with three rectangular emeralds. "We at P.C.A. are here to help you deal with your pregnancy in the right way."

"Wait just a—"

"Don't say anything yet, Devon. Just listen for a few minutes. And watch." She released my hand, then quickly reached over and punched a button on the television set.

For the next ten minutes, I sat through a propaganda film purportedly illustrating a doctor performing a late-term abortion. A computer animation simulated the fetus being hacked into pieces and sucked from the woman's womb, while the male voice-over spoke of the excruciating pain the "baby" felt as it was "literally torn limb from limb while still inside its mother."

I averted my eyes throughout most of the grisly film footage and forced myself to concentrate on analyzing the motives of Mrs. Bartz and the Planned Childbirth Association. Clearly, they'd used their Yellow Pages ad as a way of roping in women who found themselves with an unwanted pregnancy and who were looking for an abortion clinic . . . so they could brainwash them about the horrors of abortion. The end goal had to be to prevent abortions, to convince those who responded to the ad to carry their pregnancies to term. I pictured a girl Kerry's age being subjected to this pitch and shuddered.

The film ended with a crescendo of melodramatic music and Mrs. Bartz hit the rewind button. She reached for my hand again. I jerked it away and dropped it into my lap. "What you just saw is very disturbing, isn't it, Devon?"

I had no trouble agreeing with that statement.

The counselor smiled reassuringly. "I'm sorry if it upset you, but we at P.C.A. believe women need to know the truth, so we—"

"Excuse me, please, Mrs. Bartz." I got to my feet. "Do you have a rest room I can use?" I figured she couldn't refuse a pregnant woman use of the bathroom.

"Oh. Sure, down the hall, second door on the left."

In the bathroom, I wet a paper towel with cold water and pressed it against my closed eyelids while I thought about what to do next. I'd been on the verge of losing my cool, of telling Mrs. Bartz exactly what I thought of her tacky little propaganda film and her misleading ad in the phone book. Yet my more rational self knew that telling her off would change nothing. Plus, if Kerry Hammond had approached this group, my letting off steam could ruin any chance I had of finding her. I hid out in the bathroom until I'd collected my thoughts and regained my composure.

By the time I returned to the TV room, Mrs. Bartz was no longer alone. The videotape was playing again, this time for the viewing pleasure of the red-haired teenager I'd seen outside. She was sitting opposite the second desk and weeping softly into a crumpled tissue, periodically stealing a look at the television set. An extremely tall woman with her hair pulled into a salt-and-pepper bun at the nape of her neck was leaning over the girl, an arm around her trembling shoulders.

"Devon, come on over and sit down," Mrs. Bartz said.

The tall woman turned and looked at me as I entered the room. I caught my breath and took half a step backward as I recognized Helen Beale, Reverend Ed's wife. I quickly averted my eyes, hoping she hadn't recognized me.

Trying to make sense of the connections here, I took the chair opposite Mrs. Bartz and tried to keep my face hidden from Helen's direct view. I didn't know whether the minister's wife had any idea who I was, or whether she'd noticed me before today, either at the church rally in Newton Prairie or at the women's clinic protest in Minneapolis. There probably hadn't been any reason for her to single me out in either crowd. Still, there was no sense in giving her time to study my features and an opportunity to realize that she'd seen me somewhere before.

"Here's a little pamphlet we've put together explaining about your baby's development." Mrs. Bartz opened a flyer that pictured the development of the fetus at progressive stages. She spread it flat on the desktop in front of me and pointed to a picture of a two-month fetus. "See, your baby's little heart is already beating by now. And it's already decided whether it's going to be a little boy or a little girl. Look what it says right here . . ."

I let her rattle on, reading me parts of her brochure and pointing to the pictures, while I concentrated on trying to eavesdrop on what Helen Beale was saying to the red-haired girl across the room. The film had ended now, and it clearly had elicited the desired reaction from the teenager Helen called Melissa. The girl wept openly now, with heart-wrenching sobs.

"I—I guess— I guess you're right." Melissa blew her nose and choked out her words. "I better do like you said."

"You won't be sorry, Melissa. You'd never forgive yourself if you killed your baby. Especially when there are hundreds of wonderful families waiting to love it."

"It—It's just so *hard*."

"Of course, it seems hard now, but this is only a few months out of your whole life." Helen stroked the girl's hair.

"But I won't be able to graduate on time or—" The girl broke into tears again.

"Sure you will. You'll keep right on with your studies, so you don't have to miss a thing. And a year from now, you'll look back on this and feel really good about yourself and the choice you made . . . because you'll know you did right, what God wants you to."

"Devon! Devon, did you hear what I just said to you?" I pulled my attention back to Mrs. Bartz, who sounded annoyed with me.

"I'm sorry, I—I guess my thoughts wandered off for a minute. What were you saying?"

"I was explaining. If you can't care for your baby yourself, we'll help you find a good family to adopt it. Or if it's just money that 's troubling you, we'll help you apply for public assistance."

"Thanks," I said, getting to my feet. "I don't know what I want to do yet. I have to think about it." I shook the hand wearing the rings, picked up the brochure, and sidled toward the doorway, keeping my face turned away from Helen Beale.

As I left the room, I heard Melissa say something about not letting people at home know about her pregnancy.

"Don't worry about that for a minute. It'll be our secret. No one will ever know."

Outside, I sat behind the Honda's wheel and thought about what I'd just witnessed. It was obvious I'd started out on entirely the wrong track. P.C.A. wasn't in the illegal abortion business at all, so clearly Kerry Hammond hadn't gotten one here. It followed that P.C.A. couldn't be responsible for the death of the unidentified teenager whose body Monica and I had viewed, either. So who was?

There had to be some sense to be made of all this. It was clear that P.C.A.'s intention was to prevent abortions, not perform them. And, logically, with Helen Beale involved in it, P.C.A. must be financed by Reverend Ed's network of anti-abortion organizations. Yet, if Reverend Ed was involved, I was convinced there had to be a way to make a buck out of it somehow.

My eye fell on the Chrysler Le Baron parked in front of the little gray house and I remembered that Mrs. Bartz had driven Melissa here. Yet the two of them clearly hadn't known each other before today.

The bus station, that was it. Mrs. Bartz had met Melissa at the bus station. I remembered what the woman from the bus station news stand had told me—that she'd noticed a number of young girls arriving on the buses and later being met by a woman or a couple who whisked them away.

I pulled my 35-millimeter camera from the glove compartment and snapped on the telephoto lens. Then I parked the Honda a few spaces closer to the house and waited until Mrs. Bartz left for lunch. As she approached her car— this time Melissa wasn't with her—I aimed the camera through my windshield and clicked off half a dozen shots of her.

My pictures would never win a photo contest, but they should be sharp enough for my purposes. I started the Honda and drove toward downtown St. Cloud.

27

I drove directly from the one-hour photo printing service in downtown St. Cloud to the bus station, where I found Molly the newsstand clerk working behind her counter. She was wearing an oversized white turtleneck shirt with patch pockets over a pair of dark green slacks, and her brown hair was held back by a green head band a shade lighter than her pants.

There were customers waiting in line at the news stand when I arrived, so Molly had set aside her current paperback; a dog-eared copy of Joseph Wambaugh's *The Blooding* lay beside her cash register. Apparently she'd finished reading *Predator* and moved on to another violent true crime story. I waited until the current rush of customers had left with their purchases, then approached the counter.

Molly recognized me right away. "Hi, there. You're that private eye, right?"

I nodded. "Right, Devon MacDonald."

"Ever find that girl you were looking for?"

"Still working on it."

"Got your card right here." Molly grinned and punched a button on her cash register. The drawer popped open. She lifted up the black plastic coin section, pulled the calling card I'd given her from underneath it, and showed it to me. "See? Been keeping my eye peeled for that little blonde girl like I promised, too, but can't say as I've spotted her." She shoved the card back into the register and snapped the drawer shut.

A man in a rumpled brown raincoat grabbed a copy of today's *Minneapolis Tribune* from a stack in front of the counter and held it up. "How much?"

"Thirty-five." He dropped three dimes and a nickel into Molly's open palm and wandered off. She rang up the sale and put the coins into the cash register.

I pulled three of the photos I'd taken of Mrs. Bartz from my purse and handed them to the clerk. "How about this woman? Ever see her around here?"

Molly studied the photos for a minute, then turned to wait on two more customers. She set the pictures on top of her cash register while she sold a package of Doublemint gum, a Hershey bar with almonds, and three magazines, then picked them up again. "Yeah, yeah, I've seen this one around here all right, at least half a dozen times." Her voice took on an air of excitement. "She's one of the ones I told you about before, remember? Those people who meet young girls getting off the buses."

"Was she here this morning? Maybe hooking up with a red-haired girl in a gold sweatshirt?"

"Yeah—Yeah, you're right. I remember both of them now. The girl stopped off here and bought herself a copy of *Cosmopolitan* before the woman caught up to her. I remember thinking she was a little young for that kind of reading, that *Seventeen* might be more her speed."

"Hey, thanks, Molly. I really appreciate your help."

"No problem." She leaned across the counter, her elbows resting on a stack of *Newsweek* magazines, and whispered, "What's it all about, anyway? You got any idea what they're up to?"

"I'm not really sure," I told her, "but I think it might have something to do with teen pregnancy counseling."

Her eyes widened and her eager smile died. "You mean that little red-haired girl is going to have a baby?"

I shrugged. "It's just a guess."

"Lord, they just keep getting younger and younger, don't they?"

"Sure does seem that way sometimes."

"You ask me, that stuff they see on TV and that junk they read's gotta have something to do with it. I mean, what's a kid fourteen, fifteen years old doing with a magazine like

Cosmo, anyway? It's got nothing but articles on how to have a more exciting sex life, or how to steal somebody else's husband, that sort of thing. Gives kids all the wrong ideas."

Who could tell? She might've been right. I figured if anyone should know something about how people are influenced by what they read, it would be Molly. As I headed out of the bus station, I saw her scan the area for customers. When she saw none approaching her counter, she picked up her paperback, opened it, and sank back into the world of violent crime.

28

I stopped near the bus station exit and used one of the pay phones to call Dr. Barbara Hansen at her Minneapolis clinic. She'd heard of the Planned Childbirth Association before, and was able to confirm the impression I'd gotten from my morning visit. "That group's business is brainwashing pregnant teenagers," she told me. "Planned Childbirth is nothing but a front for the anti-abortion movement. But it's not only in St. Cloud. I've heard of at least three or four other towns where they've got offices."

"Remember where?"

"Let me get out my file." The sounds of metal drawers being opened and papers being shuffled echoed over the phone line. "I belong to a national abortion rights action group that's trying to get these people shut down," Barbara told me when she came back on. "Or at least force them to stop running ads where they pose as family planning or abortion services. Our group puts out a newsletter and I thought I remembered reading something about Planned

Childbirth in one of the recent issues." There was more paper shuffling. "Good, here it is. I found it. Says here that our national office has had complaints about Planned Childbirth from Sioux City, Iowa; Wichita, Kansas; Eau Claire, Wisconsin; and Pierre, South Dakota."

"All small Midwestern cities close to farm country."

"Right, but these may not be their only offices. Could be they've got dozens more. These people have piles of money, you know. They've done some real damage to some of the kids they've sucked in, too."

"Like what?"

"I know of at least two cases where they talked young women out of having early abortions, when they would have been safer. Only trouble was, these kids really couldn't cope with their pregnancies. One, a fifteen-year-old, decided she wanted an abortion after all . . . when she was already five months along. But she couldn't find a doctor willing to give her a late abortion, so she tried to self-abort. Ended up with a hysterectomy.

"The other one was sixteen. Managed to keep her pregnancy secret from her family by wearing baggy clothes and hiding out in her room. Finally gave birth at home, all by herself, then tried to flush her infant down the toilet."

"Oh, my God," I said.

"Yeah. These people may look harmless, but they aren't. Their brainwashing techniques can be fatal." I heard the clunking sound of a file drawer slamming shut. "Listen, Devon, I've got to go; I have patients waiting. But I hope you come up with something to nail these people. I'd love to see those bastards out of business."

Forty-five minutes later, I was back in Newton Prairie, pulling into the curb in front of Linda Lundberg's big yellow house. It looked like she'd almost finished painting the trim; only the front steps remained to be changed to the new weathered cedar color.

"Hi, come on in," the high school counselor said, answering the door.

I explained that I wouldn't stay long, but that I had a few more questions to ask her.

"I'm just unpacking my groceries. Come back to the kitchen, if you want. I've got to get some things in the freezer before they thaw out."

I followed her to the back of the house and into the cozy kitchen, where I squeezed into a tiny corner breakfast booth and watched her work. Like the house's exterior, the kitchen was yellow; obviously this cheerful shade was Linda's favorite color.

She pulled a sack of oranges from a grocery bag and set it on the sand-colored Formica counter. "You haven't found Kerry yet?"

"Not yet." I explained about my trip to Los Angeles to see Lucas Drew. "But Kerry wasn't there. And—Well, Lucas says he hasn't heard from her. He swears they never had sex and . . . well, I'm inclined to believe him. If Kerry's pregnant, I don't think Lucas is the father."

Linda shoved some packages of frozen vegetables into her freezer, shut the door, and sat down opposite me. She brushed her coppery bangs off her forehead, met my gaze, and sighed. "I had a hunch it wasn't going to be Luke," she said. She cocked one eyebrow at me, as if to ask whether my impression of the handsome youth was the same as hers; she'd probably long suspected he was gay. But I kept my promise to Lucas and held my tongue on that subject.

"Anyway," I said, "I wondered whether you had any ideas about other boys Kerry might have been involved with."

She stood up again and began loading packages of dry goods—macaroni, saltines, Minute Rice, Kellogg's Corn Flakes—into the tidy bleached oak cupboards. "No, I can't think of anyone at all. Like I told you before, I don't know Kerry as well as Monica. I always found her to be particularly shy, a very quiet girl." Linda opened a second cupboard and started unloading a sack filled with cans onto its shelves. "I suspect the boys were interested in her—she's such a pretty girl—but I never saw her respond to any of them."

"Well, it was worth a shot." I pulled out the photos I'd

taken that morning. "Just one more thing. Do you recognize this woman? Her name might be Mrs. Bartz." Or it might not. Bartz could well be a pseudonym.

I handed Linda the photos and she held them up to the kitchen light. "Should I know her?"

"I'm not sure. She works for a pregnancy information hotline I thought Kerry might've contacted. This group seems to have ties to Newton Prairie, so I wondered if Mrs. Bartz was a local woman."

Linda handed back the photographs. "Sorry, I don't recognize her."

"Know anything about the Planned Childbirth Association?"

"Is it like Planned Parenthood?"

"Not exactly." Although the similarity of the groups' names certainly was no mistake.

"Sorry. Guess I'm not much help today."

I left Linda Lundberg's comfortable home feeling depressed. I still hadn't found my client's sister. I still didn't know for certain whether the girl was pregnant. If she was, I didn't know who the father was. Or, if she had turned to the Planned Childbirth Association for help, where that had led her.

I got into the Honda and headed out of town. It was mid-afternoon now and, if I hurried, I could still make my seven o'clock dinner date at Sam's house. Rose had invited me, saying that Lael and her family would be there. She and Sam both seemed so anxious to show off baby Aaron that I didn't want to disappoint them.

As I left town and turned east onto the two-lane county road that would lead me back toward St. Cloud, I played out a scenario in my mind. Suppose that Kerry had called the P.C.A. number in the Yellow Pages, as I had. Then suppose she'd gotten off the bus in St. Cloud, where she was met by Mrs. Bartz or someone else from P.C.A. and brought to the little gray house for the indoctrination session. That alone might have been enough to convince a girl like Kerry that she couldn't possibly have an abortion. She was, after all, already subject to similar arguments from her family and church.

But what if an additional ingredient were added to the mixture? Suppose that she'd run into Helen Beale—her own minister's wife—at P.C.A.'s little gray house. Now Kerry's options would shrink to none. The secret she'd been trying to keep from her family and her town would be out, wouldn't it?

Unless . . . Unless Helen Beale had offered her another alternative. I tried to remember what the tall minister's wife had been saying this morning to young red-haired Melissa . . . something about finding her baby a good home.

I was so lost in my thoughts that I didn't realize the Honda was beginning to pull severely to the left until I drifted across the yellow center line. I swerved back toward the right and felt the car begin to bump and thump along on the lightly traveled road. *Hell,* I thought. I *couldn't* have a flat tire. Not after spending more than six hundred bucks on an entire new set of radials.

I pulled off onto the shoulder of the road and got out. Sure enough, my left front tire was nearly flat. I crouched down to inspect it. A shiny silver nailhead protruded between the treads—the sort of thing that makes a tire lose air slowly until it finally goes flat. At least, I thought, the tire should be repairable. I went to the trunk for the spare tire and the jack, congratulating myself that I'd replaced the ancient spare when I bought the new set of tires.

As I pulled the spare tire from the trunk, I heard the gravel crunch behind me. I breathed a sigh of relief, certain that help had arrived. If I got lucky, I'd be able to talk some nice farm lad into changing the flat tire for me.

I turned around to see a mud-spattered old pickup truck pulling onto the shoulder behind me. It stopped and both doors of the cab flew open. Two men emerged. My smile froze. Both men wore bandanas pulled up over the lower halves of their faces, while sunglasses and visored caps hid their eyes and hair from view. This did not look like help.

I caught my breath and turned back to the trunk, searching frantically for the jack. I grabbed one end of it and spun around to face my visitors.

"Bitch!" yelled the taller of the two men, rushing toward me. I swung the jack hard and connected with his upper arm.

But before I could land a second blow, the other man caught hold of the jack's end and twisted it behind my back. I felt sharp pains in my elbow and wrist and my grip loosened. The jack fell to the ground.

"Grab her, man," the shorter guy, dressed in jeans and a red jacket, shouted.

The one I'd hit with the jack tackled me and threw me to the ground. "You fuckin' bitch!" I landed face down, tasting gravel and pain. I spit out the dirt, then lay still for a second, until I felt my assailant loosen his hold on me. I twisted around in the dirt and jerked my knee up hard. I caught him in the crotch, but with less force than I'd hoped for. Even so, he moaned, then hauled an arm back and slapped me hard across the face with his open palm. My head cracked against the ground. My vision blurred and I tasted blood. My head throbbed and I felt myself retching.

The man in the red jacket bent over and grabbed one of my feet. The guy I'd kneed took the other one and together they dragged me around the side of the Honda, away from the open road. My sweater rode up and my bare back burned as my skin scraped along the gravel.

My mind raced, but I couldn't seem to get it out of neutral and into first gear. All I could think about was that there were two of them, both of them big, and only one of me, not nearly big enough. I was scared. Still, I told myself that it was broad daylight here. Not much traffic passed on this road, but surely someone would notice what was going on here. Someone would stop to help me. Wouldn't they?

I heard a car approach on the highway. "Help!" I yelled as loud as I could. "Help me!" *Please hear me. Please stop,* I begged silently, willing the passing car to stop and help. But it kept going.

The larger man threw a leg over my body and straddled

me, pinning my arms to my sides with his beefy thighs. His weight crushed my ribs, squeezing the air from my lungs. He dug his palm into my mouth and nose. Now the rancid tastes of tobacco juice and sweat mixed with my blood and I gagged. My ribs throbbed and I couldn't breathe. I fought hard against panic. "Keep that fuckin' mouth o' yers shut, bitch, or ya ain't gonna be able to open it no more."

This didn't seem the best time to bring up my First Amendment rights. He slowly removed his hand and I gasped for air, then swallowed, doing my best not to choke. If only I could keep them from taking me somewhere else, away from the open roadway, I thought, I might be able to survive. They wouldn't dare rape me, even murder me, here. Would they?

As thunder thighs continued to roost on my chest, preventing me from moving or even taking a complete breath, I heard the Honda door open. The other guy was searching my car—for what? "Shit! There's nothin' here," he declared a few minutes later. "Stupid broad ain't even got a gun."

Sam had often nagged me to buy a gun and learn how to use it, but I always fought him. I don't like guns. If I'd listened to my partner and gotten a gun to carry in the car, would I be pinned down here on the ground right now? Yeah, I decided, I'd have kept the gun in the glove compartment. So now I'd probably be lying here with one of these turkeys sitting on me and the other one pointing my own weapon at my head.

The guy in the red jacket slammed the car door shut and dropped to his knees into the dirt beside us. I felt something sharp prick the skin under my chin. Red jacket grabbed my ponytail with his left hand and twisted my head around so I was facing his bandana-covered face. With his right hand, he waved a short silver blade—it was pointed and as sharp as a scalpel—back and forth in front of my eyes. "You been stickin' your nose in where it ain't wanted, lady. Some of us don't much like that." His voice was low, almost a growl. He probably was trying to disguise it. I felt a surge of hope as I realized that, if red jacket meant to kill me, he wouldn't have to worry about my recognizing his voice later.

He held the tip of the blade against the side of my nose now. I couldn't so much as flinch without the nasty thing's cutting me. "You're pretty goddamned stupid, too, ain't you? How many warnings you gotta get before you back off, bitch? How many, huh?"

I had a terrifying vision of my face sliced up, scarred for life. Was that to be my next warning?

The hand holding the knife moved downward and the sharp tip pierced my clothes. I felt a stinging pain in my left breast. "Don't" I pleaded. Then he reached around his accomplice and pricked my belly and my crotch with the blade. "Don't, *please* don't hurt me."

I hated myself for begging, but I couldn't prevent the words from coming out of my mouth. Lying there on the ground, I'd quickly become like the millions of other women throughout history who suffered abuse and violation as the weaker sex.

I'd always felt physically strong, and I'd been self-confident because of my taller-than-average height. I'd frequently talked my way out of potentially violent situations, too. But I was no match for these two louts, each of whom outweighed me by a good fifty pounds.

"Asked ya a question, ya dumb bitch. How many warnings does it take?" He yanked my hair again.

"Wha—What do you want from me?" I fought hard to keep from trembling.

"We want you outta here. Lost. You never heard of Newton Prairie, see? We want your pretty little nose outta our business, outta our church, outta our campaign, outta our town. Get it?"

So that's who they were. I fought for a crumb of control, of self-respect. "Boy, I'm impressed," I said. "You religious fanatics sure know how to get a message across."

"That mouth's gonna get you killed, lady." I held my breath, waiting to feel the knife.

The larger man bounced hard on my chest, squeezing the air out of my lungs, while the guy with the knife pulled my hair and twisted my head around until I could see nothing but the muddy fields along the side of the road. I felt an eerie scraping sensation along the back of my neck. "Now we got somethin' to remember each other by," the man with the knife growled.

Suddenly both of them released their hold on me and bolted for the truck. I pulled my knees up to my chest and sucked in gallons of fresh air, then pushed myself into a sitting position. I began to shake violently.

As I heard the truck's engine catch, I forced myself to calm down. I crawled around the back of the Honda just in time to see the truck make a U-turn and speed back toward Newton Prairie. It wore no license plate.

My hands explored my clothes and body where the two men had touched me. The only blood I found seemed to be coming from my nose, where the bigger man had struck me. The scalpel apparently had done no more than tear my clothes and scratch my skin. There were a few bruises and abrasions from my ordeal, but they would heal quickly. Continuing my inventory of injuries, I felt tearfully grateful that I was still alive.

I reached around and ran my hand up the back of my neck. My fingers froze to the spot. There was nothing there but bristly stubble.

With a start, I realized that the man with the knife had taken something to remember me by, all right. He'd sliced my ponytail off at its roots.

My hair was gone.

29

I changed the tire and drove back to St. Paul in a daze. There was no sense in going to the local police. I couldn't identify my attackers anyway, and I'd promised Monica I wouldn't let anyone know I was looking for her sister. The last thing I wanted to do was explain to the police why I'd been hanging around Newton Prairie.

When I got home, I stripped off my clothes and threw them into the trash can. I climbed into a bathtub filled with hot water and soap suds, attempting to soak away an overwhelming feeling of having been soiled. That afternoon's experience had given me the smallest inkling of how rape victims must feel.

I soaped and scrubbed myself until my skin was red. Then I rubbed myself dry with a big aqua towel and, using a hand mirror and my kitchen shears, attempted to even up the back of my hairdo. I'd never thought of my long, not-quite-red, not-quite-blonde mane as particularly stylish, but what was left of it looked like hell. I'd never really thought of myself as a particularly vain woman, either, but now I couldn't help feeling maimed. I looked in the mirror and wanted to cry.

But I didn't have time for self-pity. I was already nearly an hour late for dinner at the Shermans' house, and suddenly I was hungry—for food, but even more for the company and protection of friends. I quickly applied makeup to hide the spot where the big man's blow had reddened my face. Then I pulled on a camel sweater and matching slacks, and drove the three miles to Highland Park.

Rose answered the door, greeting me with a kiss on the cheek. The pungent smell of roasting turkey permeated the house, making me think of Thanksgiving. It was a friendly, family gathering kind of odor, and I felt myself beginning to relax.

"Sorry I'm late," I told her. "I sort of got held up and I was late getting home."

"Not to worry, Devon. Betty Crocker says let the turkey rest a little before you slice him. So he's been resting."

"Turkey's pretty special, Rose. What's the occasion?"

"A celebration—my new grandson's very first dinner at

Grandma's and Grandpa's house. That calls for the best, even if he can't eat it yet."

Rose hung up my coat, then took my hand and pulled me into the living room. "You know Lael and David, right?" Rose's daughter and son-in-law, seated on the couch, greeted me with smiles. "And *this* is Aaron." Rose bent over a white mesh portable crib and planted a light kiss on the wrinkled forehead of a sleeping infant. "Isn't he simply the most gorgeous baby you've ever seen?"

"Mom, please," Lael said, rolling her eyes skyward. But she looked pleased with her mother's enthusiasm.

I watched as Aaron's little mouth made sucking motions while he slept. "He really is gorgeous," I said, meaning it. I reached over and gently stroked his tiny clenched fist.

Sam lumbered into the room, licking something off his fingers.

"Sam! I told you a thousand times, leave that bird alone 'til we're ready to slice him," Rose scolded. "You've been pulling his skin off, haven't you? I can always tell." Sam looked sheepish. "I tell you, Devon, sometimes I think this man I married hasn't got Aaron's sense. His cholesterol goes sky high, does he worry? No, I'm the one gets the ulcer while he—"

Sam stared at me. "Devon, what the hell did ya do to your hair?"

My hand flew to the nape of my neck and rubbed the stubble. "I sort of got scalped."

"What happened?"

I described my day, beginning with my visit to the Planned Childbirth Association and ending with my roadside encounter with the anti-abortion boys. I left out the part about being terrified half out of my mind.

Sam responded with his usual verbal bravado. When he got his hands on those pricks, he would teach them a lesson they'd never forget. He would cut more important things off their bodies than their hair. He would—

Rose flitted between me and Sam, uncertain which of us needed her administrations more. "Devon, my poor baby," she cooed, gripping my hand and stroking the length of my arm. "This nasty investigation business isn't right for a woman. I told Sam. He should've hired a man—a young man, one with muscles and smarts both. You've got the brains, but muscles, well, that's a diff—"

"Honest to God, Rose, let the girl be. I'll take care of this."

"A doctor, Devon, don't you think you should see a doctor, make sure there's no permanent damage?"

"Just five minutes is all I ask. Gimme five minutes alone with those bastards and I'll—" Sam began to grow red-faced, and Rose shifted her attention back to him.

She hovered, patting her husband's shoulder and begging him to calm down. This wasn't worth giving himself a heart attack, she insisted, especially now that I was safe, with no permanent harm done. My hair would grow back. She began to harp on her favorite theme of late—that Sam should retire now, before he gives himself another heart attack and it's too late. If Rose had her way, neither Sam nor I would be employed as private investigators.

I used to wonder how Sam could stand Rose's nudging and nagging, but then I realized it didn't really bother him; he loved having his wife's undivided attention. It was obvious, too, that he simply ignored any of her demands that he didn't agree with, doing precisely what he wanted to do.

By the time Lael and her husband had finished asking their own questions and expressing their concerns about my safety, Sam's blood pressure, and Rose's overdeveloped sense of mothering, I was beginning to feel grateful that I had no family of my own. I was smothering under the weight of all that attention. "Turkey must be getting cold, don't you think?" I asked.

Lael got to her feet. "I'll go slice it. Come on, David, give me a hand." The young couple trotted off toward the kitchen.

"They'll need my help," Rose said, seeing her control over her kitchen now in jeopardy. She hurried after the young couple, allowing me a few minutes alone with Sam to discuss our search for Kerry Hammond.

"Ya think that counselor gal let them bullies know where you were?" Sam asked.

"Uh uh, Linda Lundberg was with me the whole time and, besides, I think she's on the up and up. No, I think either Helen Beale recognized me at Planned Childbirth and called somebody to follow me after I left there, or else somebody saw my car parked outside Linda's house and decided I was becoming too much of a nuisance. He had the bright idea of pounding a nail into my brand-new tire and then following me out of town. It couldn't be too long until the tire got flat and I had to stop."

"Yeah, well I don't like the way this case's shakin' down, sweet pea. These churchy types ain't playin' by the rules and I don't like it one bit."

I wasn't exactly fond of the way things were going myself. But I reminded Sam that I had an obligation to do the job I'd been hired to do, and I had no intention of quitting now.

"I'm gonna ride along with ya, then, petunia. See ya got some protection."

I repressed a smile, fully aware that Sam's presence would undoubtedly be more of a hindrance than an asset to me. We argued until Rose called us for dinner, managing to agree only that we would trade cars if I had to return to Newton Prairie. Obviously my Honda was a magnet for trouble in that town. I made a mental note to have the flat tire repaired first thing in the morning; no way was I about to let Sam drive around in a car with no spare.

The meal was delicious. As I helped myself to a slice of dark meat and a scoop of sage dressing, I realized I hadn't eaten since breakfast. Rose had made no gravy—apparently so as not to tempt Sam, who certainly would have downed the largest portion had it been offered. But I didn't care. I ate like a stevedore and felt much better.

After dinner, Lael and I visited in the living room while she nestled baby Aaron to her breast and nursed him. We were alone for a few minutes, while the others cleared the table and loaded the dishes into the dishwasher. The baby's lusty sucking sounds brought back bittersweet memories of my own lost son. I mused wistfully about whether I would ever have another child.

"Those people really make my blood boil," Lael said, stroking Aaron's nearly bald head.

"Who?"

"Those anti-abortion fanatics. They're all so dogmatic, but the fact is, they don't even know what they're talking about."

I was surprised at the strength of Lael's reaction. "I'm sure they believe they're on strong moral grounds with their beliefs. Only problem is, it's somebody else's body they're out to control."

"I almost had an abortion a few months ago," Lael said, her face grim. "I don't know what I'd have done if it wasn't legal."

"But—I don't understand. I thought you were thrilled to be pregnant." There was no doubt she adored her new son.

"I *was* thrilled, so long as my baby was going to be healthy. We were lucky—I thank God every day for that—but we could've ended up just like Faye, David's sister."

I listened as Lael told me about her sister-in-law's tragedy. Three years ago, Faye had given birth to a baby boy afflicted with Tay-Sachs, an always-fatal hereditary disease that strikes the descendents of Eastern European Jews. "Adam lived fourteen months—fourteen months of complete hell for him and everyone around him. That poor little thing didn't have one minute of life without pain, not one minute." Lael's dark eyes misted over as she talked. "I don't know how I'd be able to survive if that happened to Aaron."

"But I thought both parents had to be carriers before you had to worry about Tay-Sachs."

"Right. We already knew David was a carrier; he had a test as soon as we found out about Adam. Then I got tested before I got pregnant. Turned out I carry the gene, too." Aaron began to fuss. Lael lifted him onto her shoulder and gently stroked his back until he burped, then returned him to her breast.

"We looked into adopting," she said, "but that's really grim these days. No babies available, except for ones with heavy problems. And that's what we were trying to avoid. Don't get me wrong—I really admire people who can adopt handicapped kids. But it takes a kind of patience I know I just don't have. Anyway, David and I talked it over and decided to risk having a baby of our own."

"So what were the odds that Aaron would have the disease?"

"One in four that he'd be born with Tay-Sachs. Two in four that he'd be a carrier." She wiped a milk bubble from Aaron's lips. "The worst part was that I couldn't have the amniocentesis test to see if my baby was okay until I was nearly four months pregnant. Then it took more weeks of waiting to get the results."

Neither Sam nor Rose had said anything to me about this; I wondered if Lael and David had told them. "You must have been frantic."

"It's the most godawful thing I've ever lived through in my entire life, that waiting, not knowing whether I'd end up with an abortion or a baby."

"I—I'm really sorry, Lael. I never realized."

Lael brushed her lips across her son's head. "It was hell. But can you imagine how much worse it would've been if abortion wasn't legal?"

"No, I can't." And I didn't want to.

"What frosts me is, who are those self-righteous idiots to tell me I have to give birth to a child, only to watch him suffer and die."

I felt my throat constrict. I knew a few things myself about watching your child suffer and die, and I would never wish the experience on anyone, not even those two creeps who'd assaulted me that afternoon.

The others were returning from the kitchen now, and I suddenly wasn't in the mood for more conversation about the new baby. I wished Lael and David the best, but being around tiny Aaron was beginning to make me sad. Something Lael said earlier had given me an idea, too, one I was anxious to pursue.

I begged off dessert, protesting that I'd eaten so much

turkey I didn't have room for another bite. Rose insisted that I wait while she packed up some leftover turkey for me to take home. I don't think I've ever had dinner at the Shermans' when Rose didn't make me take home leftovers. Sometimes I think she worries as much about my not eating enough as she does about Sam's overindulgence.

It was after ten o'clock by the time I bid everyone goodbye and headed out the door, the requisite aluminum foil-wrapped package in my hands. If I hurried, I could make it to Dinkytown and back again and still get to bed by midnight.

30

I found Monica Hammond waiting tables at the Pizza Cellar in Dinkytown. Her shift wasn't over until two in the morning, so I took a table in the corner, ordered a cup of tea, and waited until she could find a few minutes to talk to me. The Pizza Cellar was in the basement of a building near the University campus. Upstairs was a beer bar.

Several of the Pizza Cellar customers looked as if they'd had more than enough to drink upstairs. "Hey, gorgeous, commere," I heard one of them say to Monica. "Ya call this extra cheesh? I ordered extra cheesh." He grabbed for her uniform skirt, but Monica twirled away from his reach. The drunk momentarily lost his balance, fell forward, and nearly ended up face down in his steaming pizza.

"You got your extra cheese," Monica said to him, slapping his check on the table and walking away.

She eyeballed her other tables, decided they didn't need her for a few minutes, and slipped into the seat beside me.

"That creep is in here at least three nights a week and he always pulls the same crap. Thinks he can get away without paying, I guess."

"You handled him well."

"Yeah, well enough to earn the twenty-five-cent tip he always leaves." Monica sat with her eyes glued to the kitchen door. "If the owner comes in, I'll have to stop talking and look like I'm working. He doesn't like us to sit down and talk with the customers, and I can't afford to get fired."

"Can you take a break for a few minutes? We can go someplace else to talk."

"Nope, not now. I just finished my dinner break at ten."

I promised to talk fast. I gave Monica a quick sketch of my day, downplaying the seriousness of the scene with the two guys who'd punctured my tire and followed me out of town.

Monica chewed her thumbnail. "You don't think my brother could've been one of them, do you, Devon?" She looked very young and vulnerable.

"No, I don't think so. Both of them were bigger than Mike." The two might have been among Mike's cronies, the ones I'd seen at the meeting with Reverend Ed, though. But I hadn't come to see Monica for help in speculating about who'd given me a free haircut. "I wondered whether you'd heard about any kind of home for unwed mothers near Newton Prairie, maybe something your church sponsors?"

Monica half stood up as the kitchen door swung open, but sat down again when she saw it was only another waitress, carrying a tray filled with glasses. "No, I never heard of any place like that," she said.

"What about girls in Newton Prairie who get pregnant and aren't married? What happens to them?"

"Most of 'em get married, I guess."

"To their babies' fathers, you mean."

"Yeah, right."

"Any girls who keep their babies and don't get married?"

She shook her head, then stopped herself. "Well, I guess there's one I can think of—Jill Lester. She left town for five or six months, was s'posed to be visiting her aunt in England. She came back to school and all, but about two months later, the weirdest thing happened."

"What's that?"

"Jill suddenly stopped coming to school, and next thing we knew, she had this tiny baby she was taking care of at home."

"You mean it was her own baby?"

"Uh huh. Story was that she never went to England at all. She went somewhere to have her baby and she gave it up for adoption. But the parents—I mean the people who were s'posed to adopt Jill's baby—they found out the baby couldn't see, so they gave it back."

"You mean the baby was blind?"

"Yeah, right. Blind from birth. Only I guess they couldn't tell right away or something."

"So the adoptive parents backed out on the adoption when they found out."

"That's what I heard. I couldn't swear it's true."

"Poor Jill. And her poor baby." I sipped my tea, but it was already cold. "So now Jill lives at home in Newton Prairie."

"Well, right outside Newton. Her folks have a farm and she lives there with them. Or, she did, last I heard."

I asked Monica to try to remember any other girls who might have disappeared for several months, using an excuse similar to Jill's. "Anybody people gossiped about." I remembered a couple of girls like that in my own high school. One had actually been sent away to boarding school because her parents were divorcing, but that hadn't stopped tongues from wagging back home.

The drunk finished half of his pizza, tossed a quarter on the table, and staggered toward the cashier. Monica cleared his table, put the coin in her uniform pocket, and sat down again. "I've been thinking about it. I guess there's three or four girls like that," she said. She wrote down their names on the back of one of her restaurant checks. "I don't know where these girls are now, and I can't swear they had babies.

But there was lots of talk about where they really went, and why." She handed me the list. "If you see them, don't tell them I was the one who gave you their names, okay?"

"I'll try not to." I read Monica's list. "Any of them married as far as you know?" If they were, they probably would be using different last names now, Newton Prairie not being a bastion of feminism.

"I think Glenda Johnson got married. I heard she married Win Milstead from the county dairy association. Miss Lundberg'd prob'ly know about the rest of them. She keeps pretty good track of the kids from Newton High."

A group of six rowdy college men in intermural baseball team uniforms came down the steps. They pulled two empty tables together, then scraped chairs across the floor to place around them. Monica stood up. "I better go," she said. I watched as she handed out menus and sidestepped her customers' crude, beery come-ons. A dream job this was not. It saddened me to know that Monica had to live in fear of losing it.

I put her list of names into my purse, tossed a five-dollar bill on my table, and made my way back upstairs.

Traffic was light and I made it home in under twenty minutes. As I parked the car in the alley behind my apartment building, I realized I was exhausted. I'd had a long, grueling day. Even if I hadn't been physically assaulted, I'd have been pooped just from the amount of traveling and interviewing that I'd done. Under the circumstances, I could barely put one foot in front of the other as I carried Rose's leftovers up the three outdoor flights of wooden stairs to my apartment.

I'd left my porch light on and, as I reached to put my key into the lock, my foot bumped against something solid. I looked down. Next to the welcome mat was a box, about a cubic foot in size, wrapped in crisp brown paper. I pushed open the door, picked up the box, and carried it inside.

I set the box on my small dining table next to the foil-wrapped turkey and looked it over. "Devon MacDonald" was crudely lettered in blue ink across the top of the box. There was neither an address nor any attached postage.

I put the turkey leftovers in the refrigerator, got a knife from the kitchen, and stood with it poised above my strange parcel for a good ten minutes. Dared I risk opening it? I heard no ticking coming from the box, which was mildly reassuring. Yet, not all bombs could be counted on to tick. As far as I knew, letter bombs were quiet, right up until they exploded in their recipients' faces.

I considered waiting until the next morning. I could bring the box to the St. Paul Police Department and ask Sam's old friend, Lieutenant Barry O'Neil, to have the bomb squad open it for me. But then I pictured how embarrassed I'd be if the parcel turned out to contain nothing more than unsolicited reading materials or something I'd lent to a friend who'd finally remembered to return it.

What the hell. I used the knife to pry the ends of the brown paper loose and gently unwrapped it from the box. Under the paper was an unmarked brown corrugated box. Holding my breath, I lifted off the cover.

Inside was a Mason jar, the kind used in home canning, held in place by packing materials. I lifted the jar out by its lid, nearly dropping it when I saw what it held. Floating inside the jar in a murky liquid was what looked like a tiny human fetus. Bile rising in my throat at the grisly sight, I set the jar down on the table.

It wasn't until after my pulse returned to normal that I began to examine the packing material inside the box. There was no note of explanation, but I did find something else. Underneath the usual styrofoam pellets was a cloud of something silky, a pale reddish gold in color.

I reached in, grabbed it, and held it up to the light. With a gasp, I realized what it was.

In my hand was my own severed hair.

31

After I stowed the box, its wrappings, and its grisly contents in the back of a closet and managed to get my blood pressure back to normal, I checked my phone machine. There was one message, from my real estate agent, telling me she'd found the "absolute one hundred percent perfect condo" for me. Meredith O'Connor was never at a loss for superlatives. Her message announced that she had set up an appointment for me to view the place the next morning and that I should call her back to confirm, no matter what the hour. I groaned, but returned her call.

One thing I had to say about Meredith—she was always accommodating. She picked me up at the gas station where I left the Honda to have the punctured tire repaired, and drove me east on Summit Avenue, then north three blocks to the condo she had in mind. She never even commented on the silly-looking scarf I was wearing to hide my hair. The place was an end unit in a building of six brownstone townhouses, built about a hundred years ago. But, Meredith assured me, it had been "completely restored and brought up to date." The location was convenient, only about half a mile from where I now lived and within a mile of Sherman and MacDonald's offices.

"You're really going to love this place, I can feel it in my bones," Meredith said, using her realtor's key to let us in.

The living room was to the left of the small foyer. It was compact, just large enough for the owner's pair of matching loveseats placed perpendicular to the fireplace wall, with a square, glass-topped coffee table between them. The fireplace was of locally mined granite; three pristine birch logs lay on its grate. "Does the fireplace work?" I asked, picturing myself lounging in front of a roaring fire on snowy Minnesota nights.

Meredith checked her listing sheet. "Says here it does. If you decide to make an offer on this place, we'll have a professional check it out."

I looked around the living room. Whoever owned the townhouse had made excellent use of the space available. There were built-in bookshelves on either side of the fireplace and an upholstered window seat built into the bay window overlooking the street. Pale neutral colors dominated the room, making it seem larger than it actually was.

The dining room featured the house's original built-in oak china cabinet, with leaded glass doors. The oak floors had been refinished recently, giving the room a warm glow.

"Look over here," Meredith said. "They took out a closet under the stairs here and made room for the cutest little half bath." So long as none of the guests were more than six feet tall, the room seemed to be usable.

As Meredith had promised, the kitchen had been completely remodeled. There was a new granite countertop and the oak cupboards had been refinished. A top model dishwasher had been added to the original design, too. "They lost a lower cupboard when they put in the dishwasher," she explained, "but there's still plenty of storage space. Especially for one person living alone." Truth was, this kitchen was twice the size of the one in my apartment, and a dishwasher was a luxury I hadn't enjoyed in years.

"What's that sound?" I thought I heard water running. "Is the dishwasher going?"

Meredith unlatched its door and opened it. "Nope. Must be the water pipes in the next unit. They're probably in the walls between the kitchens." She closed and re-latched the dishwasher door. "Let's go up and take a look at the bedrooms. The second bedroom is pretty small, but the master is a nice size."

Meredith led the way up the stairs, stopping on the second-floor landing between the two bedrooms. "There're two bathrooms upstairs," she said. "The one off the hall here has a tub and the one in the master bedroom has a shower stall. All the plumbing was updated about five years ago."

I poked my head into the hall bathroom. The whine of running water was louder now, but all the taps were turned off. Meredith showed me the smaller of the bedrooms, which the owner had set up as a study. There was a compact desk with a computer, a bookcase, and a blue plaid easy chair with a reading lamp beside it. The window overlooked the street. The view would be green in the summertime; right now it was the variegated browns and grays of the bare trees planted along the boulevard and the building across the way.

"You get a better view from the master," Meredith said. "The master bedrooms in both of the end units in the building have windows on three sides. From this one, you see mainly the treetops, but you get a little of the downtown city lights at night, too."

I was still exhausted from yesterday's ordeal, and after my short but romantic Big Sur tryst with Doug Winthrop, I wasn't even sure I still wanted to buy property on my own. Yet I found myself liking this cozy place more and more. I caught a glimpse of the master bedroom across the hall through its open doorway. Morning sunshine was spilling through the windows onto the cream-colored carpet and the room appeared drenched with light. The condo was quiet now, too. The whine of running water had stopped.

"That's a great rocking chair over there by the window," I told Meredith, spying an antique oak rocker with a cane back and upholstered box cushion. "Think the owner'd throw it in if I bought this place?"

"Can't hurt to ask."

I felt my mood lighten as I marched into the master bedroom. I could actually see myself sitting in that chair at night, maybe sipping a glass of chardonnay, as I watched the city lights twinkle. I turned to ask Meredith a question. "How big would you say—"

"Aaah!" A skinny, balding man stood squarely in my view. Completely naked. "What the hell are—" He turned and darted back into the master bathroom, slamming the door behind him hard enough to set the pictures on the wall swinging.

I looked at Meredith, whose face registered abject horror—she probably had a vision of her real estate license being yanked for gross embarrassment of clients—and I began to laugh.

"Oh, my God! Oh, my God!" she shrieked, wringing her hands. "I *told* him nine o'clock and he *said* it was all right. Oh, my God!"

I laughed harder as the two of us beat a fast retreat down the stairs.

When she'd locked the front door behind us, I turned to her and asked, "How much extra do you think they want for the naked guy?"

She did not think my question was funny.

32

I traded cars with Sam, pulled on an old Eva Gabor wig made of some sort of synthetic brown fiber, and headed north again. Driving Sam's old tan Chevy—he calls it the perfect surveillance car because it's so nondescript—felt like piloting a boat after driving my little Honda. But the price was right and I hoped the Chevy would help me avoid attracting the wrong kind of attention.

Linda Lundberg had been able to give me addresses for three of the girls on Monica's list, and she'd confirmed that all of them had left during the school year for several months, then returned with suspicious tales of long visits to far-flung relatives.

I decided to try Jill Lester first. I found her at her parents' farmhouse, about three miles east of the Hammonds' spread. A short, hefty brunette about nineteen years old, Jill's mouth had a bitter line to it. I introduced myself, explaining that I was investigating adoption abuse in the state and had been given her name.

She stood in the doorway, eyeing me suspiciously. "Whadya mean, adoption abuse?" I could hear a television set in the background.

"Adoptive families who haven't been screened adequately by the adoption agencies and turn out later not to be suited for parenthood. Or families who begin proceedings to adopt a child and then back out for some reason. My information is that that's what happened to you."

"Pretty much, I guess. But it's over now. Me and Tiffany get along okay."

"Tiffany's your daughter?"

"Yeah, she's two, almost two and a half."

"I'm glad things are going well for you, Jill, but I'd really like to talk to you about what happened. My report may make a difference. Maybe if you tell me about what happened to you, it won't happen to some other girl."

"Are you from the welfare?"

"No. I'm an independent investigator. This has nothing to do with the welfare department." She seemed relieved. "It won't take long."

She checked her watch. "I—I guess it's okay, then. Tiffy's down for her nap and my mom went to the store. I guess you can come in." She held open the door and I entered the cluttered living room. Jill turned off the TV and cleared some magazines off a chair, dropping them on the floor. The one on top was *Soap Opera Digest*. "You can sit here." She took a spot on the sofa, next to an open magazine lying face down and a box of pretzels. A can of Diet Pepsi rested on the scarred coffee table.

I looked around the room. A one-armed doll lay in the middle of the floor, next to an old playpen. A laundry basket filled with clean diapers occupied a gold plush chair and a jack-in-the-box with its spring exposed lay sideways next to the Diet Pepsi. I couldn't help wondering how a blind toddler could possibly function in this environment. Unless Tiffany never left the playpen.

My gaze returned to Jill, who absent-mindedly chewed on a pretzel. "Oh, sorry," she said, holding the box out to me. "Want one?"

"No, thanks anyway." I took a pad of paper and a pen from my purse; might as well do what I could to make my visit look official. "Now, let me be sure I've got my facts straight, Jill. When was your baby born?"

"Her birthday's November eleventh." I wrote down the date.

"So she was two last November?"

"Yeah, she'll be two and a half in May."

The room was warm and my head began to itch under the wig. "And you originally put her up for adoption right after she was born, right?"

"Uh huh." She chewed on her pretzels as she talked. "I thought it was all taken care of. I mean, they told me she'd be in a good Christian home and everything, and that the people adopting her had plenty of money, so they'd take good care of her. I really thought everything was gonna be okay."

"So you came back home here and returned to school." She nodded. "And then what hapened?"

There was a long pause as Jill swallowed, then swallowed again. When she spoke, there was a catch in her voice. "They—They called and told me my baby—She—She was born blind." She blinked rapidly, struggling to retain her composure. "They said—They told me the people didn't want her anymore."

"But didn't the adoption agency try to find another family to adopt Tiffany?"

"Uh uh. They said nobody'd want a blind baby. That they were gonna give her to the county and put her in a foster home unless—unless I wanted to take her back again."

I instinctively reached out to Jill, but she didn't take my hand, so I put it back in my lap. "God, that must have been a nightmare for you."

She looked up at me, tears streaking both cheeks now.

"I—I couldn't just let her get passed around like that, could I? I mean, I'm her *mom!*"

Jill told me she left school in the middle of her junior year to stay home and care for Tiffany. The baby's father had already left town to join the army. He was now married and stationed in Germany, and he played no part in his handicapped daughter's life. Jill and Tiffany received some financial help from the county welfare department, and a social worker visited the house a few times a year to see how they were making out. They also depended heavily on the physical and financial assistance of Jill's parents.

"Don't get me wrong," Jill told me. "I love Tiffy and I wouldn't give her up now for anything in the world. But— Well, I—I used to dream about goin' to college, maybe gettin' some kinda career goin' for myself. And just look at me. . . ."

"Tell me about the place you went to, Jill, the place where you spent your time until Tiffany was born."

"It was a home for pregnant girls, girls who couldn't get the guy to marry them. And who wouldn't have abortions, either. There were ten or eleven other girls there with me, and all our babies got adopted out."

"Would you give me the name and address of this place?"

She twisted a strand of dark hair around her index finger. "It seems sorta strange now that I think about it, I guess. It was called the Compassionate Charity Home for Girls, but I don't have the address."

"Well, what about the town it's in?"

"I dunno."

"You mean you didn't even know what town you were living in?" How was that possible?

"Not really. I mean, when they drove me there, it was nighttime." She remembered the drive taking about three hours, but she wasn't sure in which direction they'd driven. "We weren't allowed to leave the home again until after our babies were born. We couldn't even get any mail the whole time we were there."

"Why not?"

"They said we had to keep everything secret. I mean, I only even knew the other girls by their first names, and they only called me Jill. That was so we wouldn't come looking for each other after. They told us if we didn't follow those rules, then everybody would know we were bad girls and we'd never be able to put our sins behind us and get a husband."

I shuddered, picturing how psychologically damaged a girl would be after an experience like the one Jill was describing. She'd been taught she was a sinner, one who would have to keep her transgression a secret for the rest of her life. Either that or be ostracized from her society. Even the name of the home—Compassionate Charity—reinforced the idea that the girls were being done a massive favor by being giving housing and medical care during their pregnancies. "So," I asked her, "in what—five or six months?—you never left the place even once?"

"Right."

"What about your medical checkups and when Tiffany was born? You must've gone to the hospital to deliver your baby. What hospital was she born in?"

"No, that's not the way it worked. The doctor came to see us girls right there at the home. And there was this hospital room kind of place on the first floor, where the babies were born." All Jill remembered was that the doctor was called Doctor O. He apparently sought to remain as anonymous as the girls who lived there.

"How did you find out about this Compassionate Charity Home, Jill? I mean, was it listed in the phone book or what?"

"It was my mom and dad that found out about it. I think through church."

"What church is that?" I had a feeling I knew what her answer would be.

"The one right here in Newton. Community Fundamentalist."

"Reverend Ed Beale's church."

"Yeah. My folks told Reverend Ed I was in trouble and he was real good about it—didn't yell at me or nothin'.

Promised he'd do what he could to help us out. Then, a few days later, somebody called and told my folks about this Compassionate Charity Home for Girls, so I figured he was the one set it up."

"Momma. Momma!" The cry came from the back of the house. "Up! Up! Tiffy up now."

"Tiffy's awake," Jill said. "I havta go now, gotta get her changed and dressed before my mom gets home."

I thanked young Jill and gave her one of my cards. "If there's anything else you can remember about the Compassionate Charity Home for girls, or the people there, anything at all, please call me."

Jill said she would, but as I headed for the door, I saw her toss my card onto the pile of magazines. I didn't expect I would hear from her anytime soon.

33

The second of the addresses Linda Lundberg had given me was ten miles away, in Parkland Creek. It was the upper half of a white frame duplex that backed up to a railroad track. I climbed the stairs and pressed the doorbell. There was no answer. I tried knocking, but still got no response.

I pressed the doorbell for the lower unit. I could hear movement inside the apartment, so I waited. Eventually the door was opened by an elderly woman wearing a pink terrycloth bathrobe and slippers. Her permed white hair was flattened on one side.

"I'm looking for Penny Morrison," I told her. "Know where I can find her?"

"What say?" She cupped a hand around her ear.

I spoke louder. "Penny Morrison, the young woman who lives upstairs. I'm looking for her."

"Pennies? What're you selling?"

"Penny Morrison, ma'am, she lives upstairs." I pointed a finger upward. "Do you know where she is?"

"Sorry, I was lying down. Took my hearing aid off." The old woman pulled on her earlobes, as though that simple exercise would somehow restore her hearing.

I tried not to sound impatient as I enunciated slowly. "Do you know where Penny Morrison is, ma'am?"

"Don't know what you're selling, dear, but I live on a fixed income. Can't afford to buy from door-to-door salesmen."

"Thanks, anyway." I knew a losing battle when one kicked me in the teeth. "Guess I'll wait 'til she gets home."

"Girl upstairs might buy something, but you'll havta come back later. She works up at the Dari-Mart 'til three every day."

I thanked the woman and headed back to the Chevy, silently lecturing myself about learning to have more patience with those less fortunate than I.

I figured the Dari-Mart had to be somewhere in town, so I U-turned and headed in that direction.

The Dari-Mart turned out to be a small convenience store, Parkland Creek's version of a 7-Eleven. The clerk behind the counter told me that Penny Morrison was in the storeroom, checking in the day's deliveries. He stuck his head behind a curtain and yelled. "Hey, Penny. Somebody here to see ya."

A tall, thin young woman in her late teens emerged from behind the curtain. She had dark reddish brown hair and pale, freckled skin, and she wore a white shirt and snug jeans with a green apron tied around her waist. She was holding a clipboard and had a blue ballpoint pen stuck behind her left ear. "Hi. I'm Penny," she said, sticking out her hand. I shook it.

"My name's Devon MacDonald," I told her. I handed her one of my cards. "Is there somewhere we can talk privately?"

As Penny read my card, her eyes widened and she looked frightened. Turning to her fellow employee, she asked, "Hey, Tim, cover for me for a few minutes?"

"Sure, Pen. Old Man Bowden shows up, I'll give ya a yell."

Penny led me to the back of the store, out of earshot of the front counter. Apparently she and Tim were the only employees working at present. We sat on facing folding chairs near the back door of the shop, an ashtray overflowing with cigarette butts resting on the upside down carton between us. The stench of stale tobacco assaulted my nose and I sneezed.

"Sorry 'bout that." Penny moved the ashtray about six feet away, placing it on top of an unpacked carton of canned baked beans. "Tim doesn't clean up after himself so good sometimes."

I blew my nose, then explained to Penny that I was searching for a young woman I suspected had gone to the same home for unwed mothers where she herself had once stayed. "This girl's family doesn't know where she is and they're worried sick about her."

Penny listened as I spoke, her face a complete blank. Her fingers played nervously with a charm that hung around her neck, sliding the tiny religious fish symbol back and forth on its gold chain. "I understand you gave your baby up for adoption about eighteen months ago, right?"

Penny stared straight ahead, as though she could see through me. She spoke slowly and deliberately. "I don't know what you're talking about. Maybe I missed some school for a while, but I was never at any home for unwed mothers. I went to stay with my grandma in Miami, 'cause she was real sick."

I leaned forward and lowered my voice to a whisper. "Listen, Penny. I'm not here to tell anybody your secrets, honest. As far as I'm concerned, this is the nineties, and having a baby when you're not married is a helluva long way from the worst thing somebody can do. All I want is a little bit of information from you so I can find this missing girl."

Penny sprang to her feet, nearly knocking over her chair. "I don't know who sent you here, but I don't want to talk to you. I want you to go away. Right now."

"Please, Penny—"

Her composure began to crack. "Don't you understand? I'm engaged to be married. If you start spreading rumors like this, it could ruin my whole life."

"I'm not here to spread rumors, Penny. Trust me, please. All I want is talk to you, get a little information. Then I'll leave town and never bother you again."

"No! I don't know where you got my name, but you can't prove anything. I went to my grandma's and there's no way you can prove different." Anger began to replace her fear. She stood straight and tall, her feet braced well apart and her arms crossed over her small breasts, as though her forbidding posture alone could protect her from unwanted assaults on her privacy.

I got to my feet. "The Compassionate Charity Home for Girls ring a bell with you?" I asked, watching her face carefully.

Penny winced and moved backward half a step, as though I'd slapped her. But her words admitted nothing. She stared at a spot in the middle of my forehead and insisted, "Never heard of it."

"Keep my card," I told her. "Think about what I said. I promise you, Penny, I'm not going to hurt you in any way whatsoever. But I have to find this missing girl, and I really believe you can help me." She jutted her chin out stubbornly. I was getting nowhere fast. "Please call me if you change your mind. You could help save another girl from a terrible tragedy."

Penny Morrison did not escort me as I headed back toward the retail section of the Dari-Mart. As I reached the curtain, I turned and looked back at her. Her chin was quivering and she was staring straight at me. I felt guilty for having caused her so much obvious anguish. But I also felt terribly frustrated by her unwillingness to cooperate. I was absolutely certain Penny had been at the Compassionate Charity

Home only a few months ago. But I also had no doubt that she would never tell me about it.

If the Compassionate Charity Home for Girls was where Kerry Hammond had been lured, Penny Morrison would not be the one to help me find her.

34

I drove the ten miles back into the heart of Newton Prairie feeling a little bit nervous, despite the fact that this time I was behind the wheel of Sam's car and disguised by the itchy brown wig, which was quickly driving me crazy. Scratching my head with the eraser of my pencil, I drove with my other hand on the steering wheel and an eye out for anyone who might give me trouble. Luckily, I didn't spot the dusty old pickup, nor did I see either the orange VW beetle or Reverend Ed's dark red Cadillac.

I crawled along the main street of town, then turned left onto Elm Street. The house where Win and Glenda Milstead lived was in the third block; it was a tiny brick bungalow with a detached single garage at the rear of the lot. The garage door was open, displaying the empty cavern within. I looked up and down the street before emerging from the relative safety of the Chevrolet, then walked rapidly toward the front door.

This time I was in luck. Glenda Milstead answered the door. I guessed her age at nineteen or twenty. She had hair the color of a summer wheat field, worn in a long French braid, and deep-set blue eyes. Clad in jeans and a man's gray football jersey with the number twelve printed in blue across her chest, she was at least seven months pregnant.

I introduced myself and told her I'd come in the hope that she could help me with one of my cases. Looking intrigued, she led me into the interior of the house, which smelled strongly of cooking onions. "I'm making soup for dinner," she told me. "If you don't mind, we can talk in the kitchen, so I can keep an eye on the stove."

Glenda's kitchen was minute, probably a third the size of Linda Lundberg's, and very cluttered. She steered me toward a round glass-topped table about eighteen inches in diameter, and I sat down on one of the two narrow wrought iron chairs that completed the traditional ice cream parlor set. The chair's metal curves dug into my back, and I wondered how poor Glenda could bear to sit on something so uncomfortable in her condition. My main memory of being seven months pregnant was that my back ached constantly and I could never quite manage to get comfortable.

Glenda stood at the stove, stirring hamburger and onions frying in a large soup pot. "Private investigator, huh? This is exciting." She cocked an eyebrow at me as she opened two cans of Campbell's Beef Bouillion and poured their contents into the pot.

I explained my quest as concisely as possible. "I promise I won't reveal any of your secrets to anyone," I told her. "I just want to know what you can remember about the home you went to. I think it could help me find this girl who's disappeared."

Glenda was silent as she added two cans of diced tomatoes, then piles of sliced carrots, celery, and cubed potatoes to her brew.

I let her think about what I'd said without interrupting her. Chewing her lower lip, she twirled a revolving spice rack, selecting a jar of basil, then a jar of thyme. She opened each one, sprinkled the proper amount of the spice into the palm of her hand, and dumped the seasonings into the soup. She stirred the mixture thoroughly, then turned to face me, tears brimming in her eyes.

"That place." She wiped her eyes with the back of a hand, laid down the spoon on a chipped pottery spoon rack, and put the cover on the soup pot. "I still have nightmares about that goddamned place."

"The Compassionate Charity Home for Girls?"

"Compassionate, my ass." She took the wrought iron chair opposite mine and sat down gingerly, straddling it. Her hands rested on the bulge of her belly. "They outright stole my baby—least that's the way I see it now."

"When, Glenda? When was your baby born?"

"February tenth, nineteen ninety."

"Over three years ago. Was it a boy or girl?"

Her chin quivered and her blue eyes blinked rapidly. "I— I don't even know." Her tears spilled onto the football jersey, soaking into the faded gray fabric and quickly disappearing. "They wouldn't even let me see my own baby."

"Why not?"

"Said it'd be better for me if I didn't let myself get attached." Glenda blew her nose. "Attached, shit! You have any kids?"

"I did, a little boy. But he died."

"Sorry to hear that. But maybe you can understand a little about how I feel. In my heart, I always believed my baby was a boy, too. He—It—It felt like a boy when I was carrying it. But I could be wrong about that. Guess I'll never know for sure."

I asked Glenda how she had ended up at the Compassionate Charity Home.

"Usual story, I guess. I was only sixteen when I got pregnant, and my parents didn't like the boy. Abortion was out of the question, and my folks refused to sign for me to get married. My dad said he'd rather see me dead. Even threatened my boyfriend with statutory rape charges, 'cause he was a legal adult and I wasn't. Truth is, both my folks just wanted the whole thing to go away. So, when they had a chance to ship me off to that hellhole, they did it."

"Where exactly was this place? I haven't been able to find the address."

"Doesn't surprise me none." The cover of the soup pot began to rattle. Glenda got up to turn down the flame on the stove. "I remember when I first went there. They came and got me in a limousine with dark curtains hanging all around the back. I was scared to death, and I didn't have a clue where I was going. Then, all the time I lived there, I wasn't allowed to write to anybody or even talk on the phone. Seemed a lot like prison must be."

"So the idea was that you'd have your baby, give it up for adoption, then go back home and forget the whole experience, right?"

"Right. 'Cept I can't seem to forget. I never wanted to get rid of my baby, but they made me."

A chill crawled down my spine. "I don't understand. Didn't you sign adoption papers relinquishing your rights?"

"Sure, I signed 'em, all right, but not 'cause I wanted to."

"Tell me what happened."

"Well, the whole time I was there—more than four and a half months—they kept telling us girls they were keeping everything secret for our own good, so we could go back home and pick up our lives where we'd left off, with nobody the wiser. That we'd be best off if we never told anybody we'd made this big mistake and got pregnant. It was s'posed to be like we were just erasing a few months from our lives, and that was all there was to it. Like nothing ever happened."

"Only you couldn't do that."

"No way. I don't think I could've, even if I'd had a normal birth. But I—I was in labor for nineteen hours, and my baby wasn't getting himself born. Finally, the doctor knocked me out and did a Cesarean section on me, sliced me open from here to here." She drew a finger from one side of her lower abdomen to the other. "And this guy was no plastic surgeon, either, believe me. I've got the scar to prove it. Here I am, a purple stripe all across my stomach, and I'm s'posed to believe my future husband's never going to catch on that I had a baby. Any guy that dumb, I wouldn't want to marry. Fact is, this one—" Glenda patted her belly. "This one has to be a Cesarean, too."

"So you're saying the bit about keeping the secret doesn't mean a whole lot in your case."

"Hardly. But that was never that big a thing with me, anyway."

"Why not?"

"Look, some of those girls I was there with just wanted to get it over with, go back home, and forget. Their boyfriends dumped them, or else the guy who got them pregnant never meant much to them in the first place. I was different. I loved my baby's father and I really did want to marry him and keep our baby. It was just that I wasn't old enough, and my parents wouldn't let me. My mom and dad were the ones who didn't want anybody to know, not me."

"But I don't understand how the people at the home could force you to give up your baby if you didn't want to. What's to stop you from refusing to sign the papers and taking your baby home with you?"

"The money."

"What money?"

"The money they spent on me. Twenty-three thousand dollars is what they told me."

"For what?"

"My room and board while I was at the home. That, and all the doctor's bills. Cesareans are pretty expensive, you know, 'specially when you don't have any medical insurance."

"Let me make sure I understand what you're saying here, Glenda. The home told you you'd have to repay them twenty-three thousand dollars if you wanted to keep your baby?"

"Yeah, that's right. If I signed over my baby, the adoptive parents would pay my bills. If I refused to sign, then I would have to pay." She stood up and stretched, one hand pushing against the small of her back. Lifting the cover from the pot of soup, she peeked inside. A cloud of steam escaped. "No way could I ever come up with that kind of money."

"I can understand that." Glenda's inability to pay the Compassionate Charity Home for Girls twenty-three thousand dollars wasn't the only thing I was beginning to understand.

I questioned Glenda for another half hour. She didn't

know much more about the home's location than Jill Lester. Glenda remembered being in the back of the curtained limo for no more than two hours, and she described the home itself as a three-story building with bars on the windows. None of the girls were ever allowed to leave the fenced grounds, although some days they went outdoors and did yard work. "That was only in the beginning, though. I was there in the fall and winter, so pretty soon it got too cold to be outside."

Glenda agreed with Jill that the girls exchanged only their first names, and never their home addresses or phone numbers. And both young mothers told me that the residents were continually chastised for their "sins," from which the home was supposed to be redeeming them.

"I came away from there feeling like a real tramp," Glenda told me. "I've been married a year and a half now, and there's still times I can't kick the feeling that I'm some kind of slut." She pounded her fist on the glass-topped table. "Sometimes, I'd just like to kill those people for how they screwed up my head."

The sounds of a door opened, then slamming shut again, came from the front of the house. A moment later, a tall, blond young man in a rumpled business suit and blue knitted tie entered the kitchen. "Hi, babe," he said, kissing the top of Glenda's head. "What's up?"

I stood. "Guess I'll be going now." I certainly didn't want to cause Glenda any trouble with her husband.

She held up her hand in protest. "No, it's okay, Devon. I haven't got any secrets from Win." She snuggled against his chest. "He's the father of both my babies. We got married after all, soon's I turned eighteen."

"I'm happy for you," I said, meaning it. Maybe theirs was one youthful marriage that would actually last. Certainly they'd been tested by fire early on and they seemed to have survived intact.

Glenda told Win why I was there. He gave her a sympathetic squeeze, then left to change his clothes while she and I talked for a few more minutes.

"If—If you do find the home, is there any way you can help me get my baby back?" Glenda's blue eyes were pleading. "I—I went to talk to a lawyer about getting him back once, but the guy wanted a lot of money up front, and I just didn't have it."

"I'll let you know what happens, Glenda, but I'm afraid I can't encourage you to get your hopes up. If those papers you signed were legal . . . Well, it's been three years and I don't think anybody can do much for you now."

And if the papers were not legal? I wondered. Chances were that a judge in a custody hearing would rule according to the best interests of the child. At this late date, the child's best interests would probably be to remain in the custody of the adoptive parents.

I could foresee no way that Glenda Milstead could ever get her baby back. That fact made me very sad for both her and her young husband.

35

The main street of Newton Prairie was busier now as the business day drew to a close. A few people strolled along the sidewalk, and cars were parked outside Bud's Diner, the convenience store, and Krauss Hardware.

I pressed the brake pedal as I passed Tammy Myers's beauty shop and peered inside. A woman with a platinum blonde bouffant hairdo was paying her bill at the cash register. I U-turned at the end of town, near the gas stations, doubled back, and waited for the final customer to leave the beauty shop before I went in.

"I've got a major hair emergency," I told black-haired

Tammy. "Think you might be able to fix it for me?" She squinted at me, but didn't seem to recognize me from our talk outside her shop a few nights back. "You're open here a little while longer, right?"

" 'Til six or so, most nights." She eyed my cheap wig and wrinkled her nose. "What exactly did you want me to do?"

"Let's get away from those windows and I'll show you." We headed for the back of the shop, near the shampoo station. I pulled the wig off my head and revealed the disaster underneath, then turned around. "The back here is a real mess. I tried to even it up myself, but I've got to admit I'm no beautician."

"You can say that again. What on earth were you trying to do?"

"Somebody gave me a bad haircut. I was just trying to fix the damage."

"No lie. Whoever cut *this* oughta have their license yanked." She picked up a strand of hair, rubbed it between her slender fingers, then let it fall back into place. "Your natural color's sure a lot nicer on you than that sick old wig you been wearin'." She smoothed the top of my hair with her fingers. "Okay, I'll see what I can do. Might be able to give you a Dorothy Hamill—you know, the ice skater—that's sort of a bowl cut on top, with bangs, and real short at the sides and back. Unless you were maybe thinking of goin' with a perm. That could be real cute on you."

"No, no perm." I'd worn my hair long and straight for so long now that I hardly recognized myself in short hair. Adding a mass of frizzy curls all over my head was far more change than I was willing to face. "All I want is something that doesn't look too bad while I wait for my hair to grow out long again."

"Well, let's get it washed. Then I'll be able to tell better what I've got to work with."

Tammy's fingers were strong and sure as they massaged the shampoo into my scalp. I felt the itchiness that had plagued my scalp all day begin to subside. Closing my eyes, I relaxed and allowed myself to feel pampered as she shampooed my hair a second time, then rinsed off the rich suds with a warm water spray. I wasn't crazy about Tammy's own choice of hair style, particularly her harsh and unflattering black dye job. But I figured her hair-cutting skills should be good enough to get me back to something approaching normality. Truth was, no matter what she did to my hair, I could hardly end up looking much worse than I already did.

"You live around here?" she asked, as she wrapped my wet head in a clean white towel and led me over to her work station. I sat in a black leatherette swivel chair, facing the lighted mirror, while she laid out her comb, brush, and scissors on the counter in front of me.

"Nope, I'm from St. Paul."

"So, how come you came here?" She sprayed what was left of my hair with some sort of conditioner, then combed out the snarls.

"This is where I got the bad haircut."

"What? Not in *my* shop, you didn't."

"No, not in your shop, in Newton Prairie." I reminded her that we'd met the night Community Fundamentalist Church held its anti-abortion rally, then explained what had happened to me on the road leading out of town.

As Tammy listened to what I had to say, she stood frozen, her scissors poised above my head. "Oh, shit. I thought you looked sorta familiar when you first walked in here." She moved a step away from me, as though I threatened to contaminate her. It wasn't hard to tell that the young beautician was now sorry she'd ever agreed to work over my hairdo. Yet, now that I was sitting here in her shop, my soaked hair dripping onto my pink plastic smock, she had too much pride in her professionalism to throw me out. "Look," she said, "I don't want to get mixed up in anything to do with those guys. This thing's got nothin' to do with me. Nothin' at all."

"At least tell me who they are. It's obvious you recognized the guys in that orange Volkswagen bug the other night. Who are they?"

"I got my ideas, but I plan to keep 'em to myself." Her

face grim, she began to lift sections of my hair with her comb, then snip them off at a uniform length. Wet snippets of my hair fell to the floor around me. "Yeah, I think a Dorothy Hamill's the answer, all right."

"Look, Tammy, I'm not fooling around here. I was jumped and beaten up the other night, by two of your local thugs. Know how that feels?" She flinched, then quickly recovered her composure and resumed snipping away. "Not only that. I think those guys could be the same creeps who burned down that women's clinic in St. Cloud. If they are, they're guilty of murdering two innocent women."

"I don't know nothin' about any of that stuff." Tammy's face was deadpan as she began clipping the hair around my ears.

Watching the quick movement of her hands in the mirror was almost hypnotic. Earrings, I thought, analyzing my reflected image. Maybe if I put on a pair of dangling gold earrings, my new short hairstyle wouldn't seem quite so masculine.

"The other night when we spoke, you essentially warned me to keep away from Reverend Ed and his bunch," I said. "Please, Tammy, all I want you to do is explain what you meant, why you said that." She was working on my neckline now, snipping away faster and faster, as though she couldn't wait to finish this unwanted job and get me out of her shop. "Think about it. You could help put some murderers in jail for good."

"I told you all I'm gonna. Probably shouldn'ta said what I did. You're smart, you'll keep away from Reverend Ed, 'cause he can't be trusted. That's all I got to say."

"But *why*? What do you know about him?" Tammy turned on the blow dryer, which roared in my ears. If she answered my question, I certainly couldn't hear what she had to say.

When she shut off the dryer, Tammy quickly combed my hair, then handed me a mirror and spun my chair around so I could view the back. "Not bad," I had to admit. "You do real nice repair work."

"That'll be ten bucks." She swept the red-gold remnants

of my shorn hair off the pink plastic smock and onto the floor, then unsnapped the garment around from my neck and tossed it aside.

I removed a twenty dollar bill from my wallet and handed it to her. "What about the Compassionate Charity Home for Girls?" I asked, watching her face carefully for a reaction. "Ever hear of that?"

Her expression didn't waver. "Nope."

"It's a home for unwed mothers, and I think some sort of adoption agency as well. Sounds like Reverend Ed has some connection to it."

Tammy rang up the sale and pulled a five-dollar bill and five ones from the till. "Well, you sure couldn't prove it by me." She handed me my change. I folded the five around one of my cards and handed it back to her as a tip. "Think about it, Tammy. If we can get these guys put away somewhere permanent, there's a good chance you and I both would sleep a lot better at night."

I didn't have the heart to put the brown wig back on, now that I looked human again, so I stuffed it into my purse. I checked the street carefully before emerging from the beauty shop. No doubt about it, I'd taken a big chance in going there and questioning Tammy Myers, a chance I hoped I wouldn't later regret. If her refusal to tell me what she knew indicated that she was a member of the opposition, I could be in real trouble. All she had to do was make a quick phone call the minute I left her shop, and I could be confronting those turkeys in the pickup truck all over again. With far more serious results than losing my ponytail.

I kept my eyes glued to Sam's rear view mirror as I drove out of Newtown Prairie and back toward I-94. I'd almost reached the suburbs of St. Cloud before I began to breathe easy again.

36

I reached home late that night, feeling bone tired as I trudged up the stairs to my apartment. A few steps from the landing, I saw something sitting outside my front door—another special delivery. My memory flashed back to my discovery of the grisly jar now hidden in the back of my closet, and my heart skipped a beat. Had I been spotted in Newton Prairie today after all?

I climbed the last three steps and approached the package carefully, then laughed out loud at my own skittishness. My mystery package was nothing more than a delivery of flowers. I pulled off the card that was stapled to the green paper wrapping and read, "I've been trying to reach you by phone for days, but our schedules never seem to coincide. Hope you enjoyed our stolen weekend half as much as I did. Love, Doug."

My fatigue dissolved. I've always thought it was amazing what a little love could do to revive the human spirit. I dialed Doug at the Carmel Police Department to thank him, but he wasn't in and it was too early—California time—for him to be at home. Doug was right as always; our schedules never seemed to mesh.

I pulled the telephone onto the bed, intending to try him again later. But I dozed off while running the Kerry Hammond case through my mind and, by the time I awoke, it was already six in the morning—a cool four o'clock in California. Once more, talking to Doug would have to wait.

I was in the office, a cup of decaf and the telephone sitting in front of me, before either Paula or Sam arrived. One of the things that had occurred to me last night was that the

Compassionate Charity Home for Girls should be licensed by the State of Minnesota. Adoption agencies had to be licensed and, from what Jill Lester and Glenda Milstead had told me, the Home functioned as an adoption agency. Could finding Kerry be as easy as calling the Department of Human Services and asking for the home's address?

I dialed the Department and explained my quest three or four times, as my phone call was transferred here and there and back again. Transferring incoming calls must be a basic requirement of all government bureaucracies. I don't think I've ever reached the proper person on the first try.

I was finally connected to the office of adoptions specialist Ivy Palmer, who looked up the Compassionate Charity Home for Girls on her list of adoption agencies licensed by the State. "Sorry, there's no agency with that name licensed in this state." Judging by her voice, Ivy Palmer was nearing retirement. Either that, or she had a heavy cigarette habit.

Frowning, I explained a little about what I'd learned from Jill Lester and Glenda Milstead, without identifying my sources.

"There's something wrong somewhere," Ivy said. "That just isn't the way a licensed agency works in Minnesota."

"How about this, then? Maybe Compassionate Charity arranges private adoptions of some kind. You know, the kind put together for couples by their doctor or attorney."

"Can't do that legally—not in Minnesota, anyway." Ivy explained that Minnesota was one of only a few states in the entire country where what's commonly known as independent adoption is not legal. "All adoptions between non-relatives in this state have to include a home study, either by the human services people in the county where the child lives, or by a licensed private child placement agency. No exceptions."

"But what if the baby's mother herself chooses a family that she wants to adopt her child. Couldn't she do that?"

"You mean, could she choose somebody who's not one of her own relatives—not a man she married after her child's birth, for instance, or not her own biological parents—to adopt her child?"

"Right, like maybe she picks some couple looking to adopt, simply because they've been recommended to her. Because she's been convinced they'd be good parents for her child." I wondered whether the papers Jill and Glenda signed indicated somehow that they themselves had chosen specific parents for their babies. Neither of the young women remembered much of anything about what the documents actually said.

"Sure, the birth mother could choose a home for her baby herself, but that's just the beginning of making the whole thing legal. After they got the baby, the adoptive parents would have to self-report the situation to us within thirty days. Then, as soon as we have the particulars, we would send the County Child Protection people out to the home to assess the situation." The process was beginning to sound terribly complicated.

Ivy explained that, after inspecting the home the birth mother had chosen, the county would have several options: it could license the home as a foster care home, after which the legal adoption process would begin; it could remove the baby from that home and place it into a licensed foster care home; or, it could remove the baby from that home and return it to its birth mother.

The way I understood it, in no case could a legal adoption take place in Minnesota without the proper licensed private or state agency inspecting the home and signing off. After that, the usual adoption proceedings would still have to take place and, finally, the adoption would have to approved by the courts.

What Jill Lester and Glenda Milstead had described to me in no way meshed with the stringent and difficult requirements Ivy Palmer was outlining. "Maybe Compassionate Charity Home for Girls is licensed under some other name," I suggested, grasping for some plausible explanation for the discrepancy. "Is that possible?"

"Could be, I s'pose, but I don't think it's very likely."

"Why not?"

"You said this place is basically a home for unmarried mothers, right?"

"Uh huh."

"Well, far as I know, the last of those places closed down some twenty years ago. There just isn't a stigma attached to unmarried motherhood these days."

Except maybe in some fundamentalist backwaters, I thought, but didn't say.

"I remember there used to be a Florence Crittenton Home," Ivy said, "and the Salvation Army ran one of those places, too. There were a few others as well, but they all ran out of clients and closed down years ago."

I sighed. So much for my finding Kerry Hammond with a simple phone call. "I'm confused," I said. "From what's been described to me, there's got to be thirty-five, maybe as many as forty babies a year being adopted through this Compassionate Charity place."

"You're sure it's in Minnesota?"

I thought about whether the place could be in a nearby state. Glenda Milstead had told me her ride in the curtained limo took about two hours. Jill Lester thought her ride was closer to three hours. From Newton Prairie, it would take a minimum of three hours to reach the closest town over the Wisconsin border, and much longer to reach Iowa or either of the Dakotas. "I think the place has to be in Minnesota," I said. Unless both Glenda's and Jill's memories were way off target.

"Do me a favor, if you ever find this place?" Ivy asked.

"What's that?"

"Call me right away. There were only about four hundred legal infant adoptions in this entire state last year. And a good percentage of them were minority or mixed-race babies, or ones with physical or mental handicaps. From what you're telling me, there could be another ten percent—all of them healthy, white infants—coming out of a place I've never even heard of. Like they say about the city dump—something smells."

The stench that had reached my nostrils long ago was beginning to spread.

37

I cornered Sam as soon as he came in and put him to work on his computer. He didn't complain. Whoever said older folks are computer-phobic never met Sam. He loves working with his various programs and networks almost as much as he loves eating. Actually, he usually manages to do both at the same time.

Today's project allowed him to tap into a new information service that gave us access to the state's birth and death records. I handed him the list I'd typed out. "These are the dates that Jill Lester and Glenda Milstead—her name was Glenda Johnson then—had their babies. Penny Morrison wouldn't cooperate, so I don't have an exact date for her baby. But, from what I could piece together, it had to've been born sometime between mid-November, nineteen ninety-one, and the end of that year. Think you can dredge up the birth certificates for me?"

"With one hand tied behind my back, sweet pea." Sam clicked on his computer and dialed the access number through his modem. "Gimme half an hour and I'll have 'em for ya." As his computer buzzed and flashed, he munched happily on a jelly donut. This was as close to hog heaven as Sam was ever going to get—sleuthing without having to get out of his chair.

I wandered into the outer office while I waited for the birth records. That was a big mistake. Paula quickly beckoned me over to her desk. "Devon, you're just the person I need to see." She had three color brochures and half a dozen magazines spread out across her desktop. None of them resembled the agency's work in any way whatsoever. "I gotta make some serious decisions real quick, or my dress is never gonna be ready in time." Her little-girl whisper held a note of sheer panic. "Take a look at these and help me choose, willya?"

I leaned over her desk and surveyed the bridal gowns pictured. "Gee, I don't know, Paula. This really isn't my kind of thing. When I got married, I wore a white suit I borrowed from my college roommate."

"Oh, come on, Devon. You got eyes. You go to the movies. You watch TV. You know what people are wearing. Just take a look at these dresses and tell me what you think'll look best on me."

"We don't exactly have the same taste in clothes, Paula." I do most of my shopping from the Lands' End catalogue, while Paula's clothes look more like they're from Frederick's of Hollywood.

But she wasn't taking no for an answer. She pointed at one photograph of a particularly buxom blonde falling out of the top of a white dress. "I like the neckline on this one best, but I'm not too sure about that bell shape the skirt's got. Might make me look hippy."

"What neckline?" As far as I could see, the dress stopped at the model's belly button. In this picture, the magazine's readers could see far more of the woman's silicone implants than the top of her dress.

"Honestly, Devon, you're such a prude sometimes."

"Whatever happened to wedding dresses that actually have sleeves, and full skirts, and those little seed pearls on the bodice?" The bridal gowns Paula'd selected all looked more like negligees.

"You can still get that kind, but they just don't say *me*. I'm a lot more modern. Besides, Stuart likes to show me off and, the way I see it, this is his big chance."

"That's one way of looking at it."

The phone rang.

"So, what do you think, Devon?"

"I think the phone's ringing."

"Oh, you're no help at all." Paula glared at the phone, as though it had a real nerve, interrupting her while she was taking care of important personal business. She mumbled something under her breath, then picked up the receiver and chirped, "Sherman and MacDonald, Private Investigations."

I used the interruption as an opportunity to escape to my office. Unlike Paula, I felt an obligation to do some real work while I was on the agency's time clock.

"Somethin's strange here," Sam said. He handed me a single-page computer printout. "This's all I came up with."

I looked it over. It was the birth data for Jill Lester's blind toddler daughter, Tiffany. "How come?"

"There's nothin' there for them other gals, least not under the names you gave me."

I thought a moment. "Damn, that's right. The parents' names probably were changed on the babies' birth certificates as soon as the adoptions were finalized." I remembered the problems a friend of mine from high school had had. She was adopted and she spent years and years trying to locate her birth mother. The effort was made a hundred times more difficult because my friend's birth certificate had been changed when she was adopted, and all her adoption records had been sealed by the court at the same time.

Still, I wasn't ready to give up. I sat down and studied the printout. It said that a six-pound, eight-ounce female infant had been born to Jill Marie Lester on November eleventh, 1990. The father was listed as "unknown," despite the fact that Jill obviously knew full well who he was. She'd told me he left town to join the army. Perhaps the folks at the Compassionate Charity Home for Girls encouraged their residents to testify that they couldn't identify the guys who got them pregnant; that certainly would cut down the chance that a biological father would someday show up and try to sue for visitation rights with his offspring.

As I read the rest of the birth certificate, I caught my breath. I had a strong feeling we'd hit paydirt. According to the paper I held in hand, baby Tiffany Lester was born in the town of Rockville, in Stearns County, Minnesota. And her birth was attended by one Otto Kugle, M.D.

"Hey, Sam, you got this by plugging in the mothers' names and the birth dates I gave you, right?"

"Yeah."

"Does the computer service work if you cross-reference the place of birth with the birth date?"

"Sure, any two variables'll give us a printout. Only thing is, might be more'n one birth in a city on a given day."

"Let's try it this way. Plug in the dates I gave you, but this time cross-reference them with births that took place in Rockville, Minnesota."

"You're on." Sam waddled off to his office while I grabbed the telephone.

The clerk at the Board of Medical Examiners told me that Otto Kugle was a general practitioner with a medical office at 110 Front Street in Rockville. He was no newcomer; he'd been licensed to practice medicine in Minnesota for the past thirty-two years.

I checked my atlas and learned that Rockville was in southern Stearns County. Farm country. The town's population was only four hundred and ten people; it wasn't exactly a major crossroads. Something tickled my memory. I grabbed my file on Kerry Hammond and began digging through it. There it was. I whistled out loud, grabbed my notes and sprinted for Sam's office.

"I found it!" I shouted. "I'm sure of it. I've found the Compassionate Charity Home for Girls."

Sam wore a good imitation of the Cheshire Cat's grin. "Bet it's right there in beautiful downtown Rockville, ain't it?" He handed me five more computer printouts.

"More like rural Rockville."

I looked at the printouts. They listed birth data for five different babies, all born in Rockville and all delivered by Dr. Otto Kugle. The first was undoubtedly Glenda Milstead's. Glenda's intuition had been right; her child was a boy, all eight pounds, three ounces of him. He was born on February tenth, 1990, but Glenda's name did not appear on this birth certificate. Instead, the baby's parents were listed as Lillian and Lawrence Carruthers of Apple Valley, Minnesota.

Three babies were born in Rockville during the time span I thought would cover Penny Morrison's delivery date. The first, a boy, was listed as the child of Karen and Einar Gustavson, Junior, of rural Rockville. I set that one aside; it sounded genuine. The others, both girls, were documented as the children of Phyllis and Claude Charbonneau of Duluth, Minnesota, and Madeline and George Bestor of Detroit, Michigan, respectively.

"What's this one?" I held up the last printout Sam had given me.

"Had a hunch. Checked the date Jill Lester had her kid and cross-referenced it with Rockville. Came up with a second birth certificate."

I read the document carefully. The sex, time of birth, weight, and other details were all identical to Jill's baby's document. The only difference here was that Jill Lester and father unknown were not listed as this child's parents. That distinction went to Sophia and Vito Marinelli of Eden Prairie, Minnesota. "This is the same baby," I said.

"Bingo." Sam puffed out his chest and grinned broadly at me.

"The Marinellis must be the people who gave Tiffany back when they found out she was blind." Yet something still didn't make sense here. I stared at the print on the page until it began to dance before my eyes. "Why the birth certificate in the Marinellis' names, Sam? Those records don't get changed until the adoption is legalized . . . and this one never was. These people backed out before—" Suddenly I understood the whole thing. "There never were any legal adoptions, were there, Sam?"

"That's the way I got it doped out."

"I see now how he did it. Dr. Kugle had his so-called adoptive parents all signed up before the babies were even born. Then, when the young mothers gave birth, he simply put the names of the couples he'd recruited on the babies' birth certificates, instead of the real mothers'. As the attending physician, he could certify any damned information he wanted to."

"Probably had them pregnant girls sign somethin', just so's they wouldn't get ideas about comin' around later, lookin' to get their kids back."

"You're right about that, Sam. Jill and Glenda both signed papers they thought were legal documents releasing their babies for adoption. But—But the fact is, we're not talking about adoptions here. I think we're talking about selling babies."

"Always said ya were smarter than ya look, daffodil." Sam grinned at me like a naughty schoolboy.

I threw my pencil at him, but he ducked before it connected. "That's why they told Glenda she'd have to pay twenty-three thousand bucks if she wanted to take her baby home. Somebody else had already paid at least that much to Kugle and he wasn't about to give it back because the baby's birth mother changed her mind."

"Think bigger, kiddo. Twenty-three grand's *bubkes* in this business. My guess is we're talkin' closer to fifty or sixty per kid."

"Fifty or sixty thousand dollars for a baby?"

"Easy, petunia. Lookit what people're layin' out to go to them fertility docs, tryin' all kinds of fancy things to have their own kids. That kinda stuff can run ya upwards o' thirty or forty thou, easy. When you're lookin' at waitin' ten, twelve years to adopt—if ever—and you got the money, you'll pay."

Something told me that, for people like the Marinellis, the Bestors, the Charbonneaus, and the Carrutherses, money was no problem. I started adding up numbers in my head and quickly realized that the Compassionate Charity Home for Girls could well gross a couple of million dollars a year. Not bad in a recession.

And more than enough motive for kidnapping and murder in the best of times.

38

Paula handed me a message that Meredith O'Connor had called while I was in talking to Sam. Seeing my real estate agent's message filled me with sudden anxiety. The more I thought about the last condominium Meredith had shown me, the more I liked it. I'd been dreaming about placing my furniture in its rooms and coming home to the cozy place each night after work. Yet, the more I thought about my last weekend spent with Doug Winthrop, the less certain I was that I actually wanted to buy any property—no matter how appealing—all by myself. Oh, well, I told myself, what harm could it do for me to look at the place one more time?

"I haven't got time to return this call now, Paula." I had to drive north again, the quicker the better. "Do me a favor, will you? Call Meredith back and ask her to set up a time for me to take a second look at that Ramsey Hill townhouse she showed me. Sometime over the weekend." I handed the phone memo back to Paula.

"Sure thing." She set the phone message aside and continued cutting a photograph out of one of her bridal magazines. Then she snipped the photo in two and taped its bottom half to the top half of another photo. Apparently attempting to create a unique wedding gown for herself by using portions of several of the dresses pictured in her magazines.

By the time I grabbed my coat and purse and was heading for the door, there was no sign that Paula had done anything about returning my call. "Maybe you didn't understand me, Paula," I said. "I meant for you to call Meredith now, and that I'd look at the condo over the weekend, not the other way around."

She wrinkled her nose at me, but, as I grabbed for the door handle, I turned and saw her reaching for the telephone.

Rockville was closer to the Twin Cities than Newton Prairie and even smaller, a collection of small frame houses and a handful of shops. I entered town on Maple Avenue and drove the three blocks to Front Street, turned right, and easily located number 110. Dr. Kugle's office was in a one-story white frame building with half a dozen parking places in front.

The tiny parking lot was empty except for a black Lincoln Town Car with M.D. plates. I pulled in to the curb just long enough to jot down the license number. I doubted that I would really need to have Sam check it, however; the Lincoln was certain to belong to Kugle.

The small medical building did not, however. My file on this case had already told me that the property belonged to Reverend Ed Beale—who I was now certain was up to his holier-than-thou ass in the business of selling healthy white infants to the highest bidders.

The scheme the minister and doctor had cooked up was perfect, once I put it all together. Reverend Ed's anti-abortion organizations and their crusades put him in the perfect position to recruit pregnant teenagers who couldn't handle motherhood on their own. All he and his staff had to do was convince any young women who contacted them directly—or through the bogus Planned Childbirth Association—that they would fry in hell forever if they had abortions. Then they offered the girls and their parents an apparently easy way out of their dilemma—a few months' stay at the Compassionate Charity Home for Girls and promises of absolute secrecy. The young recruits never even had to know that this solution was netting Beale and Kugle a cool fifty grand or more for every baby born at the Home.

I was willing to bet that the anti-abortion crusade served another vital purpose for this seedy business, as well. Certainly the baby selling operation had to be conducted in cash—pesky records like income tax returns, cancelled checks, and the like would attract unwanted legal attention. So, the fund-raising networks of Kids for Life and Adults for Life became the perfect laundry for all that dirty currency. And, as these national organizations were supposedly religious charities, all of their proceeds were tax-free, too. The whole thing was ingenious.

I put the Honda into gear and drove on through town, then out onto the open county road. I checked the map several times before I found the half-hidden turnoff leading to Reverend Ed's rural property. Pulling onto the shoulder of the road across from the farm's entrance, I looked the place over.

It was just as I'd pictured it. A three-story yellow brick building, the house sat behind a six-foot-high chain-link fence topped by barbed wire. Signs were posted on the fence about every ten feet, warning, "No Trespassing" and "Beware of Guard Dogs." There was, however, no sign identifying this place as the Compassionate Charity Home for Girls. There was no sign identifying it at all.

I spotted a closed circuit television camera and an intercom mounted in a brick column to the right of the heavy iron gates that closed off access to the driveway. Clearly, unexpected visitors were not encouraged here.

The windows on the second and third floors of the big old house sported sturdy black iron bars across them, the kind usually seen in high-crime inner city neighborhoods. But my hunch was that these particular bars had more to do with keeping the residents in than keeping the criminals out.

I got out of the Honda and approached the gates on foot. As I peered through the thick iron bars, I saw a long black limousine parked on the east side of the building. The back section was curtained off, exactly as advertised.

I rang the bell at the gate.

"Yes? Who's there?" It was a woman's voice, brusque and to the point.

"Is this the Compassionate Charity Home for Girls?"

The pause was a beat too long. Finally the woman answered. "Yes. What do you want?"

"I'm here to see Kerry Hammond." What the hell. Maybe they'd actually let me in. Or send Kerry out. If not, my up-front visit just might stir up something interesting.

"Who did you say?"

"Kerry Hammond."

"You got the wrong place, miss. Nobody by that name here."

"That's not the information I have. I know Kerry Hammond's there, and I want to see her right now."

"Please leave. You've got the wrong place." The intercom went dead.

I moved away from the range of the closed circuit TV camera and stood against the fence for a few minutes, my eyes trained on the house. Soon a heavy-set, gray-haired woman in a white nurse's uniform and cap opened the front door and looked out. She stared daggers at me, but we were too far apart for conversation.

The nurse went back inside, but reemerged shortly. This time she was holding a German shepherd by his choke collar. She knelt down next to the dog and spoke briefly into his ear, then released him. He bolted towards the fence, snarling viciously.

I flinched as the animal leapt against the portion of the fence closest to me, his fangs bared. The chain link rattled and shook, but held fast. Suddenly I was grateful for its existence. After all, I was allergic to dogs.

This seemed a good a time as any to make my exit. It was clear that Kerry Hammond was not coming out and, if I ever managed to get inside, I doubted that I'd be leaving anytime soon, either. At least not alive.

I jumped into the Honda and headed back toward town.

39

Like Newton Prairie, Rockville had only one café, which was located in the middle of town on the main drag. Rockville's one eatery was called—believe it or not—Mom's Place, and the food was predictably bad. I don't think any café with the word Mom in its name has ever served edible food, and this one was no exception. I stopped in long enough to choke down an undercooked omelet stuffed with some sick-looking canned spinach and a slice of gummy Velveeta . . . and to let the people at the Compassionate Charity Home for Girls think I'd left for good.

An hour and a half later, my stomach full if not particularly satisfied, I headed back out of town. It was dusk now, but not so dark that I could miss the tangerine-colored Volkswagen bug parked in front of the little medical building on Front Street. The Lincoln was no longer there. I couldn't be certain that the VW was the same one I'd seen a couple of times in Newton Prairie, but the chances seemed good. I slowed down enough to commit the bug's license plate number to memory, then continued on my way out of town.

I parked the Honda fifty yards down the road from the iron gates, in a spot sheltered by three ancient oaks. I approached the fence quietly and on foot, waiting for the German shepherd to sound the alarm. But the grounds remained silent; the nurse must have brought the dog back inside after I drove off, perhaps because the place had some more welcome visitors.

The gates were still closed, but now Dr. Kugle's Lincoln was parked behind them, in the circular drive in front of the big old house. There were two other cars there as well, both older American models, plus the limo still parked at the side of the building. No one was outside, and all the drapes were drawn against the quickly falling darkness.

I stood outside, waiting and watching, and quickly becoming chilled as the temperature dropped into the low fifties. After an hour of pacing to keep my blood flowing, I decided I could watch the house just as well from the shelter of the Honda.

I climbed inside and started the engine, turning the heater on full blast. When the interior had warmed up, I shut the engine off again. My dying of carbon monoxide poisoning wouldn't help the Hammond sisters.

By eighty-thirty, Dr. Kugle still had not emerged from the building. It seemed a strange hour for him to be doing medical exams on the residents, unless he had a full-time practice in town during the day and did his rounds here at night.

When another half hour had passed, I felt certain that something was going on inside—too much time had passed to account for nothing more than routine checkups on the five or six teenagers Jill and Glenda had told me were generally in residence. Unless Kugle was simply in there counting his money; if he'd accumulated as much as I'd estimated, that could take ages. I was cold and tired and I wanted to go home, but I decided to stick it out a while longer.

By nine-thirty, I was glad I had. A black BMW pulled up outside the gates and stopped, its headlights still bright and its motor running. An expensively dressed, middle-aged man got out of the driver's side and rang at the gate. He held a brief conversation I couldn't hear over the intercom, after which an electric motor opened the gates. The BMW drove in and parked behind the doctor's vehicle, while the gates quickly closed again.

I got out of the Honda and crept closer to the fence. The BMW had a second passenger, a short red-haired woman wearing a long camel-hair coat. The man helped her from the car, then opened the rear door and removed a small black satchel from the backseat. The nurse I'd seen earlier opened the front door of the house and ushered the man and woman inside.

The wind picked up and I shivered, wishing I had the BMW woman's camel-hair coat to keep me warm. Instead, I had only a green cotton sweater topped by a well-worn denim jacket. I also needed a bathroom—a predictable problem whenever I get chilled. Yet I didn't want to miss anything going on here at Compassionate Charity. So I gritted my teeth, crossed my legs, and bounced up and down.

My patience paid off earlier than I had any right to expect. Within half an hour, the front door re-opened, and the couple left, the woman now carrying a blanket-wrapped bundle in her arms. The small black bag the man had brought inside was nowhere to be seen. The man helped the woman and her burden into the BMW's passenger seat, and the electric gates swung open again as the BMW's engine turned over.

I sneaked back to the Honda and pulled onto the road in pursuit of the BMW. I left my headlights turned off as I trailed it back to the main road, then flipped them on was we neared the town limits.

The BMW's driver seemed completely oblivious of the fact that he was being followed. There was little traffic on the dark country roads, so I hung back, watching the car's taillights from a distance. When we reached I-94 and headed toward the Twin Cities, I closed the gap, periodically allowing another car to get between us so my tail job wouldn't be too obvious.

As we approached the Twin Cities, the BMW took the route east on I-694, then exited the freeway at Lexington Avenue in Arden Hills. I followed at a discreet distance as the black car headed into a residential neighborhood built along the shore of Lake Josephine. Finally the BMW turned into the driveway of a classic, if huge, ranch-style house. The middle of the three garage doors opened electronically and the car disappeared inside. I watched as the door closed again and lights went on inside the house.

I looked up and down the street, spotting Neighborhood

Watch stickers in most of the front windows. A dog across the street barked at my headlights. This did not seem like the best place to be skulking through backyards and peeking in windows.

I U-turned at the end of the street and sped away toward the nearest main drag, in search of a gas station with a Women's Room. I found a Shakey's Pizza instead, where I used the facilities gratefully while waiting for a small cheese pizza to go. When the pizza was ready, I headed back toward the ranch house.

It was almost midnight as I rang the doorbell. The porch light went on and the dog across the street resumed its barking.

"Who's there?" a man's voice demanded.

"Pizza delivery."

The peek hole in the center of the door darkened briefly, followed by the sound of the deadbolt being unlocked. The door swung open and the man I'd seen leaving the Compassionate Charity Home for Girls stood there, arms crossed over his chest. He was about my height, dark-haired with graying temples. He looked annoyed. "What's this about a pizza?"

"Here's the pizza you ordered, sir. That'll be twelve dollars and seventeen cents."

He shook his head. "Nobody here ordered any pizza."

I stared at the address I'd scrawled across the top of the box. "This is thirteen twenty-seven Lake Lane, isn't it?"

"Yeah, but I tell you, we didn't order any pizza."

"I don't understand. This's the address they gave me." I wore my best poor-helpless-little-woman expression.

"Sorry, can't help you, miss." He began to close the door.

"Say, mister. I know it's late, but could I just use your phone a minute to call in? This thing's going to get cold and one of your neighbors is going to be awfully mad at me if this pizza never arrives."

The man hesitated, looked me over, and decided I was harmless. That's one advantage of being a female PI—people usually don't consider me to be particularly threatening.

He let me in and ushered me through the decorator-perfect, mauve-toned living room and into the designer kitchen. This place made the condos Meredith O'Connor had been showing me look like turn-of-the-century chicken coops.

I looked around, but saw no sign of the woman or the bundle she'd been carrying. I dialed my own home phone number on the wall phone and asked my answering machine to repeat the address for the pizza delivery. I hung on the line as long as I dared, the man hovering nervously at my shoulder. "Thanks, Betty," I said finally into the receiver, and hung up.

I turned to my host and explained, "The new operator wrote the number down wrong. I tell you, she's really an idiot. You ask me—" A baby's cry came from the recesses of the house, confirming what had already been my moral certainty. "Gosh, I'm really sorry. Sounds like I woke up your baby."

"Don't worry about it. My wife will take care of him."

I thanked the man for the use of his telephone, then hurried out the front door. The pizza was still warm as I turned the Honda around in the driveway.

I flipped open the box on the passenger seat and ate two slices as I drove home to bed.

40

"That license number ya got for that VW's gotta be wrong," Sam reported the next morning. He plopped down on one of my visitor's chairs, his notepad in one hand and a steaming mug of coffee in the other. "That plate belongs to a seventy-nine Ford pickup owned by Cleveland Butts of St. Cloud."

Damn. I must have remembered one of the numbers or letters wrong, or transposed a couple of them. I silently lectured myself about being more careful. "What about the Lincoln?"

"Belongs to the doc, all right. Home address the DMV's got is six-oh-four Pine Street, Rockville." Sam slurped some of his coffee and set down his mug on my desktop. A wet brown ring began to spread around it.

I folded a Kleenex in half and slipped it under his dripping mug. My desk was no prize, but it didn't need another circular scar.

"You just can't seem to shake yer Suzy Homemaker complex," Sam said.

I didn't bother to respond; it was my desk. "That's all we got, then?"

"Not quite. Found another little tidbit you might like."

"Shoot."

"There's a sixty-five VW bug registered to a Kugle at the same address."

"All right! Give."

"Different license number, and it ain't Otto owns it. This one's registered to a Robert O. Kugle."

My mind began to put together the possibilities. "You happen to check this Robert Kugle's driver's license record?"

"Think I'm a *shlump*?" Sam glared at me. He'd been working on the agency's accounts receivable until I interrupted and asked him to access some public records on the computer. My partner was obviously in another of his famous foul moods.

He picked up his mug and drank again; the soggy Kleenex stuck to the bottom. "Got everything here, 'cept the guy's blood type. Robert Kugle's twenty-three years old, five-foot-eleven, a hundred and ninety-five pounds. He's got brown hair and eyes, and he hasta wear glasses to drive. Satisfied?"

That physical description certainly fit the guy who'd attended Reverend Ed's staff meeting after the anti-abortion rally, the one who later drove away from the church in the orange VW. I wondered whether young Kugle had also been one of my attackers. But, even with a mug shot to look at, I wouldn't have been able to identify him. The men who assaulted me had kept their faces covered. Still, Robert Kugle's height and weight were right for the smaller of the two, the sadistic bastard who'd worked me over with that silver scalpel, then chopped off my hair.

"Figure Robert Kugle's the doctor's son?" I asked. If he were, that would explain where he'd obtained that nasty little weapon.

"Prob'ly. The doc's fifty-nine years old, so the age spread's right. Could be Robert's a nephew or cousin or somethin', but father and son's my best guess."

"I wonder about that plate number I took down off the orange VW," I said. Could it be the license plate that was missing from the truck my two attackers had been driving? Maybe they'd switched it over to the VW for some reason.

Sam agreed to check on whether the truck had been reported stolen.

I turned to my own notes. "The City Directory says the new parents I visited last night in Arden Hills are George and Josephine Pollack. That jibe with the car registration on the BMW?"

"Yup. The Pollacks own that Beamer, all right. Free and clear."

From what I'd observed, George and Josephine had a lot of expensive possessions, and their list now included a healthy white infant to call their very own. I wondered how much they'd paid for the baby. I pushed back my chair and stood up. "I'll be back in a couple of hours, Sam. With luck, George Pollack'll be off wherever he goes to earn all that money. I'm going to pay a little visit to Josephine and the new heir to the family fortune."

"What for?"

"Got an idea. But I'm going to need Josephine Pollack's help to pull it off."

"Great!" Sam slapped his forehead. "Another one o' yer famous ideas. I can hardly wait to hear how much *this* one's gonna cost us."

"Know what I like about you, Sam? You always look on the bright side. 'Specially at the end of the month, when you're sending out the bills." I grabbed my coat and purse and headed for the door.

Paula was actually typing something as I walked into the outer office. Not wanting to be like Sam, I told myself that she'd finally gotten around to doing some of the agency's business. But I didn't dare look too closely. I had so few illusions left.

"Hey, Devon, hold up a minute." Paula pulled a small slip of paper from her typewriter and held it out to me. "Your real estate lady called. Left this message for you."

I read it. "Sorry. Can't see the Ramsey Hill place this weekend. It's sold to a cash buyer. Call me. Meredith."

Great. Now I would have to start all over again on my search for a new home. Provided that I really wanted a new home, that is. Feeling both disappointed that the condo I liked was already gone, and relieved that now I wouldn't have to choose between buying it and seeing more of Doug Winthrop, I scrunched up the message and tossed it into Paula's wastebasket.

Resolving my ambivalence would just have to wait.

41

Josephine Pollack was less than thrilled about letting me into her house. But after I explained that I knew where and from whom she'd bought her new baby, and that I needed to discuss it with her, she paled and opened the door. She led me into the mauve-colored living room, where the baby was asleep in an antique pine cradle. We sat next to each other on a huge silk sectional.

"There's nothing really wrong with what we did." Josephine Pollack kept her voice low so as not to disturb the sleeping infant. She was a petite woman with bright red hair and sharp features that were softened and made almost beautiful by her flawless makeup. She wore a yellow cashmere sweater and gray wool slacks that probably cost a month of my pay. "It's not like Ryan's birth mother could keep him. I mean, she's a child herself—only fifteen years old. He'll have a much better life with us." She spoke with great conviction.

"What makes you think so?"

"Because she's so young, and—and she's *poor!*" She wrinkled her nose, as though poverty had an unpleasant odor. "You know as well as I do, the family's having enough money can make a lot of difference in how a child grows up."

"Yeah, sometimes." In my book, money wasn't the most important factor in rearing children, but poverty wasn't particularly desirable, either.

"You tell me, is an unmarried teenage girl going to be able to send Ryan to a really good nursery school?" She gestured toward the sleeping infant. "Why, that cradle alone cost us six hundred dollars—it's hand-carved oak, one of a kind. Where's a young girl going to get that kind of money? Or the money to buy him nice clothes and toys, or to get his teeth straightened later on? And you can just forget about college." She lifted her chin. "Besides, the doctor told us Ryan's birth mother wanted him put up for adoption."

"Yes, well. If the mother really wants to give up her baby, the State has a few rules about who gets to adopt him."

"So, maybe George and I took a few shortcuts. What's the harm?" Josephine Pollack began to knead her small hands together. The diamond on her left hand was at least two carats in size, only slightly larger than the three stones set into the center of her wide gold bracelet. "You have no idea how long the waiting list is at those adoption agencies."

"But I do, Mrs. Pollack, really. I know there are many,

many couples who've been waiting for a baby like Ryan. For years. Now it looks like they're all going to have to wait a little longer."

"So what?" Her voice was rising now, but the baby continued his slumber. "If you couldn't have a baby, and . . . and you could afford to pay for one the way we did, I bet you'd do it."

"Look, Mrs. Pollack, I can understand why you went to Dr. Kugle instead of an adoption agency, really I can." The Pollacks were hardly the only couple desperate enough to do almost anything for a baby. "But that doesn't make what you did right—either legally or morally."

She began to chew on one of her perfect fingernails. "You *don't* understand, you really don't. You don't know what it's like, how much I wanted this baby. George and I tried everything, we went to all the doctors, we had all the tests, but nothing worked. Nothing! So we decided to adopt, but— but the agencies said no. They told us there was an eight-to-ten year waiting list, and only younger couples could get on it. I'm already thirty-five and my husband is forty-four. By the agencies' standards, we're too old to be parents."

I resented the sense of entitlement she'd displayed, but now I began to feel a little sorry for her. Obviously, her money hadn't made her happy. Still, I couldn't let sympathy deter me from my goal. I plunged ahead. "You know, Mrs. Pollack, if the State finds out about what you and your husband have done, you're going to have to give the baby back."

"No! I won't give him back! Dr. Kugle said nobody'd ever know. He guaranteed us that."

"Yes, well. Unfortunately, Dr. Kugle is in no position to guarantee anybody anything."

She sprang to her feet. "I'm going to call him right now and—"

I grabbed her arm. "Sit down, Mrs. Pollack. You're going to call Dr. Kugle, all right, but not just yet. First, I'm going to tell you exactly what to say to him."

Half an hour later, when Josephine Pollack dialed Dr. Otto Kugle's phone number in Rockville, she and I had come to an understanding. I agreed not to go directly to the Department of Human Services and turn her in, and she agreed to get me entre into Kugle's network as a potential adoptive parent.

"Dr. Kugle? Hi. It—It's Jo Pollack." Her voice was shaky, nervous. I motioned for her to calm down. "Uh, I'm fine, thanks. And you?" She listened a moment. "No, Doctor, there's nothing wrong with Ryan. He—He's sleeping right here in front of me. Just like a little angel."

Mrs. Pollack listened again. "Well, yes, of course there's a reason I called. It—It's just that—"

I glared at her, my look intended to remind her that I was ready to go straight to the authorities if she didn't play her part convincingly.

"I—I mean, it's about these friends of ours, Doctor, Mr. and Mrs. Sam Miller. They want to adopt a baby, too, like we did. I hope you don't mind, but I told them about our, uh, our arrangement . . . and they asked me to put them in touch with you."

She smoothed an invisible wrinkle out of her slacks. "Yes, Doctor, I told them. They understand. Money's not a problem."

Apparently the fictitious Millers had passed the most important—maybe the only—hurdle, the size of their bank account. Josephine had admitted to me earlier that she and her husband exchanged fifty-five thousand dollars in cash for young Ryan. Now, as she listened to the doctor talk, she flashed me a thumbs-up sign. I nodded encouragement.

"All right, then, Doctor. I'll tell Mr. and Mrs. Miller to call you directly. . . . No, no, thank *you*. 'Bye now." She hung up the phone, took a deep breath, and pulled a handkerchief from her pocket. "Did I do okay?"

"Fine," I told her. "So Dr. Kugle's expecting my call?"

"Uh huh." Her chin quivered. "You *will* keep your promise, won't you?" The baby began to stir in his sleep. "I can't even imagine losing Ryan. Not now, not after all we've—"

"I'll do what I can, Mrs. Pollack. I promise I won't turn you in—providing that you don't get any bright ideas about calling Kugle back and warning him."

"Oh, no, I'd never—"

"Good. That would be exceedingly stupid. But you have to understand one thing. Nobody can guarantee you that the good doctor and whatever files he has on these so-called adoptions won't someday end up in the hands of the police. The guy is a crook and someday he's going to get caught. You and your husband had better be prepared for that."

When I left her, she was standing over the cradle, gazing at tiny little Ryan, a look of sheer terror on her face. The Pollacks certainly had brought this problem upon themselves, but knowing that gave me no personal satisfaction whatsoever. I left the house feeling sad, for the Pollacks, for young Ryan, and for his birth mother as well.

42

"I tell ya, I don't know what you were thinkin' when you cooked this one up. You had some *meshuggeneh* ideas in yer time, but this one's gotta top 'em all."

Sam had been bitching at me ever since I picked him up at his home an hour earlier. When I'd returned to the office the day before, I called Otto Kugle. Playing the part of Donna Miller, a wealthy woman desperate for a baby she couldn't have on her own, I made an appointment with him. My husband Sam and I were to meet with the doctor to discuss adopting a baby, like our friends the Pollacks had done, at eleven this morning.

Now Sam and I were in my Honda, speeding toward Rockville, where my reluctant partner was to play the part of my husband. He didn't exactly relish the opportunity.

"You got a better idea how to get Kerry Hammond out of there, Sam? I'm all ears."

"No, I ain't got a better idea. But I tell ya, there's no way in hell we're gonna pull off this stupid charade." He ripped open a bag of Fritos and began stuffing them into his mouth as I drove.

"Give me one good reason why not."

"Lookit us. You think this guy's gonna believe you're really my wife?"

"Why not? Just because you're old enough to be my father?" Out of the corner of my eye, I saw Sam stiffen. I'd hit him smack in the middle of his vanity. If there was one thing my partner didn't want to hear, it was that he wasn't anywhere near as young as he used to be.

"Hell no! Got nothin' to do with my age. It—It's just we got nothin' in common, that's all. Any dope can see that."

"Maybe, Sam, but I've got confidence in you. I remember you once told me you could play any role if you had to."

He stuffed three more Fritos into his mouth. "Well, maybe. . . . But I still don't like this."

"What you don't like, pal, is that you're riding north with me on a Saturday morning, when you'd rather be home with Rose and your family."

"Damn right I'd rather be home. Aaron's *bris* is just a few more days. Rosie 'n' me got preparations to make. And where am I? In the middle of my partner's *mishegoss!*"

"All you have to do is back me up, Sam. Just sit there and look like a fat cat with a younger wife who wants a baby. I'll do the talking, and you pretend there's nothing you want more than to indulge my every little whim. Think you can handle that?"

"Ah, hell, I s'pose."

I parked half a block down the street from the medical building, mainly so that the doctor wouldn't be able to look out his window and see my ancient Honda parked in his lot. My little car was hardly a sign of the kind of affluence I was trying to portray, and Sam's old Chevy would have been no better. What we really needed was a Mercedes, or at least a Cadillac. But this case had no budget for renting such an extravagance, so we were forced to make do.

At least Sam and I were dressed reasonably well. I was wearing my new periwinkle blue silk slacks and matching sweater and Sam had somehow managed to dredge up a decent sweater and slacks. He certainly never wore clothes this good to the office. Maybe the outfit was something new he'd bought for the upcoming family celebration.

I checked the tape recorder I'd hidden in my purse to see that it was working properly. I wanted to keep my promise to Josephine Pollack to keep the authorities out of this, if I possibly could. Truth was, I didn't want them involved any more than she did. If I called the police or the Department of Human Services in my effort to spring Kerry Hammond from the Compassionate Charity Home for Girls, the girl's parents would be notified immediately. And I had sworn to Monica that I wouldn't let that happen.

Under the cirucumstances, a little blackmail seemed a much more workable idea. If I could get Kugle on tape, making an explicit offer to exchange an infant for a bundle of cash from the fictitious Millers, I figured I could later exchange that tape for Kerry Hammond's freedom.

I clicked a ninety-minute tape cassette into my recorder and put it back into my purse. "Come on, Sam. Let's go." He reluctantly got out of the Honda, then tossed his open Fritos bag onto the passenger seat. "You've got crumbs all over your sweater." I reached over and brushed off Sam's paunch.

He pushed my hand away. "Jesus Christ, Devon—Leave a man some dignity, willya?"

"*Donna*, Sam. My name's Donna, 'til we get out of town." I hadn't dared use my real name when I spoke to Kugle. Devon is too unusual and, for all I knew, Reverend Ed and his mob had put the word out about Devon MacDonald, private eye. With luck, they wouldn't connect her with Donna Miller, the anxious and infertile young wife of an older, but wealthy husband.

Dr. Otto Kugle himself met us as we entered his outer office. "My girl's off today," he explained as he introduced himself. I'm always so charmed by doctors who refer to their usually middle-aged nurses as "my girl."

Kugle ushered us into his inner office and offered us the two leather-covered chairs facing his desk. As I sat down, I slipped my hand inside my purse and clicked on my tape recorder.

The doctor sat down behind his desk. He was about five feet ten and sported a fringe of gray hair around his completely bald dome. His chubby, pink-cheeked face seemed at odds with his wiry body. "Now," he said. My eyes were drawn to the framed diplomas and certificates on the wall behind him, and I wondered at what point being a legitimate doctor had ceased to be enough for him. "As I told you when we spoke yesterday, Mrs. Miller, I never like to discuss adoptions over the phone. I feel it's important that I meet the couple face to face, sort of size them up before we get into the details."

"Oh, we understand that, don't we, Sam?" I reached over and patted Sam's hand. He flinched at first, then caught himself and gave my hand a squeeze.

"You, bet, sweet pea."

"What would you like to know about us?" I smiled at the doctor. "Anything. Just ask."

He narrowed his eyes at us. "There appears to be an age discrepancy between the two of you. I suppose you know that would work against you in a regular agency adoption."

I withdrew my hand from Sam's grasp and leaned toward the doctor. "We've already been to the agencies, Doctor. We know their rules and we're completely aware they're not going to give us a baby. It—It's not because there's anything wrong with *us*. It's just that we don't fit into the adoption agencies' neat little categories."

Kugle waved his hand as though to dismiss the rules and the categories. "Yes, well. That's why my colleagues and I can be extremely valuable to couples like you, Mrs. and Mrs. Miller. Extremely valuable. We can offer you a second chance." He pulled a pad of legal paper from his desk drawer and sat with his pencil poised above it. "What about religion?"

"What about it?" I asked.

"Do you belong to a church?" The doctor's eyes fell on Sam, who squared his shoulders and looked grim.

"No," I said. "Sam was raised Jewish and I wasn't raised in any particular religion. But we're moral people."

"Hmmm. Different ethnic groups, too." He wrote something on the yellow paper, then looked up at us. "It's obvious you'd never qualify through an agency." He placed his fingers together in the shape of a tent and paused, as though coming to a decision.

"My friend Jo Pollack said you use different, more realistic criteria, Doctor. Such as a couple's desire for a child, and their ability to give it some of life's—Well, uh, shall we say life's little advantages?"

"Many, many couples want babies, you know. Healthy, white babies. This kind of adoption can be expensive."

"Jo explained that to us. Didn't she, sweetheart?"

Sam nodded. "If money's the only problem, Doc, forget about it. Anything my little honey cakes here sets her heart on, I'll give it to her. You may not know it, but—" I kicked Sam's ankle to shut him up before he said too much.

"Sweetheart," I said, "I'm sure the doctor doesn't want a blow-by-blow of how you made all your money." I patted Sam's hand and turned my eyes to Kugle. "The point is, Doctor, we can afford this kind of adoption, and we're willing to pay. Now, Jo said it cost them fifty-five thousand for Ryan. Is that what we can expect?"

The doctor didn't respond immediately, and I was suddenly fearful that I'd seemed too eager to discuss money. Perhaps I should have sidled into the subject less straightforwardly.

"My dear Mr. and Mrs. Miller, I don't want you to get the wrong idea here. We're not talking about negotiating a price for a child. Nothing that crass. That would be both illegal and immoral—"

My heart skipped a beat. Had I blown it? "Of course not, Doctor. I didn't mean—"

"Fact is, we have certain expenses that must be paid. That's what the money goes for."

"Yes, that's what Jo told us."

"There's room and board for the young mothers, of course, plus their religious instruction, medical care, travel expenses. Then, every once in a while, one of the girls miscarries or there's a problem with the baby and nobody wants to adopt it. Somebody still has to pay those expenses, so we spread them out among the other adoptions."

"That's certainly understandable, Doctor."

"Then there's our overhead—you know, staff salaries, the Home's running expenses, and the like."

"I'm sure it adds up." I heard a car engine outside the medical building, followed by the slam of a door, and willed the doctor to cut to the chase before we could be interrupted.

He scribbled down some numbers. "I think you'd better figure on closer to seventy-five," he said.

"Seventy-five thousand dollars?" My mouth fell open; a split second later, I realized that I was letting my surprise show and snapped it shut again.

"You've got to realize, Mr. and Mrs. Miller. The Pollacks didn't present nearly as many problems as you two do. My organization would be taking far more risk with the two of you. And risk has to be compensated."

"That's a lot of money," I said. "What guarantee do we have that the baby will be healthy?"

"All our babies undergo a rigorous physical examination immediately after birth. I do it myself. If something gets by me . . . if your baby is later found to have, say, a serious birth defect, we could, er—Shall we say make an adjustment?"

"And the baby's birth mother? Could we meet her, get to know her a little?"

The doctor fidgeted in his seat and rolled his pencil between his fingers. "That's not the way we do things here, Mrs. Miller. The mother's privacy is of utmost importance to us. You won't know who she is and she won't know who you are. We've found that works out best."

"Makes sense to me," Sam said, anxious to hurry the transaction along. "Seventy-five it is, then. So, when do we get the baby?"

Dr. Kugle smiled. "We've got three or four girls who'll be delivering their babies within the next two or three months. I'd say you'll have one of them by the end of June, maybe sooner. If you don't have a sex preference, that is."

"And, if we do?" I asked.

"Then it might take a little longer, and cost a little more."

"I don't really care whether it's a boy or a girl, just so long as it's healthy, do you, Sam dear?"

"Nope. Whatever you want's okay with me, rosebud." Sam leered at me and began to paw my sleeve. I cringed; once my partner really gets himself into a role, he has a terrible tendency to overact. "Now, how's this deal work, Doc?" he asked.

"We work in cash and cash only. We'll need a deposit from you, of course. Let's say half up front and the remainder when—"

The door behind Sam and me burst open. I jerked around to see Reverend Ed standing there. His giant form nearly filled the door frame. "Sorry I'm la—" His eyes riveted on me. "You! What the hell, Otto. Don't you know who this woman is?"

I sprang to my feet, clutching my purse to my side.

The doctor's confidence crumbled and he looked like a flustered employee caught by the boss in a major screw-up. "What do you—"

"This is that investigator I told you about, Otto, that MacDonald woman from the Cities. The one who's been poking around the church and Planned Childbirth. What the hell have you told her?"

"I—I thought—"

Ed rushed me, snatching at my purse. I managed to hold onto it for only a moment.

Sam lurched to his feet. "Give that back to her!" He reached for my bag, but Ed held him off with a blow to the chest. Sam fell back, caught his balance and started toward the minister a second time. "You thief, you bast—"

Reverend Ed shoved him again, harder. Sam folded back into his chair, gasping for breath. I placed a hand on his shoulder, an attempt to calm him before he did something really stupid and had another heart attack.

The big minister's face turned crimson with rage. He snapped my bag open and yanked out the tape recorder. He pried out the tape and dropped the recorder on the floor, where it landed with a crack.

"Give me that tape. That's my property."

"Yeah?" Reverend Ed's big hands cracked the cassette in two without effort. The filmy recording tape inside quickly unraveled into a useless pile on the floor. Sneering at me, Ed ground his shoe into the ruined tape. "It's all yours." Now that he'd found what he wanted, he tossed the purse back to me. I caught it. "What's your game, lady? And who's fatso here?"

"My partner and I want Kerry Hammond," I told him. No sense beating around the bush. The hard evidence I'd hoped to use for a trade was gone now, but maybe I could still bluff my way through.

Dr. Kugle backed up, as though to distance himself from the enraged minister. If I'd had any doubts about who ran this show, they were now history.

"We haven't got her," Reverend Ed said.

I squared my shoulders and moved between the minister and Sam. I didn't want my partner pulling any more amateur heroics on my behalf. "I think you do. I think you're holding her prisoner out at that farm of yours."

The minister began to laugh. It was an evil, threatening sound. "You really got some nerve, lady. Even if we had the Hammond girl, what makes you think we'd give her to you?"

"Because I've got something to trade for her. Something you don't want in the hands of the authorities."

The laughter died. "Such as?"

"Tapes. And affidavits. From some of your best customers."

"She's bluffing, Ed," the doctor yelled. "If she really had

that stuff, why would she come up here and pose like this?"

"Hey guys, I'm not bluffing. I know all about your slick little business here. I know about the Pollacks and the Carruthers and the Marinellis and the Bestors and the Charbonneaus." The expressions on the minister's and the doctor's faces froze as they listened to my list. "And Sam and I can find the rest of the people you sold kids to, too. 'Cause we know exactly how you did it.

"We know all about the birth mothers you tricked out of their babies, too. Remember Glenda Johnson, a pretty young blonde? Well, guess what? She wants her baby back. And then there's Penny Morrison and Jill Lester. Remember them?"

"So what, Ed? She can't—"

"Shut up, Otto!" At the minister's sharp words, the doctor grew silent. Reverend Ed grew cold and businesslike. "What exactly are you proposing here, Miss MacDonald?"

"A simple trade. You turn Kerry Hammond over to us, and you don't tell anyone—including her parents—where she's been since she took that bus out of Newton Prairie. In return, we keep quiet about the nice little scam you've got going here." I knew I had to offer something substantial or there would be no deal. Whether I would keep my side of the bargain was something I'd think about later.

"Why should the doctor and I believe you'll keep quiet if we agree to your terms?"

"Because all we care about is getting Kerry Hammond back. We don't give a damn about the rest of it. That stuff's not our problem."

"Don't believe her, Ed. She can't—"

The minister silenced the doctor with a glance. "We'll discuss it," he said. "Where can we find you?"

"We'll be at that motel down the street. What's it called, Borg's?" The two men nodded. "We'll give you until four o'clock this afternoon to call us there. We don't hear from you, we'll have no choice but to take our evidence to the proper authorities."

Reverend Ed stood aside as Sam and I headed out the

door. Sam was red-faced and breathing hard. I was worried
about him. Ever since his second heart attack, he'd been
unable to handle stress. His blood pressure tended to shoot
up dangerously high.

I paused a moment and looked back at the two men in
the doctor's office. "Don't get any cute ideas, fellows. We've
got copies of everything. Anything happens to either one
of us, our attorney goes straight to the cops."

I grabbed Sam's arm and helped support him as we walked
back to my car.

43

Borg's Motel was spartan at best. We rented an end room,
from where I could keep an eye on both the parking lot and
the main street of town. The Honda was parked in clear
view of our window. I was tired of people tampering with
it. If anyone approached my car now, at least I would know
about it.

I sat on an old pine ladder-back chair, looking out the
window at the gathering storm clouds above the rooftops
across the street, and waiting anxiously for the telephone to
ring. Sam lay spread out across the lumpy double bed, al-
ternately dozing and chewing me out.

"For God's sake, Sam, put a lid on it, will you? I'm tired
of hearing how pissed off you are. Do both of us a favor—
rent yourself a car, drive home to Rose, and let me handle
the rest of this thing by myself."

He pushed himself up on his elbows and peered at me
across his bulging stomach. "Whadya take me for? Ya really
think Sam Sherman's gonna run out and leave a woman to

handle two *shmucks* like them all by herself? Not as long as I'm still breathin'."

That was the problem—I was scared Sam wouldn't be breathing a whole lot longer if he didn't go home. I didn't know what to expect from Kugle and Beale, and I was afraid Sam's heart wouldn't be able to take much more stress. Not that I wouldn't have been grateful for some backup; it was just that Sam promised to be far more hindrance than help. Still, I had to let him keep his pride, so I avoided being too blunt with him.

The parking lot and street outside had been quiet all afternoon, as though the townsfolk had decided to stay home to avoid the rain forecast for late afternoon. A kid with a dog strolled by once, and every so often, a car would pass, but I saw no sign of Kugle, Beale, or the orange VW I figured might belong to Kugle's son, Robert. I was bored.

I looked over at the ancient clock radio on the nightstand. It was digital, but not electronic—the kind with the numbers on little hanging rectangles that flip over to change the time. It read three-forty-five—only fifteen minutes left until my deadline. Thunder cracked overhead and the first raindrops pelted the motel window.

I tried not to squander mental energy guessing what was taking the minister and doctor so long. Or thinking about what I would do if they didn't phone by my drop dead hour. I have a bad habit of wasting time figuring out every possible combination and permutation in life, indulging my need to be prepared for every eventuality. A therapist friend of mine once told me I did this to achieve a false confidence that I could maintain control over the uncontrollable.

"Anywhere ya can get a decent meal around this town?" Sam asked, returning to his favorite subject. "We ain't even had lunch yet."

I sighed. Sam had done little but snack from his personal stash of junk food since we'd left St. Paul. "If I ever ask you along on a job again, Sam, do me a favor and have me lobotomized."

"Fine thanks."

The phone rang. I grabbed for it. "Yes?"

"Miss MacDonald?" I recognized Reverend Ed's deep voice.

"Right."

"We've made the arrangements. Come to forty-nine Elm Street tonight at exactly seven o'clock. That's a house on the south side of town. You and your partner. Nobody else."

"Kerry will be there?"

"You bring what we discussed, you get the girl."

"Seven o'clock."

"Sharp." The line went dead.

I smiled at Sam. "They've agreed to our terms, partner. We get Kerry Hammond at seven o'clock."

44

For nearly two hours, the rain fell in thick sheets of water, accompanied by staccato bursts of thunder and lightning. But the clouds had moved on by the time I pulled the Honda into the curb at 49 Elm Street. I parked in front of Reverend Ed's dark red Cadillac.

The address was that of a tan one-story frame house on the list of rental properties the big preacher owned. The porch light was not on, but the number 49 next to the front door was illuminated by the street light on the corner.

I reached into the backseat and pulled out the envelope I had prepared for the anticipated exchange. It held three tapes of "adoptive parent interviews" that Paula and I had faked earlier at the office, plus Xerox copies of a few of my case notes—enough, I hoped, to bluff Beale and Kugle into making a quick trade for Kerry Hammond. By the time they discovered my package was not exactly what I'd promised, I hoped Kerry would be in Minneapolis, safe with her sister.

"Ya shoulda let me bring my thirty-eight," Sam complained as he peered through the dripping car window. "This don't look right."

"Then I suggest you stay right here in the car and wait for me." Night was falling quickly and the little house was very dark. I didn't much like the looks of things myself, but this was no time to chicken out. I left the keys in the ignition and opened my door. "If I'm not back with the girl in ten minutes, Sam, take the car and go for the police."

"The hell." Sam's door flew open and he stepped out of the car, directly into a wide stream of frigid rain water running in the gutter. He swore out loud, then stomped his soggy shoes on the sidewalk in an attempt to squeeze out the water. If I hadn't been so nervous about what lay ahead, I probably would have laughed out loud. I reached back inside the car, grabbed my keys from the ignition, and stuffed them into the pocket of my pants.

My own shoes were soaked by the time we reached the front door. My feet grew cold, and I no longer found Sam's landing in the gutter quite so humorous.

The house had no doorbell, only a big brass door knocker. I hammered away with it, but got no response. Standing on tiptoes, I peered through the door's small high window into the dark interior of the house. I could see nothing clearly, but there did appear to be a light at the rear of the structure.

From what I could see, the house looked empty, yet Reverend Ed's car was out front. We'd come to the right place, at exactly the assigned time. I knocked again and waited. Still no response. I tried the door handle. It turned easily and the door creaked open.

I stepped inside, with Sam close on my heels. "Hello!" I called. "Hello! Reverend Ed? Hello, there!"

We were standing in a tiny hallway. The living room to our right was completely empty of furniture. Long white drapes covered the picture window facing the street, cutting off most of the illumination from the light on the corner. I flipped the electric switch on the wall and the porch light came on, but it did little to illuminate the interior of the house.

I listened. No one answered my call, but I could hear soft whining sounds, almost like the mewing of a cat, from the direction of the light. I headed toward it, my stomach turning nervous flip-flops.

At the end of the hall was a dining room, every bit as bare as the living room. We squished across its hardwood floor, leaving wet footprints in our wake, as we headed toward the source of the light. The whimpering sounds grew louder as we reached the swinging door at the back of the dining room. I held my breath and pushed against it.

It took a split second for my eyes to adjust from the darkness to the bright fluorescent lighting of the kitchen, and a moment longer to take in the scene before me. Like the other rooms, this one had no furniture, but it had something else.

In the middle of the blue linoleum floor was Reverend Ed, lying face down. I sprinted toward him and saw that the back of his head was a bloody pulp. Beside him was a metal mallet—the kind generally used to chop ice. It was coated with blood. I stared in horror, my stomach churning.

I heard the whining sound again. It wasn't coming from the minister. I spun around and saw a weeping young woman sitting on the floor in the far corner, her knees pulled up under her chin. The frightened kitten sounds came from her throat.

My heart jumped. I recognized her instantly. "Kerry! Kerry Hammond." Struggling to understand what had happened here, I sprinted toward the girl, dropped to my knees, and threw my arm around her shoulders. "Sam, see if you can do anything for Reverend Ed."

Sam knelt down and placed two fingers on the side of the big minister's neck. "He's still breathin', barely. Pulse's slow."

Kerry shrank back from my touch, her eyes filled with terror. "It's okay, hon, I'm not going to hurt you. You're all right now. Monica sent us."

The girl's skin was pale and her blue eyes had a sunken quality. I'd seen that look before—raw fear. Had this frail teenager managed to fell this man nearly twice her size? Or was she merely a witness to violence? Either way, she was terrorized.

"Preacher here's not gonna last much longer, we don't get help," Sam said. "See a phone anywhere?"

"Place is empty, Sam. We'll have to get a neighbor." Kerry didn't appear to be physically injured, but she was shaking hard. "Can you stand up, Kerry? We've got to get help. You can tell us what happened later."

I managed to yank the thin, blonde teenager to her feet, but she was noticeably wobbly, clearly dazed and disoriented.

"You hurt?" I asked her.

"Huh?"

I grabbed her arm, shook it, and shouted at her, trying to focus her attention. "Are you hurt, Kerry?"

"I—I—No, I—No, I guess not."

"Come on, then. Let's go." I grabbed Kerry by the hand and spun her around. "We'll go for help, Sam. You stay here with him." But, as I pushed open the swinging door to the dining room, there was a loud crash at the front of the house. In a split second, the acrid smell of burning gasoline assaulted my nostrils and a brilliant, red-orange ball of fire lit up the darkened living room. "Firebomb!" I shouted.

I spun around, yanking Kerry toward the back door. But I couldn't get it open. It was bolted shut with the kind of lock that requires a key to open, and the key was missing.

I looked around frantically, searching for a way out. The kitchen had only one window, over the sink. A quick glance told me it was nailed shut. Black smoke began to seep under the door between the kitchen and the dining room, and Sam began to cough. We didn't have much time.

Kerry stared straight ahead, chanting, "We're all gonna die, we're all gonna die, we're all gonna—"

"Shut up!" I tore off my jacket and threw it over my arm as a shield. Then I grabbed the bloody mallet and smashed at the window, over and over again. Cold, wet air gushed in as I pushed shards of glass from the splintered wooden frame. "Kerry, quick! Come here!" I grabbed the girl's arms, then boosted her onto the counter and pushed her through the window frame. She landed with a thud on the wet ground outside. "Move away from the house!"

I turned to Sam. "Sam! Come on, move it." My partner was wheezing from inhaling the smoke now, and he held his right fist clenched over his heart. "Come on, Sam! This is no time to crap out on me, damn it." He boosted his wide hips onto the kitchen counter and I half-pushed him until he was standing in the sink. "Get your feet out the window, *now!*"

There was another crash, this time at the side of the house. Another firebomb or something in the house exploding from the original fire? I'd probably never know. Certainly I wouldn't unless I got Sam through that window damned soon and myself out after him. There was nothing we could do for Reverend Ed.

I climbed onto the counter and shoved Sam through the window frame. His jacket caught on a remaining shard of glass and he got hung up. No! This was not how I intended to die. I threw all my weight against Sam and shoved. The jacket ripped, and he cleared the window frame with a jerk, landing hard on the ground outside.

I followed, just as flames burst through the kitchen door and began to lick at the edge of the gas stove. I fell to the ground next to Sam, greedily sucked in a lungful of fresh air, then forced myself to my feet.

"Kerry, help me with him. Quick!" She and I each grabbed one of Sam's thick arms and we dragged him away from the burning house.

"Le—Lemme alone. Just lemme go!" Sam was breathing erratically, but at least he could talk now. I was breathing a little easier myself.

"Stay with him," I ordered Kerry. "I'm going for help." As I rounded the side of the burning house, another flash of orange crossed my field of vision. But this time it wasn't a burst of flame; it was the orange Volkswagen, skidding into a U-turn on the rain-slicked street. I sprinted for the Honda, pulling the keys from my pants pocket as I ran.

I slid the ignition key into place and twisted it. The engine caught on my first try. By the time the taillights of the VW rounded the corner at the end of the block, I was flooring my accelerator in hot pursuit. I wasn't sure what I would do if I caught up—I had no weapon. But I wasn't about to let the VW's driver get away without at least knowing who he was and where he was going.

I slid around a second corner onto Oak Street, then took the right onto Maple, now only half a block behind the VW. As we passed through the bright lights of Rockville's main street, I could see that the tangerine-colored car carried only its driver—Dr. Kugle? Or perhaps his son?

A siren wailed somewhere behind me. I could see no cops in my rearview mirror, nor had I any intention of pulling over. I kept my foot to the floor. But the siren soon faded; the emergency vehicle was heading in the opposite direction. Good, I thought, someone had called in a fire alarm. Help for Sam and Kerry was on its way.

The VW accelerated at a crazy pace now, jumping a curb, then fish-tailing around a corner. I tried to keep my own speed at a slightly saner level, and the distance between us grew. But at the next corner, the VW's driver lost control on the wet asphalt and his car spun completely around. By the time he had righted it, I'd almost caught up.

We were on Front Street now, half a block from the medical clinic. It was no longer raining, but the dripping tree branches overhead made visibility poor. I turned on my windshield wipers. As he reached the medical clinic, the other driver suddenly cramped his steering wheel sharply to the left. He slid into the clinic's small parking lot—empty except for the doctor's Lincoln—then hit standing water and planed sideways across the asphalt.

I jerked the Honda to the left as hard as I could, almost missing the turn. I skidded into the parking lot. The air split with a deafening crash as the orange VW careened broad-side into the parked Lincoln. Metal ripped into metal and a flash of even brighter orange caught the corner of my eye. Sparks flew and, in an instant, the VW was engulfed in flames.

My heart in my mouth now, I felt the Honda hit the water and begin to plane sideways. I had a momentary sensation of flying toward a ball of fire as I pumped my brakes frantically, but my car did not slow. My tires could find no traction on the wet pavement. The Honda's rear end broke loose and I spun halfway around. Suddenly the new rubber tread of my tires caught the asphalt and my brakes held. I came to a tooth-rattling halt within a yard of the fire. My engine died.

With shaking hands, I forced my door open. My only thought was that I had to get out of my car, fast, before the fire reached it. As I put a leg out and felt with my foot for the pavement, a blast threw me headlong into the parking lot. I rolled a full car length and came to rest face down in murky water.

I heard a blood-curdling scream split the air, followed by another, filled with unforgettable anguish. "Bobby! *Bobby*!"

I pushed myself up and out of the water and turned to look. A wave of heat scorched my face, and I scrambled backward as fast as I could.

Inside the Volkswagen, a lone figure beat against the windows that trapped him in flames every bit as bright as his car's quickly charring paint.

Dr. Kugle frantically tried to reach the trapped man, but the flames forced him back again and again. "Bobby! Bobby! Oh, my God, *Bobby*!" I knew I would never forget that cry as long as I lived.

There was nothing either the doctor or I could do but watch in fascinated horror as the gas tanks of the Honda and the Lincoln quickly ignited and a series of larger explosions ended Bobby Kugle's misery.

45

"I'm glad they're dead, both of 'em. Maybe it's terrible to say, but I'm glad they're dead." Kerry Hammond sat on one of the two single beds in our room at Borg's Motel, her fists clenched and her eyes brimming with tears. She'd called her sister Monica on the telephone as soon as we got to the motel. Now Kerry and I were talking, while Sam rested in the adjoining room, having refused to let the police take him to St. Cloud for medical observation.

Kerry, Sam, and I had spent the last four hours being questioned by the local sheriff, and it was now much too late to drive back to the Twin Cities—not to mention that my Honda was history, so I would have to rent a car before I could drive anyone anywhere. We decided to stay the night.

"I can see where you'd be angry with Reverend Ed and Bobby," I said. "Ed held you against your will at the Home, and Bobby actually tried to kill you tonight." Along with Sam and me.

"You don't know the half of it." Kerry picked up a pillow and began to punch her fists into it. "I hate them. I just hate them!"

The girl's anger was palpable. "Why don't you tell me about it?"

She gave the pillow one last punch, then threw it against the wall as hard as she could. It fell to the floor. "He raped me! That pig Bobby Kugle raped me. He raped me and made me pregnant. And—And nobody would help me. Nobody! Not even my own mother." A sob caught in her throat. "I hate her, too. Sometimes I'm so mad I just hate everybody."

I went over to her and put my arm around her. Her thin

shoulders were trembling. "It's okay, Kerry. It's okay now. It's all over." But it wasn't. Not really. Sam and I might have sprung Kerry from the Compassionate Charity Home for Girls, but she still had the same problem she'd had when she left Newton Prairie—she was sixteen years old, pregnant, and afraid to face her parents.

"Do you think God's going to punish me, 'cause I'm glad they're dead?"

"I think the way you feel is very human, under the circumstances. Certainly God must understand that." I listened as Kerry told me what had happened to her.

"Bobby was Reverend Ed's assistant at the church," she said. "He got put in charge of Kids for Life, and I went to all the meetings. Only thing was, he started bothering me, making remarks about—well, you know, about my body, and stuff like that. Making me stay at church after all the other kids went home. I—I didn't want to stay. I told him no. But he said he'd tell my brother Mike I was—that I was a—a whore. And—And then my family would kick me out, the way they did Monica."

"So you stayed."

"I tried to talk to my mom about what Bobby was trying to do to me. I told her he touched me when I told him not to, and I didn't like it. But she said I must be making things up, that Reverend Ed wouldn't have somebody like that working for him. Far as my folks're concerned, Reverend Ed's practically God Himself. My mom said if Bobby was really trying something with me, it was my own fault. 'Cause I must've led him on."

I felt tears of rage spring to my eyes as Kerry described the last Kids for Life meeting she'd attended. Bobby made her stay late again, and this time his attentions did not stop with touching. He overpowered her and raped her in the church basement, then told her he'd ruin her if she ever told anyone about it.

After that night, Kerry said, she never returned to Kids for Life. On Wednesday nights, when the group held its meetings, she went into town, but she didn't go to the church anymore. She hung out at Bud's Diner, often calling Monica from the pay phone there. She waited until she saw the other teenagers leaving the church. Then she went home and pretended she'd been at the meeting.

But a few weeks later, Kerry took a home pregnancy test. When it came out positive, she panicked. As I had suspected, she found the advertisement for "abortion counseling" in her local phone book and called the Planned Childbirth Association for help.

"A nice lady met my bus in St. Cloud," she said. "Least she seemed like a nice lady. She took me to this little house I thought was where I was gonna be able to get an abortion." She chewed her fingernails, looking even younger than her sixteen years. "But that wasn't what it was at all. The people there showed me all these horrible pictures of dead babies and—"

"I know," I said. "I know. I saw them myself. The film, too."

"They made me feel really awful, like I was going straight to hell if I didn't want to have my baby. But that wasn't even the worst part."

"Let me guess. Helen Beale was there."

"How'd you know?"

I explained how I'd tracked her to the Compassionate Charity Home for Girls.

"Once Mrs. Beale knew I was pregnant, what could I do? I mean, she said she'd help me out, but she wouldn't help me get an abortion. And, she said, if I didn't do what she told me to, she'd tell everybody about me."

"Did you tell her that Bobby Kugle had raped you?"

Kerry bit her lip and looked at her lap. "No. But I—I told Reverend Ed later, after I was already at the Home. But he said I was a liar, that nobody would ever believe me. He said I'd better keep my mouth shut about Bobby, or I'd be real sorry."

"So when you met with Helen Beale in St. Cloud, you agreed to go to the Home and have your baby adopted?"

"No, I never did, not really. I told Mrs. Beale I'd try it

out for a few days, just while I thought things over. But when I got there, the people running it wouldn't even let me call Monica and tell her where I was. When I finally said I wanted to leave, they locked me in my room, except for mealtimes. Until two nights ago, anyway."

"What happened then?"

"They took me away to that house where you found me. They kept me locked in a bedroom in the back." I realized what event had precipitated Kerry's being moved. She'd been taken out of the Home right after I'd gone there and demanded to see her. If somehow I had managed to come back with the police, Kerry wouldn't have been there.

The teenager told me the bedroom where she'd been kept at the house had an adjoining bathroom and she'd been given a sleeping bag on the floor to keep her warm. Otherwise, she was in solitary confinement.

Dr. Kugle had come three times a day to bring her food and water, but she was able to find no way to escape. The windows of her rooms were nailed shut and had bars over them, and the bedroom door was always kept locked. Until tonight.

About six-thirty tonight, Kerry said, she heard male voices in the house and recognized them as Bobby Kugle's and Reverend Ed's. A short time later, she heard a thud, followed by someone's unlocking the door to her room. Terrified of both the men in the house, she cowered in the corner of her room, waiting for them to enter and not knowing what to expect. But no one came, and the house grew silent. So she ventured out and went into the kitchen.

"And that's where you found Reverend Ed."

"Uh huh. I guess Bobby must've hit him over the head. I tried to get Reverend Ed to stand up. I shook him and shook him, but—but he wouldn't wake up." The girl was so traumatized by what she saw that she was too terrified to move.

Obviously Bobby Kugle had planned to incinerate all four of us—Kerry, Reverend Ed, Sam, and me—inside the house on Elm Street. And, if an autopsy ever proved that the preacher had been bludgeoned before the fire, Bobby probably figured the cops would attribute his murder to one of the rest of us. Since we'd all be dead by then, case closed.

What I wasn't sure about was just why Bobby Kugle wanted Reverend Ed dead. But I had a feeling I would find out soon. The sheriff told me that the grief-stricken Otto Kugle had folded as soon as he saw his only son die. He'd been spilling his guts to the authorities for the past couple of hours now.

I wondered what would happen to the other residents of the Compassionate Charity Home for Girls, now that the authorities knew about the scam the place was running. Certainly it would be closed down. I asked Kerry, "Did you get to know any of the other girls while you were there?"

"No, I wasn't there very long, and they didn't like us to get too friendly with each other. There was just this one girl named Wendy. I really liked her. She had the room next door to mine."

"Is Wendy still there?"

Kerry bent over and pushed the heels of her hands against her eye sockets, as though trying to blot out a painful image. "I—I think something bad happened to her."

I caught my breath. "What do you mean?"

"Wendy told me her mom made her go to that place, even though she wanted to get an abortion. Her mom wouldn't sign for her to get one, and she didn't have anybody else to help her. Wendy's dad ran off when she was just a little kid."

"But what makes you think something happened to her?"

" 'Cause she told me she wasn't gonna stay there. That nobody was gonna make her have her baby. She said if she couldn't get somebody to sign for her to get an abortion with a doctor, she'd take care of it herself. That she had a way."

"So what happened?"

"After I was there a few days, Wendy didn't come down to breakfast like usual. So I went up to her room looking for her. She wasn't there, either, and—"

"And what?"

Kerry's chin trembled. "I—I saw something."

"What? You can tell me." I squeezed her hand. It was cold.

"Her—Wendy's mattress was—It was all soaked with blood. And—And when I asked about her, the matron said she'd gone home. But—"

I stiffened, my memory flashing back to the young girl's charred corpse that had been found in the rural dump. The one Monica and I had viewed, fearing it might be Kerry's . . . until we realized that the dead girl was much shorter than Kerry. "Tell me, Kerry, what does this Wendy look like?"

"Real short blonde hair, blue eyes. Wendy told me she used to be a cheerleader."

"What about her height? Is she as tall as you?"

"Oh, no. Nowheres near as tall as me. I guess Wendy's about five feet, maybe five-one. Real petite, really tiny and cute."

Not anymore, I thought. Little Wendy was not cute anymore. I could see how it happened. Young Wendy had tried to abort herself. With what, a knitting needle from the crafts room, a knife stolen from the dining room? She'd bled to death in her bed, which must have presented a nasty little problem for the Home. The last thing the Compassionate Charity Home for Girls wanted was for the police to come nosing around about a dead teenager. So somebody, probably firebug Bobby Kugle, had taken her body to a rural dump, poured gasoline over it, lighted a match, and driven off. Another problem solved. I decided not to discuss what I suspected with Kerry. She was being forced to absorb enough tragedy already.

I steered the conversation around to her immediate future. I could see no way Kerry could live with Monica in that dismal rooming house by the University, and I certainly wasn't about to force her to go back to her parents' home. The girl obviously needed counseling—both for the rape and for her problem pregnancy—and she'd never get it if she went back home. "I'll take you back to the Cities and you can see Monica," I told her. "Maybe you can stay with me for a few days, just until we figure out what to do."

"I—I just don't want to go home." Kerry lay down on her bed and pulled her knees up under her chin. "Please don't make me go home." Her eyelids began to close.

"We're both tired now. We'll talk about it in the morning," I promised. I wasn't sure what the legalities were, but we could worry about them later. "I won't make you go home."

In less than a minute, Kerry was asleep. I grabbed a blanket and gently tucked it around her as she slept.

46

"You're really just a big old marshmallow inside, Sam. You can't fool me." I grinned at my partner from across his desk. His doctor had checked him out and pronounced him none the worse for wear, except for a few bruises here and there.

"The hell. The girls owe us money and this's just a way for 'em to pay it off." Sam did his best to look gruff, but he couldn't quite hide the mischievous twinkle in his eye. "It's a business decision, pure and simple."

"Yeah, right. You may be a *mensch* after all, Sam." He looked secretly pleased at my analysis, but he would never admit it. It was Monday afternoon, and I'd just returned from taking Kerry Hammond to Sam's daughter Lael's house, where the teenager was to live and work as an *au pair* for as long as she wanted to stay there.

Kerry was adamant about not going home to Newton Prairie and, true to form, her parents didn't seem particularly anxious to see her return. The teenager had been due back from camp yesterday, so Monica screwed up her courage long enough to call the senior Hammonds and explain what had happened. The last thing any of us wanted was to have the Hammonds call the police and report Kerry missing.

Monica later told me that the elder Hammonds seemed far more concerned about Reverend Ed's death than about their own daughter's predicament. For Kerry, they had mainly sharp recriminations.

Kerry's *au pair* services were supposedly Sam's gift to Lael, who needed help with baby Aaron. But I knew that wasn't all there was to it. This arrangement would give Kerry a temporary place to live in a supportive family home, plus an opportunity to try caring for a newborn at least partly by herself. Staying with Lael and her family would offer the teenager time to go to school as well as to psychological counseling, until she decided what she wanted to do about her pregnancy. And about the rest of her life. At the same time, Lael would get some much-needed household help.

"So, ya talk to that cop yet?" Sam asked, transparently changing the subject. He obviously didn't want his reputation as a tough guy to become too tarnished. He'd spent far too many years polishing it.

"Yeah, spent over an hour on the phone with him yesterday afternoon." Stearns County Sheriff Frank Amery and I shared what we knew about Otto and Bobby Kugle, Reverend Ed Beale, and the various scams the three had operated. "Apparently Dr. Kugle spilled his guts. Said he didn't much care what happened to him, now that his son was dead. Far as the doctor was concerned, the sun rose and set on that kid."

"Damned good thing the doc don't care what happens to 'im, 'cause he's prob'ly gonna be in prison for a good long time." Sam pulled on his chin. "Copped to the whole thing, huh?"

"Sure did. Admitted he and Beale had been selling babies for close to ten years. Beale was running a small version of the business back in the early eighties, when he got himself in an embarrassing jam—seduced a teenager and got her pregnant.

"So he turned to Dr. Kugle and asked him to give the girl an abortion, on the Q.T. After that, Kugle became a full partner in the baby-selling business, and it was his expertise that made it grow." The girl Ed had seduced, Tammy Myers, had managed to get a good living out of keeping Ed's secret, too. The preacher sent her to beauty school and set her up in her own beauty shop in Newton Prairie.

Sam jotted a few numbers on a piece of paper. "Ten years, huh? Adds up to a few bucks."

"Yeah. Sheriff Amery thinks Beale and Kugle probably grossed in the neighborhood of fifteen million bucks in the baby-selling business alone. Plus what they pulled in on the anti-abortion crusade."

"So where's the dough now? Can't see how those two guys coulda spent that much."

"Swiss bank accounts. Caribbean banks accounts. Precious gems. The stock market. Remember, Sam, Ed was able to launder most of that cash through his anti-abortion fund-raising, so it wasn't as much of a problem for them as it might've been."

"I still don't get why Bobby killed the preacher."

"Apparently Bobby got to be a bit of a problem for Ed. Dr. Kugle had insisted on Ed's letting Bobby into the church hierarchy a few years back. Probably so the kid could report back to Daddy. Ed went along with it, but he and Bobby had a few clashes, particularly when that women's clinic in St. Cloud burned.

"Turns out Bobby and another of Ed's inner circle, a huge, but not too bright guy named Will Slauson, torched it without Ed's knowledge or approval. The boys got a little overzealous for the cause, I guess. Anyway, Ed was definitely not pleased."

I repeated to Sam what Sheriff Amery had pieced together about that crime. Bobby and Will had driven to St. Cloud in Bobby's Volkswagen bug. They bought several containers of gasoline at local gas stations, then waited outside the clinic until they thought everyone had left, and fire-bombed it. Their way of getting rid of the competition.

When the two later realized that the clinic director and another woman had been killed in the blaze, and that they could be prosecuted for murder if they were caught, they tried to cover their tracks. For starters, Bobby had the color of this beloved classic VW changed from gray to fiery tangerine, in case anyone reported having seen it near the clinic on the night of the fire. And he replaced its license plates with ones from a stolen pickup truck—the same truck I was now sure he and Will drove the day they attacked me on the road outside of Newton Prairie.

"So Ed and Bobby weren't gettin' along. Still, why would he wanna kill the golden goose?"

"Because the goose was about to give up laying eggs. Ed was pissed off at Bobby for a whole lot more than the clinic fire. The kid was out of control. He'd raped Kerry Hammond and made her pregnant, and because of my poking around, Ed figured the whole house of cards they'd built was about to self-destruct. After you and I left the doctor's office on Saturday—"

"Ugh! That fiasco!"

"Yeah, well." I didn't want to get into another argument about how stupid my idea about our playing adoptive parents opposite Dr. Kugle's baby-seller really was. I hate to argue with Sam, particularly when he's right. "After we left, Ed told the doctor that he'd had it with Bobby, and he'd had it with the business. He had accumulated more money than he could ever spend, and he was pulling the plug. Ed wanted to give Kerry to us, then close down the Compassionate Charity Home real quick, before the cops showed up."

"And the Kugles didn't go along with that."

"Bobby didn't, anyway. He talked his old man into letting him handle it his way. Bobby followed the minister to the house on Elm Street, bashed him over the head, and waited down the block until we showed up. Once we were all inside the house, he went into his firebombing routine, probably figuring he'd take care of all three problems at once—his feud with Ed, Kerry's embarrassing pregnancy, and our investigation."

"Almost did, too."

I couldn't argue with that. I still had the stench of burning gasoline in my nostrils. And, for the past two nights, I'd had nightmares about being burned alive. They would fade with time, though. The important thing was that all of us had survived. Bobby Kugle might have, too, if he hadn't had a last leaky can of gasoline in his VW when it crashed.

"So," Sam said. "Gotta admit ya done good, sweet pea. Even if we ain't gonna get *bubkes* for this one." He scribbled circles on his pad of paper, avoiding looking me in the eye. "Never thought I'd havta thank somebody for pushin' me out a window."

"So don't. It's all in a day's work." My eyes misted up. "And speaking of a day's work. I'm taking the rest of the week off."

"Yer what? Hey, come on, kiddo. This ain't the only case we got around here, ya know."

I leaned across Sam's desk. "The others can wait a few days, Sam. I'm going out and buy myself a new car." There went my nest egg that I'd been planning to put toward a condominium; I would need a good chunk of it to replace the Honda with something newer and better. "And then I'm going to start driving."

"The hell. Where to?"

"West. Maybe I'll go skiing or something, before all the snow's gone."

I wasn't about to admit it to Sam, but I had in mind a lot more "or something" than skiing. Doug Winthrop and I figured Aspen was close to halfway between St. Paul and Carmel, and he'd managed to rearrange his work schedule for a couple of days. If I started driving first thing in the morning, I could make Colorado before midnight, easy.

My romance with my Carmel cop wasn't exactly traditional, but maybe it would work for us. I was willing to give it a shot. I sorely needed a few hugs to help me fight off the demons that had been chasing me for the last few days, and Doug seemed perfectly suited for the job.

Thinking about cuddling with Doug on snowy nights in a lonely Colorado mountain cabin made me feel better already. I absent-mindedly ran my hand through my hair and along the back of my neck.

Damn! I'd neglected to warn Doug that most of my hair was missing. I just hoped he didn't have any hangups about dating a woman with a boy's haircut.